BILLY BU

AND THE BOO

Gary Robinson

7th GENERATION
Summertown, Tennessee

Library of Congress Cataloging-in-Publication Data available upon request.

7th Generation
Book Publishing Company
PO Box 99, Summertown, TN 38483
888-260-8458
bookpubco.com
nativevoicesbooks.com

Printed in the United States of America

ISBN: 978-1-939053-47-3

28 27 26 25 24 23   1 2 3 4 5 6 7 8 9

ACKNOWLEDGMENTS

I want to thank my best friend and significant other, Lola, for her support in all things. I couldn't do this work without her. She has been my biggest supporter, by my side for many years. No words printed here could express my true gratitude.

NOTE TO READERS

siyo (hello). Please note that this is a work of fantasy fiction. I've blended elements of Native American culture and history with fictional tribal culture, religion, and history. Some parts have been adapted to protect the secrecy of certain medicine practices and ceremonies. Others have been invented to create a more interesting and dramatic story. I point this out so some critical readers won't dismiss the book because it lacks accuracy—and also, so other people won't think I am revealing too many Cherokee cultural secrets.

Everything mentioned on the pages of this book regarding Cherokee medicine, history, and culture has previously appeared in nonfiction books,* so nothing new is being revealed to the public here. This includes books about the Cherokee syllabary; books about Cherokee medicine formulas, spells, and medicinal plants; and similar works. Hundreds of handwritten pages of Cherokee spells are available from Yale University's Beinecke Rare Book and Manuscript Library.

Additionally, the magical texts that were recorded in Cherokee books of spells many generations ago have been declared to be "ritually dead" by Cherokee medicine people themselves. That is, their powers to heal or harm anyone have expired over time and are now null and void.**

Finally, the term *medicine* is often used differently in a tribal context than it is used in mainstream American society. In addition to referring to a healing process, the word can also mean "power" or "a person's ability to affect nature as well as other people's health and behavior," as in "She has strong medicine."

Wado (thank you).

Gary Robinson

*Bibliography of sources can be found at the end of the book.

**Alan Kilpatrick, *The Night Has a Naked Soul: Witchcraft and Sorcery among the Western Cherokee* (Syracuse, NY: Syracuse University Press, 1997).

CONTENTS

Call to the Original People

ecil Lookout awoke abruptly with words from a dream message still fresh in his mind. *It is good that you have remembered the old ways, practiced the traditions, and recited the prophecy after all these many years,* the message said.

A few members of Native Nations still managed to hold on to ancient traditions and pass on ancient prophecies. In Cecil's tribe, the Osage, it seemed that only his family continued to remember wisdom imparted by elders and ancestors some thirty generations ago.

The eighty-year-old elder sat up in bed, listening quietly in case there was more to the message. It had been so long since he'd last heard from the ancestor spirits; he had to be sure he'd heard what he thought he heard. Or was it merely his imagination? The lines of communication between the land of the living and the land of the dead could become faulty after long periods of disuse.

As the Keeper of the Center and the leader of the Intertribal Medicine Council, it was his responsibility to hold fast when others had ceased to believe, when others had given up hope and taken the easy path of religious and cultural assimilation.

1

But not Cecil or his grown son Ethan. Not his grandson Cody, or his granddaughter Lisa. They had stayed the course and remained true to their calling. And hopefully, not for the thirteen members of the Intertribal Medicine Council scattered among the various tribes.

Cecil sat on the edge of his bed, still quietly listening for more, either an external or internal message. He'd give it a few more moments.

Then it came, penetrating his mind.

The time of fulfillment has come.

There it was! Of course, the message had to be verified through ceremony, but Cecil was certain it was a true and accurate communication from the ancestor spirits.

It was just before sunrise on an August day known as the first day of the Full Green Corn Moon. Cecil rubbed the sleep from his eyes as his thoughts turned to the immediate task at hand.

"Cody!" the elder called to his grandson, who was still asleep in the house's other bedroom. "The time has come! The command was delivered! I need your help!"

"What did you say, Grandpa?"

This response came from the other room more as a moan than a question. Moments later, Cecil's fifteen-year-old grandson burst into the elder's bedroom.

"Did you say what I think you said?" the boy asked with excited anticipation in his voice.

"Yes, you heard right. The voice of the ancestor spirits spoke to me just now. We must prepare."

Cody knew that meant Cecil would need his ceremonial headdress, eagle feather fan, and beaded moccasins, all of which were kept in a cedar-lined closet near the back door. The teen had been training to take over his grandfather's position as the Keeper of the Sky Stone's centerpiece for the past two years.

He was now both excited and disappointed that the call from the ancestors had come today. Excited because of its significance, disappointed because it meant he would never take his place in the thousand-year-old tradition of the Keepers.

Cody retrieved the ceremonial regalia from the closet, carried the items to his grandfather, and helped him dress.

As the old man began dressing, he said, "Repeat the signs that we, the Original People, have already seen."

"First, the light-skinned strangers arrived on Turtle Island," Cody said, "bringing their cravings for domination. Second, the foreigners spread like locusts across the land, devouring everything and everyone in sight. Third, the Original People were hunted almost to extinction, our means of physical and spiritual sustenance stolen. Fourth, the very essence of existence was threatened as the Red, White, and Blue Nation unleashed an explosion of unholy power on the Yellow Nation. Fifth, the Eagle flew from Earth and landed on the moon. Sixth, a Black man was chosen by the people of the Red, White, and Blue Nation to live in their White House. And seventh, the Crown Disease spread across the face of Mother Earth, decimating the world's population."

"Very good," Cecil said. "Now, according to the prophecy, what will unfold next?"

Cody collected his thoughts before speaking.

"Ancient forces will awaken," he said. "The veil separating the worlds will become thinner. Inhabitants of the Underworld shall rise up, become manifest here in the Middleworld, and try to take control yet again. Spirit beings of the Upperworld will join the Chosen One to combat the dark forces here in the Middleworld. The future of mankind will hang in the balance."

"Very good," the old man said. "And our Native American brothers and sisters will be called on to return to their ancient traditional teachings to help support and empower the holy beings to subdue the denizens of the deep."

But Cody was left with one unanswered question.

"Who is the Chosen One?" he asked.

"Ah, that is the question," the elder answered. "That is yet to be revealed. We must begin the search and remain patient until they are found."

Unsatisfied, Cody nevertheless remained quiet. His grandfather always seemed to know best.

Fully cloaked in his tribal regalia, Cecil headed through the kitchen toward the back door. Followed by his grandson, the elder stepped out into the backyard of his modest home. The elder's house was located on Ohio Street in St. Louis, very near the western shore of the mighty Mississippi River.

Generations of Keepers of the Center before him had dedicated their lives to staying in this region of the country, long part of the original homelands of the Osage tribe, also known as Niukonska, the Children of the Middle Waters.

Next door to the elder's house stood a centuries-old man-made earthen mound known to the locals as Sugarloaf Mound. In reality, it was the last remaining mound built by his people hundreds and hundreds of years ago, one of dozens of mounds and flat-top earthen pyramids that dotted the nearby Indigenous landscape.

Before ascending the grass-covered slope, Cecil turned to his grandson.

"I am proud of you, Cody," he said. "You have remained faithful to your duty. After we've finished this morning's ceremony, I want you to call your cousin Lisa and all your cousins so they know what has happened this morning."

"Yes, Grandfather," the young man replied. "I will do as you ask."

Then, aided by his grandson, Cecil climbed the slope of the grass-covered structure and made his way to the center. Turning eastward toward the rising sun, the old man cast his vision across the river.

With Cody at his side, Cecil began the fulfillment ceremony with a prayer to Grandfather Sun in the Osage language, as he'd been taught by his own grandfather, asking for a blessing upon his family, a blessing on the spirits of his ancestors, and a blessing on his descendants yet to be born. He asked Creator for extra guidance and assistance on this significant day for himself.

Finally, he sat down cross-legged on the mound and asked for the Thirteen Ancestors to appear to him and speak the words of fulfillment, if that was truly their intent this day. Then the old man closed his eyes and waited.

Slowly, an all-encompassing vision faded into view, completely engulfing him. While his body sat on the ground, his mind and spirit body were caught up into a whole other world. In this other world, he stood in the middle of a circle of Native men and women who were seated on buffalo robes, looking back at him from inside a tipi. Without counting, Cecil knew there were thirteen of them from different tribes, each dressed in their own particular ceremonial regalia.

The glowing translucent form of an unspeakably old Native man, dressed in ancient tribal regalia, stood and approached Cecil. The man spoke, using only his mind.

"The time, foretold a thousand years ago, has arrived. The signs have all come to pass. The milestones have all been reached. And the Thunder Beings will soon select the Chosen One. As the Keeper of the Center, you must call the Intertribal Medicine Council together, locate the Chosen One, and prepare to reassemble the Sky Stone."

It was an event Cecil had waited his whole life to witness. It was the message generations of Original People had known was coming but had probably forgotten.

Confident that they'd been heard and understood, the thirteen visitors faded from view.

As the designated Keeper of the Center, it was now Cecil's job to carry out the command. He must call the Keepers and the other members of the Medicine Council together. The Keepers would bring their hidden and guarded sections of the Sky Stone together. Then, when the Fire Crystal was fit into its place in the center, the reassembled Circle would activate, empowering the Chosen One to fulfill his destiny.

After his supplication, the elder lingered on the spot for a short while, basking in the aura of the spiritual energy created by the spiritual appearance. In his mind's eye, the elder could see beyond the river a few miles farther to the northeast, to the remains of the ancient mound city now called Cahokia, the largest Native American city ever built.

That city had been the spiritual center of a religious and cultural movement that had spread among the Indigenous peoples of North America, one that had never been witnessed before or since. One of the results of that phenomenon was the construction of thousands and thousands of earthen ceremonial mounds in an area that stretched from the Gulf Coast to the Great Lakes and from the Atlantic Ocean to the Mississippi River and beyond.

Known as Solstice City to its original twenty thousand inhabitants, the centerpiece of that vast cultural kingdom a thousand years ago had once been home to the "Son of the Sun." This demigod, known to some as the Falcon Priest and to others as the Sun Priest, was the human representative of the Upperworld on earth.

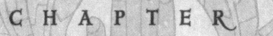

CHAPTER 1

Summer's End

The muggy August air clung to Billy Buckhorn's brown Cherokee skin like a wet blanket. He and his best friend, Chigger, were night fishing on Lake Tenkiller in eastern Oklahoma. This region, part of the western branch of the old Cherokee Nation, was filled with rivers, creeks, and lakes all nestled between heavily wooded hills.

"Drop that light down closer to the water," Billy said in a loud whisper.

Chigger let out a few more inches of rope until the camping lantern almost touched the water's still surface. "How's that?" he asked.

"Just fine," sixteen-year-old Billy replied.

Chigger, also sixteen, tied off the rope and picked up his fishing pole.

Night fishing was one of Billy's favorite things to do in the summer. Well, really, he liked fishing any time of day or night, any time of year. And hunting too, for that matter. He liked Cherokee bowhunting the best. Billy had learned these skills from his Cherokee grandfather, Wesley.

From somewhere off in the distant darkness along the lake's shoreline, the boys heard the snap of a breaking branch and a rustling of leaves.

"What was that?" Chigger whispered nervously. Unlike Billy, he wasn't such a big fan of night fishing. Or doing much of anything at night that involved being outside in the dark, because of all the scary old Cherokee legends he'd heard. But he'd follow Billy anywhere, anytime.

"Probably just a possum or badger hunting for food," Billy replied calmly.

Chigger picked up a flashlight from the seat next to him. Turning it on, he pointed its beam in the direction the sound came from. A pair of glowing red eyes peered back at him from the lake's edge.

"What the—!" Chigger exclaimed with a jump, dropping the flashlight into the lake.

"Not so loud," Billy demanded in a loud whisper as he watched the light sink out of sight. "Now look what you've done."

"There was somethin' evil looking over there, watching us!" the scared Cherokee boy declared. "It could be one of the Water Cannibals my grandparents talked about, come ashore to hunt human flesh."

A Water Cannibal was one of the many supernatural creatures said by traditional Cherokees to live in the Underworld and come up to the Middleworld from time to time.

"You're letting your imagination get the better of you again," Billy said, clearly impatient with his gullible friend. "It was a possum, just like I said."

Peering down through the water, Billy was more concerned with his drowned flashlight than the harmless animal on shore. As the light floated toward the lake's bottom, Billy thought he momentarily saw the moving form of some underwater creature he hadn't ever seen before. *I'm tired—maybe my mind is playing tricks on me,* he thought.

"Their eyes glow red when you shine a light in them," he said, continuing his logical explanation for the shoreline illusion.

"Oh," Chigger replied sheepishly. "I knew that."

The two boys had known each other since the first grade. Most days after school they had played together outdoors. In those days, Chigger's dad worked at a plant nursery near the shores of the lake. On Saturdays he'd often taken the pair with him to work on the plants, trees, and shrubs the nursery grew.

Of course, the boys had often ended up playing hide-and-seek among the long rows of greenery. And their favorite fishing spot was the inlet of water where they were now. It was near the old nursery, which had gone out of business years ago.

Chigger's fishing pole jerked in his hands.

"I think I've got a bite!" he whispered excitedly.

They always whispered when they were fishing. Even though the water muffled human noises, Grandpa Wesley taught Billy that it was best to avoid sudden movements or sharp sounds. Such things could spook the fish.

Chigger yanked the line up out of the water. He found nothing but a water turtle hooked on the end of it.

"Ah, another turtle," Chigger said. "That's the third one tonight! They musta chased off all the fish."

"Have you forgotten that turtles are good luck?" Billy asked as he unhooked the five-pound reptile from his friend's line. "After all," he continued, "it was Grandmother Turtle who brought up the mud from the bottom of the waters so Creator could make land."

He let the turtle slip back into the dark water. It paddled quickly away. Billy scanned the lake's nearby surface just to make sure no other less familiar creatures were watching them tonight from the legendary Underworld.

"And that's why we call this land Turtle Island," Chigger said, repeating a phrase he'd heard over and over since he was a kid.

"I remember that old Cherokee story just as good as you do. What's that called? A legend? A myth?"

"One man's myth is another man's religion," Billy replied, using one of the sayings his father often used. "But the Grandma Turtle story is more of a fable. You know, a traditional story that teaches us something."

"Ooh! Did you just go all college professor on me or what?" Chigger laughed.

Billy's father was in fact a college professor who taught Cherokee history and culture at the nearby college. Chigger liked to bring his friend, the professor's son, back down to the grassroots level whenever he started sounding too smart.

"Myth, fable, whatever," Chigger said.

"For someone who says he doesn't believe in ancient Native American folktales, you sure do spook easily," Billy offered.

"Old Indian stories are one thing," Chigger said, "but ghosts and hauntings and glowing red eyes in the night are something different. That eerie stuff has been documented on reality TV."

"Ha!" Billy said, much louder than he intended to. "Reality TV is mindless mental mush. But there's something behind old Cherokee legends. Hidden wisdom that's true at a deeper level."

"Enough, professor. You're making my head hurt."

Billy knew he'd pushed it too far. "Let's call it a night," he said.

"Might as well," Chigger agreed. "Ain't nothin' bitin' but terrapins."

Chigger untied the rope and pulled the lantern up into the boat. They were in a fifteen-foot skiff with a flat bottom. The flat bottom let them get in and out of shallow, reedy water where fish liked to hide.

Though the fishing boat had a motor, Billy didn't like to disturb the silence of nature on nights like this one. Another habit he'd learned from his grandpa. He and Chigger used a pair of oars to propel the vessel toward the shore.

"What could be better than this?" Billy asked as they glided along the surface of the lake. High above them was a dark, velvet sky filled with twinkling stars.

"A bowl of homemade ice cream would taste pretty good right about now," Chigger replied.

"No, seriously," Billy said, giving his friend a sharp look. "Two Cherokees on a summer night surrounded by the wonders of nature?" He looked up at the sky, finding the six stars of the Pleiades constellation, known to the Cherokees as "the Boys." "What could be better?"

"Nothing," Chigger had to admit as he gazed upward as well. "Absolutely nothing."

The only sounds to be heard that night were about a thousand chirping bullfrogs, a million clacking cicadas, and the splashing of two oars lightly stroking the water.

The boys soon arrived at the concrete boat launch. Chigger, nervously checking the shoreline for any more eerie creatures, held the boat steady while Billy walked up the slight hill to fetch his pickup truck and boat trailer.

Moments later, he backed the trailer down the ramp and into the shallow water. Chigger guided the skiff onto the trailer and then cranked the trailer's winch to secure it in place. With the boat firmly tied down, the pair headed for home.

Billy knew the Oklahoma back roads of the Cherokee Nation like he knew the back of his own hand. Every twist, turn, pothole, and crack was etched into his mind.

Almost every day of his life, he and Grandpa Wesley had driven those roads and hiked the nearby trails in search of wildlife and wonder. Each trip had included the telling of an old Cherokee legend or teachings in the spiritual ways of Native medicine.

While other kids grew up hearing stories of Goldilocks or Little Red Riding Hood, Billy heard about the ancient customs and beliefs of his people. His grandpa was like a walking, talking library of Native knowledge and outdoor lore.

Chigger, on the other hand, had grown up immersed in the world of superhero comics. Every flat surface in his bedroom was covered with stacks of them. One of the boy's favorite conversation topics focused on superhero powers.

He often asked Billy, "If you could have any superpower, what would it be?" to which Billy often replied, "Not now, Chigger. I have more important things on my mind."

But every now and then, he'd play along, just to make his friend happy, and say something like "I'd want to be able to travel back in time to witness history as it happened" or maybe "I'd like to be invisible so I could visit people without them knowing it."

Chigger thought these superpowers were unimpressive when compared to such abilities as X-ray vision, electromagnetic force fields, telekinesis, or elasticity. *All the coolest superheroes can do those things,* he thought.

Fifteen minutes after leaving the lake, the pair reached Chigger's family's mobile home. It was up a rough dirt road northeast of the capital of the Cherokee Nation.

"Did you register for the blowgun contest at this year's Cherokee Holiday?" Chigger asked before getting out of Billy's truck.

"And the cornstalk bow-and-arrow shoot," Billy confirmed. "What about you?"

"Yep," Chigger replied. "Just like last year. Only difference is, I'm gonna beat you at both of 'em this year."

He slammed the truck door and ran toward his mobile home before Billy could respond.

"You're on!" Billy shouted loud enough for his friend to hear. Then the teen sped off into the night. In another twenty minutes, Billy reached his own home near Park Hill, south of Tahlequah.

He pulled into the tree-lined driveway that led to his two-story log home. Parking beside the driveway in his usual graveled spot, he opened the truck's glove box. He took out the pocket watch he kept there. It had belonged to his great-grandfather Jim "Bullseye" Buckhorn. His grandfather was a famous bow-and-arrow hunter in his day.

The watch's antique hands pointed straight up. Midnight. Later than he said he'd be home. Giving the watch stem a couple of winds, he put the well-worn timepiece back in the glove box.

Being as quiet as he could, Billy slipped out from behind the steering wheel of his forest-green 1985 Chevy Silverado pickup. The vehicle was way past its prime, but the teen didn't care. It had belonged to his father's younger brother, Franklin, who had been killed in action during the war in Afghanistan. Billy would never forget the tribe's touching tribute to his hero uncle when his body arrived back in Tahlequah for burial.

As he slipped out of the truck, Billy looked up at his family's log house. The lights were still on in his father's upstairs library study. Billy knew he was busy preparing for the classes he taught at the college.

Stepping quietly onto the porch, he took off his muddy wet boots and left them outside. He tried to keep from making any noise as he moved into the front of the house. He didn't notice the dark shadow of someone sitting on the couch.

"Home kinda late, aren't you?" a woman's voice said from the darkness. Billy nearly jumped out of his skin.

"Ma, you startled me," he replied, trying to catch his breath. "Why are you sitting in the dark?"

"Just collecting my thoughts," she said, turning on a nearby table lamp. She was still in the white nurse's uniform she wore during her nightly shift at the hospital. The whiteness of her uniform contrasted with her black hair and bronze Cherokee skin. "I know you still think it's summer, young man," she said in a calm tone. "But classes have been going on for a week now.

I received a message from your school today. It said you haven't quite been attending on a regular basis."

"Ma, you know I can never get serious about classes until after Labor Day weekend," Billy protested. "That's when summer is really over. It's not fair that they robbed us of the last two weeks of summer."

"It's too bad you inherited your stubborn streak from my side of the family," his mother commented. "Of course, your tendency to rebel against authority is from your father's side."

"And they never cover anything important in the first few days anyway," Billy added to his defense.

"I'll put this to you as directly as I can," she said, ignoring his protest and standing up. "I expect you to be in class all day, every day this coming week. If you miss even one class, then you won't be able to take part in any of the activities you've planned during the following Labor Day weekend. No bow-and-arrow shoot, no blowgun competition, no all-night stomp dance, and no fishing contest."

"But Chigger's counting on me to—"

"You should've thought of all that before you skipped class."

"But—"

"But nothing!" his mother said firmly. "Now go to your room and get in bed. And tomorrow you'll stay home until you've written your summer reading report."

"Aw, not that," Billy moaned.

"You have read the book, haven't you?"

"Not exactly."

"Of course you haven't," she said, almost in despair. "All the more reason for you to stay home." She walked toward Billy with her hand out. "Give me your truck keys."

"What?"

"You heard me. Stubborn and rebellious. Put the truck keys in my hand right now!"

He pulled the keys out of his pocket and dropped them into her outstretched hand. One of the things Billy loved about his parents was the freedom they'd always allowed him. It had given him a sense of confidence and self-reliance at an early age. But he figured he'd pushed it just a little too far this time.

"You can have them back after you've finished the report," she said as she headed for the stairs. "If it's not done by Monday morning, your father or I will take you to school."

His mother marched up the stairs, twirling his set of keys around her index finger.

Billy's shoulders slumped. His head drooped. He trudged toward his room in the back of the house. His summer had come crashing to an end.

Sitting on the edge of his bed, the boy pulled off his dirty clothes. His jeans were wet from the knees down from when he'd jumped out of the skiff near the boat ramp. After throwing on one of the old T-shirts he slept in, he stepped into the neighboring hall bathroom.

He gazed at himself for a moment in the mirror, seeing the same dark brown eyes he saw at the end of every day. His longish black hair was tousled as usual, and splatters of gray mud from the lakeshore spotted his neck and face. *Who is this guy staring back at me?* he wondered, just as he'd been doing for as long as he could remember. *Will I ever find out?*

Quickly he rinsed his neck and face with a couple of splashes of water from the sink. A few careless swipes of his teeth with a toothbrush rounded out his bedtime routine, followed by the fast swipe of the hand towel hanging nearby.

Back in his bedroom, he flopped down on top of his bedcovers and looked up at the ceiling. "Another day bites the dust," he said, as if his room was a close companion who could hear him.

Curiously, just as he was about to fall asleep, an image popped into his mind of his grandmother Awinita. "Get ready," she might have said before her image quickly faded.

Did Billy hear and see what he thought he did? Was it just a figment of his imagination?

He attempted to shake it off.

"Go to sleep, Buckhorn," he muttered to himself. "Book report tomorrow." The dread of it made his chest and his eyes feel heavy. Forcing his mind to turn to happier thoughts, he envisioned the approaching Cherokee Holiday. Sleep came easily, and he was grateful for it.

The tribe had been putting on the annual Cherokee National Holiday during Labor Day weekend for at least sixty years. It included a lot of old-time Cherokee activities, such as the cornstalk bow-and-arrow shooting contest and the blowgun competition that Billy liked so much. Most of these events took place at the Cherokee Nation cultural grounds located near the tribal offices.

But there were dozens and dozens of other Native cultural events, displays, and activities that brought thousands of Cherokees from all over the United States back home at that time. On top of all that, there were also plenty of other events to occupy a person's time, such as a classic car show, a softball tournament, bingo, and a powwow.

But Billy preferred to focus on four specific activities during that weekend, activities he'd learned from his grandpa Wesley. Only two of them were official events of the holiday: the cornstalk shoot and the blowgun contest. The other two, the stomp dance and the fishing contest, took place at other spots away from the Cherokee headquarters.

Taking part in these events was the highlight of Billy's year. That was why it was important for him to obey his mother's orders completely in the days before the big weekend.

He finished the summer reading project and wrote the report in one day. Then he made sure to arrive at school on time every day and stay until the final bell rang. On Friday he even asked the school secretary to call his mother and tell her he'd attended class all week.

However, there was one more event Billy had to survive before he could enjoy the coming activities. Every year on the Friday evening before the holiday weekend, both sides of his family gathered for dinner at his house. And that could be a very tense time indeed. Actually, it could be like World War III.

Billy's father, James T. Buckhorn, came from a long line of full-blood Cherokee people who had resisted taking up the white man's ways for many years. But early in life he'd chosen teaching as his path. He felt it was important for new generations of his people to understand their own history and identity. "You can't know where you're going unless you know where you've been," he always said.

Billy's mother, whose maiden name was Rebecca Sarah Ross, came from a family of Cherokee country preachers. They were all descended from a famous mixed-blood chief of the Cherokees named John Ross. They had long ago adopted many of the white man's ways, including religion, partly as a way to survive. Rebecca's brother, Billy's uncle John Ross, was a well-known preacher in Native church circles.

From direct experience, Billy knew that when these two families got together, an unholy war of words was possible. His own mother and father, both more accepting in their outlooks, acted as buffers between the two extremes of his family.

Thankfully, Grandpa Wesley had been able to come to this year's dinner. He had fallen recently, had hurt his knee, and wasn't as active as he used to be. Now he walked with a cane.

"Our Heavenly Father, we pray for the sinners among us tonight," Uncle John began the prayer before supper. "May they see the light before it's too late."

"And may both sides of this family come together for the sake of our children," Billy's mother suddenly added. "Amen."

She ended the prayer much sooner than her preacher brother had intended. He could pray for hours.

"Now let's all enjoy the food that the mothers, aunts, and sisters of these families have prepared for us," Billy's father added. "And may we use it to feed our bodies in a good way so that we may help others."

Billy followed his grandpa as they filled their plates with large portions from the buffet spread across a long table. The boy didn't notice the approach of his uncle.

"Billy, I understand you've begun high school this year," John said in a booming preacher's voice that almost caused Billy to drop his plate.

"Yes, Uncle, I'm in tenth grade." The boy put down his plate for a moment so he could shake the man's hand. Being polite to his elders was something he'd been taught from a very young age.

Grandpa Wesley happily continued to move on down the buffet line, and Billy felt like he'd been abandoned to speak to his uncle alone.

"I certainly hope you won't be taking part in that devil dance out at the Live Oak stomp grounds this year," his uncle said. "Nothing good can come of it."

Having overheard this comment, Wesley stepped back to Billy's side.

"Actually, he and I will be dancing briskly all night Saturday," the old man said, loud enough to be heard all around. "Renewing our pledge to the old ways will bring good fortune and health to the entire family."

Moving quickly, Billy's mother appeared beside her preacher brother and said, "Could I speak to you for a minute outside?"

John nodded, reluctantly put down his plate, followed his sister through the sliding glass door, and stepped out to the back porch.

Billy couldn't hear their words, but he knew what they were saying. It was a quarrel they'd had for years. His mom would say that she'd raised her son to make up his own mind about cultural and spiritual matters. And her brother would argue that his nephew would not make it to heaven if he didn't put aside those old Indian beliefs and come to church. On and on it went.

Meanwhile, Billy's dad came to his son's side, and they both watched the quarrel unfold through the glass door.

"One man's myth is another man's religion," they said simultaneously and laughed.

"Come out on the front porch with me for a moment," his dad said.

They went out to the front of the house for a father-son talk.

"Your mother and I are pleased that you focused on your school duties this past week," Mr. Buckhorn told his son. "Your classroom education is every bit as important as the cultural education you get from Grandpa." He reached into his pocket and pulled out two twenty-dollar bills. "As a reward, here's a little spending money for you to use this weekend," he said with a smile.

Billy took the cash, folded it, and put it in his back pocket. "Thanks, Pops."

Billy had begun calling his father "Pops" years earlier, because Corn Pops cereal had been a favorite in the Buckhorn household when Billy was little. James had easily accepted the endearing term because it was something he and his son uniquely shared.

"We'll be there for the blowgun match tomorrow afternoon," James said, then added, "Good luck," before going back inside.

And so the holiday weekend had begun with only a minor skirmish between the Buckhorns and the Rosses. Billy was definitely ready for better things to come.

The next morning, Billy met Chigger early for the bow-and-arrow shooting contest.

"Where's your grandpa?" Chigger asked. "He usually comes to see you shoot."

"He's taking care of his hurt knee today," Billy replied. "He soaks it in a tub of herbal medicine and drinks a nasty-tasting tea. Straight out of the Cherokee medicine book."

"Why doesn't he just go to the Indian clinic and get medication?" Chigger asked. "After all, your mother *is* a nurse."

"You know he doesn't believe in white man's medicine," Billy answered. "Only for emergencies—serious emergencies."

"Oh, right," Chigger said.

"And he wants to be rested and ready for tonight's stomp dance," Billy added.

"You two haven't missed that for years, have you?" Chigger asked.

"No, we haven't," Billy said. "It's part of the old Cherokee religion that Grandpa insists we do. He says Grandma usually visits him during this ceremony."

Billy's grandmother Awinita had passed away ten years earlier. Her name meant "young deer" in Cherokee. Billy barely remembered her because he was only six when she died. Grandpa said he continued to see her spirit from time to time, wandering through the old house they'd shared or hanging around the small garden in back of the house.

Grandpa also said he always saw her during the Labor Day weekend stomp dance. Billy had never seen her, though many people at the stomp dance claimed to have seen loved ones who'd passed away. It was one of the reasons that some people still danced the old dance.

Billy and Chigger had a good day of friendly rivalry. The bow-and-arrow shoot allowed the use of only handmade bows and arrows, so it reinforced that part of Cherokee culture.

The same was true for the blowgun contest. Only handmade blowguns, made of ten- to twelve-foot river cane, could be used. Not very many people could still craft these weapons or the six-inch darts that served as ammunition.

The two friends had hunted, fished, and camped together for the past five years or so. It was how they'd gotten to learn and practice these skills. Sometimes Billy's father and grandfather had taken the boys for a weekend adventure. Other times it had been Chigger's dad or uncle who had gone with them.

But during the last couple of years, it had been just the two boys taking these outings. Their parents and relatives had gotten too busy or too old. And the teens were feeling more like they wanted to do things on their own.

But the stomp dance was an activity Billy did only with his grandfather. Besides, Chigger's family wasn't into the "old Indian religion."

The day's competitions ended with Billy and Chigger sharing the third-place prize in the bow-and-arrow event, which gave them each fifty bucks and a trophy with an archer on top. The trophy, it was decided, would live at Billy's house half the year and Chigger's house the other half.

But in the blowgun contest, nobody could beat or even match Billy Buckhorn. He took first place, ahead of Cherokee men of every age. He got to keep that two-hundred-dollar prize and trophy all to himself.

Chigger came in fourth place, just out of the prize money—again. He was almost sure that Billy had some secret skill he'd learned from his grandpa that made him so good at the blowgun. Like a sixth sense or something.

Or maybe the elder Buckhorn had blessed his grandson with a special magic spell. The conjurations in a medicine man's collection could be used to harm or help others, but Wesley only performed his "doctoring" to help others. *Helping his own grandson hit blowgun targets is in the realm of possibilities*, Chigger thought.

"Someday you'll have to tell me your winning blowgun secret," Chigger said.

"Someday, maybe I will," Billy said with a smile. "Someday."

"It's a good thing we're on the same team for Monday's fishing tournament," Chigger said as the boys parted ways at the end of the day.

"Good thing," Billy echoed.

CHAPTER 2

The Thunders Speak

As Billy waited at dusk on the front porch for his grand-father to pick him up, the teen remembered one of the things the elder had told him repeatedly. "The world doesn't operate the way most people think it does," Wesley would say. "We shouldn't cling too tightly to our notions of reality." Billy had never gotten a precise explanation for this statement, but he was sure it must be true. His grandfather said so.

Wesley arrived at seven to pick up his grandson, and they headed toward the Live Oak ceremonial dance grounds several miles south of town. The Cherokee stomp dance grounds were hidden away from outsiders. No billboards or directional signs pointed the way. Only those who belonged within the circle attended.

The Cherokee stomp dance was a very old ceremony practiced by Billy's people, and other neighboring tribes, for centuries. The sacred fire was at the center of the event. It was built within an outdoor fireplace constructed of large logs pointed in the four directions. Each of the seven original Cherokee stomp grounds was known for something special. Live Oak, one of only two grounds still in use, was known for putting people in touch with their ancestors.

The singers and dancers circled that fire all night, singing songs that honored elements of nature and the spirit force behind all of creation. The seven Cherokee clans were represented within the ceremonial grounds by seven brush arbors that encircled the dancers and the central fire.

Billy and Wesley arrived before the dancing began. As a known medicine man of the Red Paint Clan, the elder took his traditional seat in his clan's arbor. Since the age of thirteen, Billy had joined his grandpa in that arbor and was accepted as a member of the same clan. He took his usual seat next to his grandpa.

Clan membership was usually determined by what clan your mother belonged to. Billy should have been a member of the Wolf Clan because his mother was of that clan. And the mother's brothers were usually in charge of teaching a boy the Cherokee ways. But Billy's mother's brother was a Baptist church leader and not involved in the old-style ceremonies. So Wesley had taken over Billy's lessons in tribal traditions.

These days not many teens took part in the ceremonial dances. Billy was one of the very few. Most were busy with their social lives and interested in the same things non-Native teens were interested in. It was just one of the many ways Billy was different from others his age.

When the night sky had become good and dark, the call for the first round of dancing went out all over the camp. Unlike a powwow, where a drum group provides both the singing and the beat, a stomp dance's rhythm comes from the turtle shell rattles worn by the women dancers. Rows of these rattles, tied to pieces of leather about the size of a cowboy boot, are strapped to each woman's legs just above the ankle. Small pebbles within the shells create a rainlike rattle sound with each step a dancer takes.

Billy fell into line behind the circle of dancers as they moved around the center fire. The song leader at the head of the circle sang out the song's first line. The dancers who followed repeated his words like an echo. Thus began the pattern that would last all night.

After a few songs, Wesley joined the dancers, in spite of his bad knee. Throughout the night, singers and dancers drank an herbal tea prepared by stomp dance leaders. That mixture included natural medicines that kept muscles from cramping while also helping the dancers stay awake.

After midnight, the ancestor spirits began arriving. They'd been called from their resting place in the land of the dead to the west, according to tribal teachings. Though not visible to everyone, some of those spirits took their places in the line of dancers. Others found room in the arbors, each according to their clan. In that way, the spirits of the living and the spirits of the dead were connected.

By about two o'clock in the morning, Billy was feeling strange. Leaving the spiraling circle of dancers, he took a seat in the Red Paint Clan arbor and closed his eyes. Soon he entered the trance-like state of mind that was part of the ceremony. This was when it was possible to have a vision or receive messages from ancestor spirits. Each person's experience, if they had such an experience, was their own.

It wasn't long before an image appeared in Billy's mind. He was on a ladder that led into a low set of glowing clouds just above him. He counted a total of thirteen rungs on the ladder, and he stood on the third rung from the bottom.

As he looked at the ladder, the fourth rung began to glow. It seemed to be inviting him to step up to it. As he began to take that step, the ladder shook. The movement caused him to miss the next rung, and he fell. He woke up from the vision as he hit the ground next to the seat he'd been sitting in.

At about the same time, but unknown to Billy, Wesley was having a vision of his own. The spirit of his beloved wife, Awinita, appeared to be standing in the middle of the fire. That was the vision he'd hoped he would have, and she appeared only to him. She reached her arms out toward Wesley and spoke to him in his mind.

This is what he heard.

"Strange changes are afoot, because an ancient evil has returned to the Cherokee Nation. An evil that must be defeated and removed. You are much too old and crippled to face this alone, Wesley. Therefore, Billy must be called on sooner than expected. But he will need your help to take the big step before him so that he may, in turn, help the Nation."

Then, with great energy, she sent a wave of love directly into her husband's heart. The power of that wave caused the old man to pass out. He fell to the ground within the circling line of dancers a few feet from the fire. Without pomp or fanfare, several nearby Cherokees turned, picked him up, and carried him back to his arbor.

Billy was just coming out of his trance as they brought his grandfather in and laid him on a bench. One of the men told Billy what had happened. One of the women placed a rolled-up towel under Wesley's head to make him more comfortable.

Billy knelt beside his elder and replayed the ladder vision in his mind so he wouldn't forget it.

Wesley began to stir. He opened his eyes and found Billy at his side. "Your grandma put in an appearance and told me strange changes are afoot," he said with a smile. "Her message was mostly about you and the future of our tribe."

Billy had not expected to be part of his grandma's message to Wesley. "I had a vision as well," he said.

Each told the other of his vision. Each sat in wonder at what they'd experienced.

"What does it all mean?" Billy asked.

"Only time will tell," Wesley replied. "Nature will give us a sign over the next few days that will confirm these messages. We'll just have to wait and watch. Now, to give thanks to the spirits for what has been revealed to us, we must go back to the fire and resume dancing."

"Where's your cane, Grandpa?" Billy asked as he helped the elder to his feet.

"It's leaning over there in the corner. But I won't need it until morning when the ceremony is over."

With that, the pair joined in the next round of dances. Billy's mind raced with questions, but he knew that only patience and time would reveal the answers. He and his grandpa danced until dawn.

Luckily, Sunday had been planned as a day off. The teen needed the day to rest after the all-night dance, and that's what he did most of the day—rest.

Monday, the Labor Day holiday, was the day of the fishing contest. At the crack of dawn, Billy was up and had his skiff hitched to his pickup. His fishing gear was already loaded in the boat. Chigger arrived around six thirty with his fishing gear.

"I made some biscuits and gravy for you boys," Billy's mother said as she came out of the house, carrying a paper sack. "You need to eat a hearty breakfast to keep up your strength today."

"Thanks, Ma," Billy replied, taking the sack and giving her a little peck on the cheek. "Chigger also brought some dried deer jerky, so we won't go hungry."

She almost told them to be careful as they jumped in the truck to leave. She held her tongue though, knowing that sixteen-year-old boys don't want to hear a mother's concerns. But Mrs. Buckhorn was definitely feeling some sense of worry as she watched the pair head out. *What is that about?* she wondered, but she had no clue.

Earlier that morning, Billy had done his usual pre-fishing check of the weather and found a typical forecast for a late summer day: a high of eighty-nine degrees and a fifty-fifty chance of late afternoon thunderstorms. As he drove toward the lake, the teen scanned the western skies, the direction thunderstorms would be coming from, and found them cloudless. *Let's hope that holds,* he thought.

About two dozen Cherokee fishermen had registered for the contest that morning at Cherokee Landing State Park at the tip of Wildcat Point. Cash prizes would be given for the most fish caught, the largest fish caught, and the smallest fish caught. That last category was included to get younger fishermen to compete.

Billy and Grandpa had won a little prize money in previous contests for either the largest fish or most fish caught. This was Billy's first year to do it without his grandfather, and he kind of missed seeing the old man that morning. At the same time, he felt okay about fishing the contest on the lake with Chigger.

Promptly at eight o'clock, the contest began. Boats sped off in every direction as each team of anglers headed for their favorite spot on the lake. The competition would end at six in the evening. Anyone who hadn't returned to the main dock by that time would be disqualified.

Billy and Chigger headed southwest toward an inlet that on a map looked like the head and mouth of a wolf in profile. He couldn't figure out why no one had named it Wolf's Head Inlet or Wolf's Mouth Bay. It was a place where he and Wesley had caught many a fish.

As the motorized skiff skated across the water, Billy's thoughts once again turned to stories he'd heard from Wesley in years past. Bodies of water such as ponds, lakes, and rivers were doorways to the Underworld, according to the ancient beliefs of the Cherokee. Dangerous and powerful creatures inhabited those regions, regions also accessible through deep underground caverns.

Billy's professor father had corroborated Wesley's recounting of the matter.

"The ancient Inca, Maya, and Aztec peoples of Central and South America all believed that the Underworld was the repository of souls, along with powerful beings that had to be honored and placated," he'd explained once. "Even the Greeks and Hebrews had their own versions of this belief."

A flash of early-morning sunlight reflecting off the water's surface and into Billy's eyes abruptly brought him a moment of clarity.

Buckhorn, you're not a typical teenager, are you? he thought. *Why do your thoughts continually gravitate toward mythology instead of reality?*

"Chigger, do you think I'm weird?" he asked his friend, whose hand was on the outboard motor's tiller.

The teen pondered the question for a moment before answering. "Unusual, yes. Weird, no. Why do you ask?"

"I just found myself thinking about Grandpa's teachings on the Cherokee Underworld and my father's intellectual theories on the subject instead of the things normal teens like you think about."

"You mean girls, cars, superheroes, and how to get out of doing homework?" Chigger replied honestly.

"Exactly."

"I think you're just fine the way you are, Billy," Chigger said. "Why don't you leave the shallow thinking to me. I do enough of that for both of us."

Billy chuckled at his friend's frankness and said, "I am surprised you didn't bring any comic books to read today for when the fishing gets boring."

Chigger sheepishly opened his backpack and produced a half dozen of the graphic novels.

Billy simply said, "Ah, I should've known," smiled, and turned his gaze toward the lake ahead of them.

"Today, the superhero I'm pretending to be is Fish Catcher, able to call and catch underwater gill-breathers of all weights and sizes!" Chigger said and laughed.

"If that were only true," Billy replied with a smile.

In a matter of about twenty minutes, the fishing duo approached the wolf's head and picked out a spot to drop their first lines. As soon as they hit the spot, they began working the shallow, reedy area with a cane pole. The pair moved along parallel to the shoreline for an hour, only getting an occasional nibble. *We have to change tactics,* Billy thought. *And maybe bait too.*

Switching to rods and reels, the boys tried casting spinner lures just beyond the edge of the reeds. That was what those largemouth bass were looking for. These spinners were made of shiny metal pieces that twisted and turned as they moved through the water.

Billy and Chigger began getting strikes about every other cast. By late morning they had caught a dozen bass of various sizes.

As the sun climbed in the sky, the boys moved farther from the shoreline. They knew that as the water heated up, some of the larger fish would move into deeper, cooler water. They put something called stink bait on their hooks and dropped their lines down about forty feet. That was where the catfish would be hanging out, near the bottom of the lake.

Billy liked the way the day's fishing was going. He and Chigger were pulling in almost as many fish as he and Grandpa had caught together last year.

Won't Grandpa be surprised, he thought.

That was when they heard the first distant thunder. They looked to the west, the direction the rumble had come from. Large thunderclouds were gathering and building. This was a common sight in eastern Oklahoma this time of year and confirmed the weather forecast Billy had seen.

Billy defocused the physical scene before him as he remembered that Cherokee legends told of the great Thunder Beings who lived in the western skies and sometimes visited human beings for both good and mischief. In fact, the Upperworld, the

Sky World, was filled with superbeings far different from those found in European-based folk tales or religious stories.

Give it a rest, Buckhorn, he thought as he refocused his vision on the lake.

"Those tall, flat-bottomed clouds always look like stacks of cotton balls sitting on top of dinner plates," Chigger told Billy, who laughed gratefully at the childlike idea.

Billy checked his pocket watch and saw it was almost three o'clock. Looking up at the clouds again, he noticed they were turning darker and moving rapidly toward them. Just then a bolt of lightning jumped from cloud to cloud.

"Guess we'd better start moving toward the shore," Billy advised. "And get off the water. Don't want to tempt the Thunders."

"I'll drive," Chigger suggested. "You can fish as we go."

Billy nodded his agreement. Before heading toward the shore, the guys put on their lightweight rain ponchos. Chigger started the motor and set it to a slow speed. Then Billy, sitting in the front of the skiff, released a little bit of line from his reel and let it trail behind the boat. Momentarily forgetting the gathering storm clouds, the teen focused on the shiny spinning lure wriggling through the water as it followed behind them.

Suddenly, the wind came up just as a sheet of rain pushed from the shoreline out across the water. It seemed as though thunderclouds had appeared overhead out of nowhere. A flash of lightning burst across the darkened sky, followed immediately by a crash of thunder—a loud crash. The storm was already on top of them.

"We'd better get off the water right now," Chigger yelled over the howling wind and pounding rain. "Pull your line in."

With drops of water splattering in his eyes, Billy began reeling in his metallic spinning lure. Chigger looked across the lake to locate the nearest shoreline. There was a rocky finger of land that jutted out into the water not too far away. He saw other anglers already landing their boats in that area. He had to turn their skiff directly into the wind to reach that point. He'd just made the turn when Billy stood up in the front of the boat, trying to prevent the fishing line from getting tangled in the boat's motor. The unstable move caused the skiff to wobble in the water momentarily.

Chigger was about to tell his friend to sit down and hold on so he could give the boat motor full throttle. But he never got a chance to say or do anything.

All at once a bright flash of light engulfed the boys. At the same time a deafening BOOM washed over them. A single bolt of electricity hit the water near the front of the boat. It raced along the surface of the water and into Billy's metal spinner as he pulled it up out of the water. Then the electric pulse jumped from the spinner to Billy's rod and into the boy's body.

The electric shock ran through Billy's flesh and bones and up into his brain. At that moment, the world around him seemed to switch from positive to negative. Colors reversed themselves. Time shifted into slow motion. Billy had never felt anything like it. Then he blacked out.

The jolt lifted Billy up and threw him backward in the skiff. He landed right on top of Chigger, who was sitting in the back. The force of the impact knocked Chigger out cold and slammed him into the motor's tiller. The steering mechanism's abrupt right-angle change of direction set the boat spinning in a tight circle.

When he woke up, Chigger was in the back of an ambulance. He moaned and looked around. He saw two emergency medical attendants working on Billy, who was lying on a hospital gurney.

"What . . . what happened?" Chigger struggled to ask.

"You'll be all right," one of the attendants said. "I can't say the same for your friend here. He took a direct hit, and he's lucky to be alive. But we've got to get him to the hospital fast."

While in the ambulance, Billy went in and out of consciousness. At one point it felt like his whole body was on fire. At another point it seemed like every muscle in his body had contracted and clinched so tightly he couldn't relax them. And there was that smell. The smell of burning flesh.

After that, Billy slipped into a temporary coma. A strange array of images floated through his mind while he was unconscious. Memories from his childhood, bits of stories his grandpa had told him, a fleeting glimpse of his grandma Awinita, and the ladder he'd seen at the stomp dance. All these images drifted past him or swirled around him as he floated in a sea of darkness. He couldn't tell if it was the darkness of outer space or the darkness of some deep underground world, but it seemed to exist somewhere just out of his knowing.

Billy awoke from the coma a couple of days later and found his mom and dad both there in his hospital room. Someone else seemed to be in the room too, but that someone stayed just out of view. It was more like Billy felt his presence rather than saw him. It was certainly a him, though.

"Oh, Billy, you had us so worried," his mother said. She was wearing her nurse's uniform. "I'm so glad I was on duty when they brought you in."

She checked the digital screen on one of the machines that stood near Billy's bed.

"Glad to see you're back, son," his father said as he approached from the other side of the bed. "We've kept watch over you twenty-four hours a day for two days."

"Where's Grandpa?" Billy asked.

"Your grandpa was here earlier, but we sent him home to get some rest," his mother replied. "He said to call him when you woke up."

Billy's mouth was dry, and he began smacking his lips. Noticing that her son was thirsty, Mrs. Buckhorn grabbed the glass of water sitting on a tray table beside the bed. She held the glass close to him, and he sipped water through the straw. As he drank, he realized he didn't even know why he was in the hospital.

"What happened?" he asked after swallowing a big sip. "I don't remember."

"A group of people standing on the shore saw you get hit by a bolt of lightning," his dad reported. "They jumped in their boat and sped out to get you and Chigger."

"One of them called here to the hospital, and we sent out an ambulance," his mother added.

"Chigger. What about Chigger?" Billy was more awake now.

"He's just fine," Billy's father answered. "The lightning didn't hit him, but he's at home taking it easy for a couple of days."

Then Billy's mother gave his dad a funny look. He nodded to her.

"Billy, there's something I need to prepare you for," his mother said. "You have burn patterns in a couple of places left there by the lightning."

"Burn patterns?" the boy asked. "What kind of burn patterns?"

His mother opened a nearby cabinet and pulled out a hand mirror. She returned to the bed and pulled back the sheet that covered Billy's right hand. For the first time, he saw that a bandage covered the back of his hand.

Then she held up the mirror for him to see that there was a larger, similar bandage on the side of his neck. He reached up and touched the neck bandage.

"Why don't I feel any pain here?" he asked as he probed the burn areas.

"We've covered both places with numbing medicine," his mother answered. "When the doctor comes in to check on you, he'll let you see the burns."

"Okay," Billy said, gently rubbing the bandage on his hand.

"Now that I know you're all right, I have to get back to the college," his dad said, placing a hand on his son's shoulder. "A substitute has been filling in for me. I'll check in on you this evening."

As his father left the room, Billy's doctor stepped in and moved toward the bed. He was an Anglo man in his fifties, wearing a white coat and dark-rimmed glasses.

"I'm Dr. Jackson," the man said, extending his hand. Billy reached out to shake it. The doctor shook Billy's hand gently and then turned it sideways to look at the bandage. "Did your mother tell you about the burn marks?"

"She said there was some kind of pattern," Billy replied. "Can I see it?"

"Sure," the doctor replied. He carefully pulled back one side of the gauze on the back of Billy's hand to reveal a red pattern that looked a little like a cross between a spiderweb and a tree branch. Jagged red lines, like bicycle spokes, radiated out from a dark red spot in the center. Sets of finer red lines connected all the spokes.

"They're known as fractal patterns," the doctor said. "You see them occurring in nature quite often, as well as on victims of lightning strikes."

As Billy stared at the markings on his hand, Dr. Jackson pulled back the bandage on the side of his patient's neck. Billy's mother handed the mirror to the doctor, and he held it up for Billy to see. A larger version of the branching pattern spread across his neck.

"Oh my god!" Billy blurted. "I look like a freak."

"Young man, you're lucky to be alive," the doctor said. "And until the burns heal, we won't know how visible the scars will be."

"Scars?" Mrs. Buckhorn said with motherly concern. "There'll be scars?"

"I'm afraid so," the doctor confirmed. He turned to Billy's mom. "Nurse, I think it's time for your patient to eat something and get some rest. Would you mind calling down to the kitchen and asking them to send up a tray of food?"

"Sure thing, Doctor," Billy's mother replied in a very businesslike fashion. She stepped out to go to the nurses' station to order some food.

"How bad do you think the scarring will be?" Billy asked Dr. Jackson after his mother had gone.

"As I said, you're lucky to be alive. And you'll always have these markings as a reminder of that. I wouldn't worry too much about the scars."

The doctor checked Billy's medical chart, which hung from a clip on the end of his bed.

"All your vital signs look good," he said, returning the chart to its place. He then stepped back to the side of Billy's bed and said reassuringly, "Looks like you're healing just fine. I'll check in on you later."

He left, and Billy was alone in the room. Well, almost alone. He could still "feel" that someone else was around.

"Who's there?" he called out.

There was no answer.

"I know you're in here. I can't see you, but I can feel you."

"If I show myself, will you promise not to freak out?" the small voice of a man asked.

"If you don't show yourself, I'll call the nurse to come in here and chase you out," Billy answered. "I'm going to count to three. One. Two—"

"Just like when you were a little kid," the voice said as a small Native American man stepped out from under Billy's bed.

The man was only about two feet tall and had a long braid of black hair. He wore a pair of fringed leather pants and moccasins. A look of shock spread across Billy's face at the sight of him.

"You've really lost it now, Buckhorn," Billy said to himself in a whisper.

"No you haven't," the little man said. "Remember? Your mother would count to three before making you go to bed at night or eat your vegetables."

"You're not real," Billy stated firmly. "My father said there was no such thing as Little People. That was just an ancient myth—a way to explain odd things. The Irish have leprechauns and the Cherokee have Little People."

"That's not what you told Chigger the other day," the little man replied. "What happened to the idea that there was a deeper truth beneath the legends?"

"How do you know about that?"

"I know a lot about you, and it hurts me deeply that you don't remember me," the little man said. "You don't remember the times we spent exploring the woods behind your house when you were five years old?"

When he said that, a mental image flashed in Billy's mind. He was out in the woods behind the old frame house where he used to live. A game of hide-and-seek was underway. Billy was hiding in a big pile of fallen leaves. A voice called out.

"Come out, come out, wherever you are!"

As the mental movie played on, the leaves parted, and the five-year-old Billy was looking out at a face. The face of the little Indian man who now stood in his hospital room.

"Now I remember," the sixteen-year-old Billy blurted out. "Little Wolf, is it really you?"

"Bingo, Billy!" the little man said excitedly. "You remembered!"

"But I thought I had imagined you," the teen said with confusion in his voice.

"It happens all the time," Little Wolf said. "Kids grow up, lose interest, and forget about their childhood pals. It's because, as you get older, you spend less and less time in your mind and more and more time in the outside world."

"Then why am I seeing you now?"

"Things have changed," Little Wolf replied. "You have changed."

"Because of the lightning?"

"Because of the lightning," Little Wolf confirmed. "And because of who you are becoming."

"What do you mean by that?"

Just then the door to his room opened. Billy looked up to see his mother bringing in a tray of food. He looked back down to where Little Wolf had been standing. The little man was gone.

"Who are you talking to?" Billy's mother asked as she set the tray down on the mobile table beside his bed.

"Ah, no one," Billy said. "I'm in here alone."

"Oh, I thought I heard you talking to someone," she said, wheeling the food within Billy's reach. "Are you okay?"

"Yeah, sure," Billy said and then took a bite of lunch. "Why wouldn't I be?"

"People have some strange experiences after being hit by lightning," she said, checking the monitor beside the bed. "It takes the brain a while to fully recover from the electric shock. People have reported weird visions and odd dreams."

"That's good to know," Billy said, not willing to admit his own experience. "I'll let you know if anything like that comes up."

"Good," his mother replied. "After you've finished lunch, another doctor, Dr. Abramson, will come to visit with you."

"Another doctor?" the teen said, continuing to eat. "What's this one do?"

"Um, he's someone you can talk to if you need it," she replied.

After she left, Billy looked around the room. He leaned over far enough to check under his bed. No sign of Little Wolf. He was able to eat his lunch in peace.

A couple of minutes after he'd finished his food and rolled his table away, the door to his room opened again. In stepped an older man with gray hair like Albert Einstein's. He wore a lab coat and wire-rimmed glasses. Billy expected the guy to talk with a German accent, but he didn't. He was British.

"Young man, I'm Dr. Abramson," he said, extending his hand. Billy reached out with his bandaged hand, and the man gently shook his fingertips.

"Are you a shrink?" Billy asked.

"Yes, but don't worry, I don't think you're mentally ill," he said with a smile and a twinkle in his eye. "Not yet anyway."

"My mother said you're someone I could talk to *if* I needed it."

"Anytime during your recovery here or later at home, you can give me a call, and we can have a confidential conversation. How does that sound?"

"Good," Billy replied.

"Good," the doctor said, then he handed the boy his business card and exited the room.

Alone again, Billy scanned the room one more time, searching for signs of Little Wolf. Still gone. But he was starting to remember other things about his childhood friend. One thing was that no one but Billy could see him. He and Billy would be playing together outside, and one of Billy's parents would come find him. But they could never see Little Wolf, even though the little Indian might be standing right next to him.

Of course, now that Billy thought of it, they'd always been outside. Never inside. And there had been a couple of times when Little Wolf had said they should go somewhere else to play. One time they'd moved to the other side of the house just before a dead tree fell right where they'd been playing. Billy would've been crushed.

Another time Little Wolf told Billy he should go inside. A few minutes later a mountain lion was seen prowling in their backyard. That had to be more than chance. Could an imaginary friend do those things? The answer to that question would have to wait. Memories of the little man made Billy sleepy. Soon he was fast asleep in the middle of the afternoon.

CHAPTER 3

The Birdman

Billy was released from the hospital a few days later. He told no one about the return of Little Wolf, at first hoping it was one of the aftereffects of the lightning his mother had spoken about. Yet almost everywhere Billy went, he thought he saw the little Indian lurking in a corner or peering out from behind a bush.

The main outward reminders of Billy's encounter with lightning were the scars that had formed on the back of his hand and the side of his neck. The weblike fractal pattern had not faded. Dr. Jackson had explained that the center points were the places where the electricity had entered Billy's body. If you didn't know better, you'd think they were tattoos with ragged edges. They gave him a kind of eerie look.

When Grandpa Wesley saw the weblike scars on his grandson, he said, "What could be more perfect?"

"What's so perfect about them?" Billy asked. "I look like I belong in a freak show."

"Have you forgotten that it was Water Spider who brought Fire to the Cherokee people?" Grandpa asked.

Grandpa must have told him a hundred times the story of how Fire came to humans. In the beginning of the world, the only ones who had Fire were the Thunders, who lived up beyond the sky. One day they sent Lightning down to a tree in the center of an island, and that's where Fire began on earth. All the animals wanted to go get the Fire and bring it to the mainland for everyone to use. Many animals tried and failed. It was the lowly Water Spider who cleverly devised a way to bring Fire across the water for all to use.

"So it looks like the Thunder Beings sent Fire again to the Cherokee people through you," Grandpa said. "Maybe it's a sign the spirits are ready for you to take the next steps on your medicine journey. It seems you'll be aided by supernatural powers on that journey."

This left Billy speechless.

"Why me?" he eventually asked. "I'm nobody special."

"Who knows?" Grandpa responded. "Maybe you are."

While Billy was home recovering, his grandfather wasn't his only visitor. He was, of course, thrilled to see Chigger, who came by most days after school.

"I can see it now!" the boy said one day as he burst into Billy's bedroom. "They'll print a comic book about you as some kind of action hero with superpowers. I know—you could electrocute your enemies by shooting lightning bolts from your fingers!"

"Honestly, Chigger, that's the worst idea you've ever had," Billy said and meant it.

Ignoring his friend's response, the comic book enthusiast continued. "What could your name be? Most of the good ones about electricity and lightning are already taken. But you'd have to be a Native superhero. There aren't enough of those."

Billy could see his friend was really fired up, so he let him carry on a little longer. Meanwhile, the subject of this superhero fantasy closed his eyes and tried to block out the chattering noise.

Less thrilling was the visit Uncle John paid him the following day. Billy's mother escorted her brother into Billy's bedroom, then went back to the kitchen to make the man some iced tea. When the preacher was sure his sister was out of hearing range, he spoke in a loud whisper.

"I warned you not to go to that stomp dance, didn't I?" he said. "Well, this is God's punishment on you, boy."

Billy remained silent.

The man took Billy's hand in his and pointed to the scars. "And now you have the mark of the beast for all to see!" His voice was no longer a whisper. He put a hand on Billy's head. "Get down on your knees and beg for forgiveness!" he shouted loud enough for Billy's mother to hear. She rushed to Billy's room.

"All right, that's it," she said angrily to her brother. "It's time for you to leave."

"I'm only trying to save this house from the wrath of the Almighty," the pastor protested. "Repent and ye *shall* be saved!"

"Leave or I *shall* call the police," Billy's mother said.

Her brother looked at her in disbelief.

"You have sealed your own fate," he said and left.

"I'm so sorry for that," Billy's mother said as she sat on his bed. She hugged her son. "He's gone too far and won't be invited back."

"Thanks, Mom," Billy said and closed his eyes. "I'm exhausted now."

She left the room so her son could rest.

A week after the lightning strike, the doctor said Billy could go back to school. His first day back was kind of weird. Students gathered in groups in the hallways, whispering and staring whenever he walked by. Some teachers did the same thing. You might've thought he'd just landed from outer space.

The school's Cherokee principal, Mr. Sixkiller, noticed how disruptive this behavior was and decided to quiet everyone down so they could get on with the business of learning.

"You have no doubt noticed that Billy Buckhorn is back in school after his horrific accident," he said during morning notices heard on speakers all over the school. "He is lucky to be alive, and we're lucky to have him back. I want everyone here at Tahlequah High School to make him feel welcome back in our community."

That helped a little. Not so many students stood around gawking as he walked by. A few actually greeted him and shook his hand. That was when they got close enough to see the burn scars and backed away.

That's just great, Billy thought. *Now I'm a social outcast.*

At least he and Chigger had gym class together. When they got to the gym that afternoon, they learned that a substitute teacher had taken over the class.

"My name is Mr. Ravenwood," the substitute said as he stood in front of the thirty or so boys in the class. He was a tall, thin white man with longish jet-black hair. Billy thought his slightly hooked nose made him look like a bird.

"Your original gym teacher, Mr. Wildcat, suddenly got sick last week and won't be able to return for several weeks," the man continued. "I was happy to fill in on short notice. I did a little coaching with the Eastern Cherokees in North Carolina, so I am familiar with your tribe."

Billy took an instant dislike to the man. He didn't know why, but something about the guy bothered him.

"Did you get a weird vibe from the new gym teacher?" he asked Chigger after class.

"Not really," his friend answered. "He just kinda looks like a stork or something."

Having missed a week of school, Billy had quite a bit of reading and homework to do to get caught up. He didn't have time for much else during the next few days. By the middle of the week, he felt dazed and overworked. He studied for his first math test until after midnight on Wednesday.

Then he fell asleep sitting at the desk next to his bed. He'd rested his head on his open algebra book. When he woke up the next morning, he had a terrible neck ache. But there was something else he woke up with. He understood everything in the chapter he'd been struggling with. He wasn't sure how that had happened.

That day's math test actually turned out to be easy for him. He was the first one in class to finish it. That had never happened before.

"I didn't realize that high school would be so much harder than middle school," Chigger told Billy later that day. "The homework is killing me. When are we ever going to have time for anything else?"

"What do you think I'm going through?" Billy replied. "I have a whole week's extra work to catch up on." He didn't say anything about acing his math test. He was sure it was a fluke.

That night he needed to study for his first history test. He had a theory he wanted to try out, so he did all his other homework first. On purpose, he didn't look at his history lesson. Then, when it was bedtime, he opened his history textbook to the chapter he needed to study. He placed the book on top of his pillow and laid his head down on it. It was a little uncomfortable, but if his experiment worked, the discomfort would be worth it. There he slept all night.

He woke up with a clear head, a sore neck, and a good feeling about his history lesson. And when it came time for the exam, it was like a repeat of the math test. He cruised through it and finished first.

Wow, he thought. *What's going on here? Whatever it is, I think I like it!*

What he didn't like, though, was what was going on in gym. It seemed that Mr. Ravenwood often gave Billy long, strange looks. It was like he was studying the sixteen-year-old. Then, when he realized that Billy might have noticed the long stare, the teacher quickly looked away. Or was it all just in the teen's mind?

Billy thought too many strange things had been happening since the lightning strike. He decided it was time to check in with his grandfather to see if he had any idea of what might be going on. He headed to the old man's house that Saturday morning.

As was usual on a Saturday, a group of Natives sat on Wesley's front porch or in their cars parked in front of the house. They were among the hundreds of people who came to get doctored by the old medicine man on a regular basis.

Cherokee medicine people were known for fixing more than physical ailments. They also had spells and herbs to attract a mate, to provide safety when traveling, to rid a neighborhood of a bad influence, and to protect oneself from a curse—a curse cast by a malevolent medicine maker.

Yes, among the Cherokee and other tribes there were those rare individuals who used—or rather misused—their powers and abilities to do harm, often after being paid by someone. Many cultures called such men and women witches, sorcerers, or conjurers–whatever you called them, they were a bad bunch. And thankfully, there weren't many left, at least not many that the general tribal public knew about.

Billy worked his way past the people on Wesley's steps and porch and went inside. After checking some of the front rooms, he found his grandfather out back gathering herbs to help his patients. Down on all fours, the elderly man was pulling up some roots.

"You have to go deeper and deeper into the woods these days to find many of these medicines," Wesley said as Billy stepped into the garden. "All the houses, roads, and buildings disturb the natural order of things."

After brushing off most of the dirt from the root he'd just pulled up, the elder took a small bite of the brown tuber. Almost immediately he spit it out.

"This one's not ready yet," he said, spitting a couple more times and wiping his mouth with his shirt sleeve.

Needing help to stand up, the elder reached out his arm to Billy. The boy grabbed the wrinkled brown hand and gently but firmly pulled. As his grandpa got up, Billy thought he saw Little Wolf out of the corner of his eye. He was hiding behind a row of sunflowers. But when the boy looked again, the little man was gone.

"It's a busy morning," Wesley said, brushing the dirt from his clothes. "I need an able helper more with each passing day. Can you stay awhile?"

"Sure, Grandpa," Billy said. "But I need to talk to you first."

"Okay. Let me take these herbs to Mr. Hummingbird and tell him how to use them," Wesley said as he headed back toward the house. "Then I'll pour us a cup of coffee and we can talk."

"As long as you have donuts or fry bread to go with it," Billy said with a smile.

While Wesley was gone, Billy poured them each a cup of coffee and found a couple of not-quite-stale donuts that he put on plates. After taking the herbs to the front porch, Wesley returned to the kitchen. Then the two sat down for a serious talk.

"Stuff has been going on since the lightning," Billy began. "Stuff I can't explain."

"That's to be expected," Grandpa said after taking a sip of coffee. "You've entered a new phase of your medicine path. But I may not be able to help you with it much now."

"Why's that?"

"I wasn't chosen by the Thunders," he said. "You were. And I don't have the lightning gifts, but you do. In some tribes, people struck by lightning go on to become weather wizards, able to control clouds and throw thunderbolts."

"Wow!"

"But it takes extra training from a medicine person trained in such things," Wesley added. "Now tell me what's been going on with you. I might at least be able to point you in the right direction."

"Do you remember my childhood friend Little Wolf?" Billy asked after taking a bite of donut.

"Sure I do," Grandpa answered. "If you remember, your grandma and I were the only ones who believed he was real."

"He's back," Billy said. "First he appeared to me in my hospital room. Since then he's been showing up in random places. I just saw him now at the edge of your garden."

"The Little People have made themselves visible to you again," Grandpa said. "That's a very good sign. Now I can tell you the rest of that story."

"What?"

"Little Wolf has been one of my medicine helpers since before you were born," Wesley replied. "In fact, he first appeared to your grandma right out there in that garden when we were doctoring people together. We sent Little Wolf to you for your own safety."

"Really? Why didn't you tell me this before?"

"Sometimes it's best to let these things unfold naturally," Grandpa answered. "Things need to be revealed in their own good time. What other stuff has been happening?"

"I know this will sound weird," Billy said, "but I can sleep on top of my schoolbooks, and when I wake up the next morning, I've learned the lesson for that day."

"That's a new one on me," Wesley admitted. "I'll have to look in my old files to see if anything like that was recorded in the pages of the *Tsalagi Nuwodhi Digohweili, The Cherokee Book of Medicine Spells and Formulas*. That's what the old ones called the original pages, handwritten in the Cherokee alphabet. I inherited an unbound copy of the pages from your great-grandfather. All medicine people have made handwritten copies for themselves. It's part of our ancient sacred knowledge."

As he listened, Billy took another couple of sips of his coffee and a bite of his donut. That gave him time to think about what he was going to say next.

"The last thing is something that's going on at school," he began. "There's a substitute teacher who took over gym classes—a white man, Mr. Ravenwood. He just moved here."

"So? There are plenty of non-Indians working at the school."

"I got a bad feeling about him the very first time I saw him," Billy said. "And he looks at me funny. He doesn't really talk to me, but something just doesn't seem right about the man." He paused and shook his head. "I must be seeing things. No one else seems to think there's anything wrong."

"Don't do that to yourself," Wesley advised. "Don't dismiss your intuition, your inner feelings about a situation. You must learn to trust those instincts more and more. They will grow stronger and seem more real."

Wesley paused to think and drink more coffee.

"If something doesn't feel right to you, then we can't ignore it," he added. "Remember your grandma's message to me at the stomp dance? Something evil has come into the Nation from somewhere outside. We have to keep our insight turned on so we'll recognize it when we see it. Who knows what form it takes?"

"You think that might have something to do with this new teacher?" Billy asked.

"Maybe so, maybe not," Grandpa answered. "We can't rule anything out at this point, so listen to your inner voice. And allow Little Wolf to help you out if he offers."

Billy sat in silence for a moment, taking in all this new information.

"Speaking of the medicine book," Wesley said as he rose from his chair, "I've got something for you."

He headed down the hallway toward one of the back bedrooms. The old wooden floor creaked with his every step. Momentarily he returned carrying two books of different sizes. He placed the larger one in front of his grandson.

"This is my copy of the book of spells and formulas, written by my own hand in Sequoyah's syllabary," Wesley said.

Billy was surprised by its appearance. He had pictured a big thick book bound in leather, maybe with some sort of lock to keep prying eyes from seeing the pages. Instead, it was dozens of aging lined pages stapled together, with a red cover depicting a Native American man along with the words *Big Chief Writing Tablet*.

Its pages were filled with handwritten rows of Cherokee writing, with little extra notations in some of the margins. He was still taking it all in as Wesley placed the second, smaller book down on the table next to the larger one. This one was a brand-new booklet with the words *Composition Notebook* on the front. It was filled with about fifty empty lined pages, similar to ones he'd seen older students use for taking notes in class.

"What's this notebook for?" Billy asked.

"For practice," Grandpa said. "It's time for you to begin learning the formulas, memorizing the syllabary, and writing the spells. It all eventually leads to the creation of your own copy of the spell book. And you'll be helping keep the language alive."

"Ugh," Billy grunted with a grimace.

"You can also use it for a journal," Wesley continued. "It'll be good for you to take notes about people you help me treat, what herbs are used, what words are spoken. It'll all come in handy when you begin doctoring people on your own."

Billy blew out a blast of air. "I already have enough homework as it is without you adding on more."

He pushed the two books off to the side. Wesley gave the teen a disapproving look.

"One more thing you need to keep in mind," the elder said as he scooted the books back in front of his grandson. "As important as the written formulas are, the words mean nothing without the spirit of the healer behind them." Grandpa punctuated each word with a sharp tap on the Big Chief tablet cover. "As a medicine person, you give the words their power when your mind is focused and your breath is filled with spirit."

Billy blew out another breath. Then a thought struck his brain, and a small smile emerged on his face.

"Let me sleep on it," the boy said as he stacked the composition notebook on top of the medicine book. He gulped down the last bit of coffee and stuffed the rest of the donut in his mouth.

Wesley, likewise, took the final sip of his coffee and said, "Back to work. Will you go out and ask Mrs. Deer-In-Water to come in so we can see what's ailing her?"

Billy was glad to get out of his own head for the rest of the day. Helping other people, being of service, was a good way to do that, Grandpa always said. He pushed his grandfather's homework assignment out of his mind.

Word of the boy who'd survived a lightning strike began to spread like wildfire throughout eastern Oklahoma—especially after the news story appeared in the local daily newspaper, the *Tahlequah Sun*. A photographer from that paper had sneaked into Billy's hospital room. He'd taken a photo of the weblike burn marks on his neck and hand. Billy was asleep at the time and didn't know someone had snapped the photo until it appeared in print.

Other area newspapers ran similar stories in the days and weeks that followed. At the end of September, a long feature story appeared in the Sunday edition of Tulsa's daily newspaper, the *Tulsa World*. Some people called Billy's survival a miracle. Others, after seeing the scars, called it demonic, as Billy's uncle had.

"Ignore the news stories," Billy's father said. "It's just media hype designed to sell newspapers and keep people's eyeballs glued to social media. It will all be forgotten in a couple of weeks."

Billy hoped his father was right.

Back in school the following week, Billy started noticing something else strange going on. It happened when he touched people, shook their hand, or patted them on the back. A series of images flashed in his mind. Sometimes the images were in black and white. Other times they were in color. The pictures formed a quick little movie starring that person. It even happened when a person handed him something. If both his and the other person's hands touched the object at the same time, the movie started.

A girl Billy barely knew dropped a book near him. He reached down to pick it up for her. When he handed the book to her, his hand brushed hers by accident. Quickly he saw a black-and-white picture in his head. She was being slapped across the face by a boy at school. It stunned Billy for a moment.

Later, his English teacher was returning graded papers to students in class. She and Billy both had a hold on his paper for a brief instant. The color image that flashed in his mind showed her arguing with a man, another teacher, in the parking lot.

The images came and went quickly. But the flash of each movie passed through Billy like a mini-jolt of lightning. It caused him to jerk and stop what he was doing.

But in gym class Billy got the biggest mini-jolt of all. Mr. Ravenwood passed out basketball jerseys to the boys in the class. He handed one to Billy without looking at him. Billy took it directly from the man's hand, and a black-and-white image flashed in the boy's mind.

The gym teacher was in a darkened room. He stood over a teenage Native girl. She was screaming as Ravenwood gagged her mouth. In a quick flash, Billy saw the teacher's face, and he looked just like a bird—a raven.

The image was so abrupt and shocking that it caused Billy to drop the jersey on the floor. Once the item left his hand, the movie stopped running in his mind.

"I hope you can hold on to the ball better than that, Lightning Boy," the teacher said in a gruff tone. "Now pick it up."

The teacher continued to hand out the shirts, but Billy didn't want to pick up the article of clothing. It seemed to be poisoned. Poisoned by the picture in Billy's head.

What's going on, Billy thought. *Am I losing it? Did the electricity scramble my brain?*

Billy finally got up enough courage to tell his parents and his best friend about the strange thing happening to him. Each had a different reaction.

His father said, "That both fascinates and worries me. It reminds me of the strange case of Bearpaw Perkins a hundred years ago. According to papers in the college archives, he was struck by lightning up on Wild Horse Mountain."

"What happened to him?" Billy asked.

"Eyewitnesses claimed he went on to become a famous medicine man. But later they said he was taken by aliens."

"Right, Pops," Billy said as he went to see what his mother might say.

"It's probably just a medical condition that will eventually go away," she said at first. But after a few moments of thought, she placed her hand on his forehead to see if he had a fever. Then she shined a small flashlight in his eyes to see if his pupils dilated like they should.

"No signs of concussion or brain swelling," she observed. "We could make an appointment with Dr. Abramson, if you'd like to talk about what's going on."

"No thanks, Mom. I'm not a nut case."

So much for guidance from the professor and the nurse. Billy hoped Chigger would be more open to listening and giving him helpful feedback.

"That's the coolest thing I've ever heard," Chigger exclaimed. "You didn't like my comic book superhero idea, but with all the publicity you've been getting, you could have your own reality TV show in no time!"

"Chigger, this is serious stuff," Billy scolded. "I don't want a lot of people knowing about this. It makes me sound crazy."

"Sorry," Chigger replied. "I get carried away."

"I'm trying to figure out why some of the images I see are black and white and why some are in color," Billy said with a serious tone. "Maybe the black-and-white images show things that have already happened. The color images might be future events. What do you think?"

"I think WOW," Chigger said. "My best friend can sleep on his books to study for tests. He can see the past and predict the future. Can I be your manager? This is gonna be big!"

"You're getting carried away again," Billy reminded him. "I told you I don't want any attention."

Secretly, the teen had agreed earlier with his mom when she suggested an appointment with the shrink. But Billy didn't want the world to know of his interaction with the guy, including the world of his own family or his talkative best friend.

That night Billy worked up the courage to call Dr. Abramson from the phone extension in the hall near his room. The teen was realizing it could be helpful to talk to someone outside his usual circle of family and friends. As cover, he told his parents he'd be on the phone getting help with homework assignments he'd missed while in the hospital.

Unfortunately, Billy only got the doc's voicemail. So he left a message.

"Doc, this is Billy Buckhorn," he said. "I wanted to talk to you privately about stuff happening to me, but I guess I'll have to try another time." After a brief pause, he added, "You know what, this was probably a bad idea. Please don't call me here at home, because someone else may pick up the phone, and I don't want them to know I've called you."

He hung up the phone and pulled at the ends of his hair, his most common move when stressed.

Later that week, he and Chigger were leaving school at the end of the day, and they headed for the parking lot. Thirty or so kids had just boarded a school bus parked at the rear of the school. The driver, an elderly Cherokee man, prepared to make his daily trip over winding, hilly back roads, returning the kids to their homes.

Out of the corner of his eye, Billy saw Little Wolf scurrying about. First he was in the bushes near the school. Next he peeked out from behind a car. Then the little Indian ducked under the school bus. Billy looked at Chigger to see if his friend had seen the miniature man. Chigger seemed clueless.

The two boys passed by the back of the bus. Without thinking, Billy put his hand out and touched the back door of the bus. Instantly an image popped into his mind. In a close-up color view, Billy saw liquid dripping from the engine of the bus. Because he'd worked on cars with his dad, Billy knew the fluid was coming from a brake hose.

In the next image, Billy saw the driver lose control of the bus as he crossed an old bridge. The bus, and all the kids inside, toppled off the bridge and into the water below.

Billy pulled his hand away from the bus and dropped his books. He grabbed his friend's shirt sleeve.

"I have to warn the bus driver," Billy said. "I think this bus is going to crash today."

A look of shock spread across Chigger's face and froze there.

"I told you the things happening to me sound crazy," Billy said. "But I can't let thirty kids get hurt if there's even the smallest chance it might be true."

Billy sprang into action just as the driver started the bus. As the bus doors were closing, Billy thrust his arm between them.

"Hold on!" he yelled at the old man. "You can't leave."

The driver opened the doors wide enough for Billy to climb inside.

"I believe this bus is going to crash today," Billy said with excitement. "You've got to get these kids off and put them on another bus."

"Son, I don't know what drugs you've been taking," the driver said. "You need to step out of the bus. Right now."

The driver's voice was firm but controlled. Then he saw the fractal pattern on Billy's neck.

"You're that kid got struck by lightning," he said loudly. "They said your mind might not be right because of it. Now I know for sure." The old Indian reached for a two-way radio attached to the dashboard. "This is bus number two-fourteen, still on the high school grounds. I need security here, now! I've got a student causing a ruckus."

Realizing that he wasn't achieving anything, Billy retreated down the steps.

"Let's get out of here before we get in trouble," he said to Chigger. "I'm probably out of my mind anyway."

Chigger helped him pick up the books he'd dropped at the back of the bus. Then the boys headed for Billy's truck.

"This is exactly what I was afraid of," Billy said as the boys walked quickly across the parking lot. They pulled out of the parking area just as a security guard was stepping onto the bus. The boys didn't stick around to find out what would happen next.

At home, Billy didn't mention the school bus incident to his parents. He hoped the whole thing would be forgotten and ignored. He at least wanted to have time to talk to Grandpa about it.

However, at around seven o'clock that evening, someone knocked on the Buckhorns' front door. Opening it, Billy's father found a policeman and the principal of Billy's school standing on the porch.

"Mr. Sixkiller, what's this about?" Mr. Buckhorn asked. "Is Billy in some kind of trouble?"

The principal reached out and shook hands with Billy's father. "No trouble, Mr. Buckhorn. I want you to meet Lieutenant Swimmer of the Tahlequah Police Department."

The officer also shook hands with Billy's father.

"May we come in?" the principal asked. "We need to talk to your family about what happened today."

Puzzled by this statement, Billy's father invited the two men inside and called the family to the living room. Billy and his mother took seats on the couch. Then the principal began to explain why they were there.

"What happened today was both amazing and troubling," the principal started. "We're here to thank Billy for his actions this afternoon and ask him a few questions. I assume he told you about the school bus."

"Billy has said nothing about any school bus," Mrs. Buckhorn replied. She looked over at her son.

Lieutenant Swimmer told them about Billy's efforts to stop the bus from leaving the school grounds.

"Billy, why didn't you tell us about this?" his father asked sternly.

"Because it sounded too crazy," Billy said. "Even to me."

"Luckily, the security guard inspected the bus, looking for defects," the policeman said. "To see if there was any reason the bus could possibly crash today."

"And what did he find?" Mr. Buckhorn asked.

"He found that the brake line had a leak," Mr. Sixkiller answered.

"Actually, our crime lab found that it had been cut," Lieutenant Swimmer added.

"What?" Billy said, standing up. "You mean I was right?"

"Yes, son, you possibly saved the lives of the bus driver and thirty kids," the principal said.

"What we want to know is how you knew there was something wrong," the policeman said. "Two detectives on the police force think you're the one who cut that line. That you did it just so you could get attention and become a hero. Or that you cut the line but later had a change of heart. Maybe you couldn't go through with it."

"Now see here," Mr. Buckhorn protested as he stood next to his son. "Billy would never do anything like that." He looked at his son. "Would you, Billy?"

"I've been 'seeing' things lately," Billy blurted out. "Ever since the lightning strike. Little movies run in my head that show me something that has happened to someone. Or maybe something that's about to happen to someone."

There was silence in the room. Billy's parents hadn't taken their son's reports of visions seriously. Now, in the presence of a policeman and a principal, they had to. No one knew what to say.

"I haven't told many people about it because it sounds too weird, too crazy," Billy continued. "You'd probably do the same thing if you were in my shoes."

"No doubt," the principal said.

"So are you here to thank Billy for saving those kids?" Mr. Buckhorn asked. "Or are you here to arrest him for damaging the bus? Which is it?"

The two visitors stood up.

"As I said, we're here to thank your son," Lieutenant Swimmer answered. "I believe he saved those kids and did nothing to ruin the brakes."

Both Mr. Sixkiller and Lieutenant Swimmer shook Billy's hand and gave him a pat on the back. Billy half expected to see the flash of some image with each touch. He was pleased that no movies ran in his mind.

"But that leaves us with the problem of finding out who did it," Lieutenant Swimmer said as the two men turned to leave.

"Who would want to harm a busload of schoolkids? In my opinion, that would have to be some kind of monster."

Billy and his parents escorted the two visitors to the door. Just as the men were about to leave, the policeman said, "The news media have picked up on this story. Our office has been swamped with calls. We want to hold a press conference to answer their questions. What do you think about that?"

"It's a terrible idea," Billy said. "I've already had too much attention focused on me because of the lightning. I don't want any more. I just want to be a normal kid."

"Okay," the officer replied. "We'll try our best to keep reporters away from information about the incident. Try to keep a lid on it."

None of them knew that the lid on this story was about to blow wide open.

CHAPTER 4

Abnormal

The following Saturday morning, Billy decided to pay Grandpa Wesley another visit. Although he'd spent zero time practicing his Cherokee writing, the teen brought the Big Chief tablet and the notebook with him, tucked away in a leather satchel with a long shoulder strap. Maybe he'd have time to work on it at Wesley's.

When he got to the elder's house, the teenager found the usual group of Cherokee people waiting on the porch. Some of them rose from their seats as Billy came near. Others bowed a little as he passed by. *What a strange way to act,* he thought.

Moving up the steps and across the porch, the teen greeted each one with a polite nod as he moved past them and entered the house. He found Wesley in the kitchen brewing a pot of strong herbal tea.

"What's with the folks on the porch today, Grandpa? They stood up when I arrived."

"They're all waiting for you," Wesley said as he took two coffee cups down from the cupboard. "They all know you're my grandson, and they want to see the boy who saved a busload of children."

"No one was supposed to know about that," Billy said. "The police said they'd keep it quiet."

"I suspect the police didn't have anything to do with it," Wesley said as he poured coffee into the two cups. "The bus driver told a couple of his Cherokee friends what happened. And those two Cherokees told ten or so other Cherokees about it. And those ten Cherokees each told another twenty or so Cherokees. You get the picture."

"What do they want from me?"

Wesley put a cup of coffee down on the kitchen table and motioned for Billy to take a seat. He sat down.

"There's no question in my mind," Wesley said, taking a sip of the hot liquid. "The Thunder Beings have given you the rare gift of 'seeing.' Important duties and responsibilities go along with a gift like that."

"But I didn't ask for it," Billy protested, pushing away from the table. "I didn't ask for any of it." A mix of strong feelings rose up inside of him. "I don't want those kinds of responsibilities."

He ran out the back door and into Wesley's garden to be alone so he could think.

"Is it anger or fear you're feeling?" a familiar voice asked.

"Little Wolf, are you out here somewhere?"

"At your service," the pint-size Cherokee said, stepping from behind a tall sunflower. "Which is it, anger or fear?"

"I don't know," the boy answered. He calmed down some. "Maybe both."

"That's a good, honest answer," Little Wolf replied with a smile. "There's hope for you yet."

"I'm not so sure." Billy began pacing up and down the path in Wesley's garden. "I see things that normal people don't see, including short Indians who live in the woods. Some people say I'm gifted. Others say I'm possessed by something evil. My mother thinks I merely suffer from a medical condition."

"You need time to process it all," Little Wolf advised. "You should get back to the morning ritual your grandfather taught you. Quiet your mind and pray to the seven directions. Do you remember what they are?"

Billy stopped pacing to remember.

"Yeah, sure, I remember." He pointed to each direction as he described it. "First, there are the four map directions—north, east, south, and west. Then there's upward toward Father Sky. That's number five. Then downward to Mother Earth. That's six. Finally, there's inward, into your own heart. That's the seventh direction."

"Good," the little man said. "Placing yourself in the center and praying will help you know what to do. Help you decide which way to go."

This calmed Billy greatly.

"Thanks," he said. "I guess you can be useful to have around."

Once he was back inside, Billy said, "Grandpa, I'm sorry, but I can't stay to help you today. Little Wolf said I need time to process everything that's been happening."

"I'm sure he's right," Wesley said. "Why don't you go on home. I'll tell people that you're not up to seeing anyone now. You can leave by the back door."

"Thanks. I knew you'd understand."

Instead of going home, Billy spent the rest of the day by himself in the woods. The whispering wind in the nearby trees soothed his troubled thoughts. The chirping birds and chattering squirrels blotted out the babble in his brain. And the lone call of a snowy crane calmed his swirling emotions. They reminded him he was related to all things. And all things were related to him.

Feeling calmer and stronger, the young man sat down on a tree stump and pulled the Big Chief tablet and lined notebook out of the satchel. He first opened the medicine book to page one and, for the first time, noticed an extra sheet of folded paper glued to the back side of the front cover. Unfolding the paper, he found a chart displaying all of Sequoyah's Cherokee characters.

He'd seen these charts wherever he went in the Cherokee Nation all his life. They were more common than the eye charts you see in an eye doctor's office. But he'd never really focused on them until now. Of course, every Cherokee child knew the three characters that spelled the word *Cherokee*, or more accurately, Tsa-la-gi: ᏣᎳᎩ. Those characters could be found on every office door at the tribe's headquarters.

Knowing he was meant to follow in his grandfather's footsteps, Billy decided to follow the elder's instructions. Not knowing the meaning of the words, he nevertheless began copying them. Some of the characters were similar to English letters, while others were obviously very different. He counted eighty-six symbols, each representing a different syllable.

Of course, the English alphabet only had twenty-six symbols, each mark representing the sound of a single letter. *How did Sequoyah come up with his system?* Billy wondered. A question for another time.

For now, the boy just immersed himself in the sounds of the woods and the sights of the syllabary. That night, he literally slept on it, as he'd told his grandfather he would. Placing the Big Chief writing tablet on his pillow, he gently laid his head on top of the papers.

That night he dreamed of the Cherokee man who'd invented the writing system. Ink pen in hand, Sequoyah wrote line after line of the syllabary characters on Billy's forehead. As he wrote, he spoke the Cherokee words. When the man dipped the fountain pen in a nearby inkwell to get a fresh supply of ink, the letters would fade away as they sank into the teen's brain. Then Sequoyah would write another line of text and repeat the cycle. No telling how long that process went on.

When he woke up the next morning, Billy's mind was clearer, but there was definitely some additional knowledge packed in there. Additional Cherokee knowledge. He put his hand to his forehead, in the area Sequoyah had been writing on all night. Surprisingly, it felt as though he was touching raised letters. It made the teen wonder if that was what it felt like to read braille.

He opened his mouth to speak, and this was what came out.

"Anidawéhi Gohésdi Unadanohisedii." (If you want to learn these ways, you must do it at night.) *"Nvnohi Unégv Aquadé-dowadi."* (I am going down the white path.)

Until that moment, the only Cherokee the boy had spoken was *Osiyo* (hello), *Wado* (thank you), and *Tsalagi* (Cherokee), so he was more than surprised at himself. He was downright shocked!

Billy recognized the phrases as part of the ceremonial instructions for learning the medicine ways. Not only could he pronounce the Cherokee words, but also, he understood what they meant! Amazing! But how long would the understanding last? A day? A week? A month?

Billy immediately went to the backyard and performed the seven-directions ceremony Little Wolf had reminded him about. When he'd finished, he listened quietly to see if any message or sense of direction came. When nothing did, he remembered something else his grandpa had told him.

"This isn't a one-time prayer ceremony you perform and then—boom—you get an answer," Wesley had said. "It's something you do every day to center yourself. It prepares you to be guided. But it takes time."

Feeling calmer and more confident, Billy decided he would give it time.

He continued seeing the mini-movies and flashes of pictures in his head. But not always. He realized he was only seeing the conflicts or dangers in other people's lives. He wasn't seeing visions of them having quiet family gatherings or happy times with others. He only saw the bad times—the bad times they were causing someone else, or the bad times being caused by someone else.

And he was getting more and more used to it.

But there was one alarming thing he noticed as the week wore on. Oddly, his gym teacher seemed to be growing younger and healthier. Day by day he looked as if he'd been taking some miracle drug. Or drinking some magic energy drink.

Billy knew he wasn't imagining this, because Chigger noticed it too.

"I've never seen anyone change like that," Chigger said. "It's like he found the famous fountain of youth or something."

"Now I have even worse feelings about the guy than when I first met him," Billy said. "Something tells me that someone is suffering just so he can look better. Does that make sense?"

"Remember what your grandpa said about your inner voice," Chigger advised. "If you feel that strongly about it, we need to check it out. And by *we*, I mean *you* need to check it out."

"What do you suggest I do?"

"Go up to the man and create an excuse to touch him or hand him something," Chigger said. "There's no other way."

"There has to be," Billy said with a shiver. "The thought of touching the Birdman creeps me out."

"You got a better idea?"

Billy knew Chigger was right. He'd have to brush up against the guy or hand him something so they'd touch it at the same time. He thought hard about it until he came up with a plan.

The next morning before school, Billy ripped his basketball jersey up one side. He showed the torn cloth to Chigger just before gym class.

"At the beginning of class, I'll show Birdman the rip and hand him the jersey," Billy explained. "Hopefully there'll be a moment when we both touch the cloth."

"That should work," Chigger said. "Good luck."

As they entered the gym, the boys saw Mr. Ravenwood standing near the door to the boys' locker room. Most of the kids in class were headed toward their lockers to put on their basketball outfits. Billy stopped at the doorway. Chigger stayed just behind him to see what would happen.

"Mr. Ravenwood, I've ripped my jersey," Billy said. "Can you get it fixed or give me a new one?" He held the jersey out toward the teacher.

"How in the world did you do that?" the teacher asked sharply. "The world-famous Lightning Boy must really be clumsy." He sighed a big sigh, as if this was such a big deal. "Hand it over so I can take a look."

Birdman reached out for the jersey. Billy put it in the man's hand but didn't let go of it. Both of them had their hands on it for a brief moment. That was when Billy got the familiar minijolt that started the movie in his head.

In black and white, he saw a teenage girl tied to a hospital gurney like the one he'd been on in the ambulance. Her mouth was gagged, and she was in a state of panic. The shadowy figure of a man entered the scene. His dark, blurred outline wouldn't come into focus, and he seemed to have bird claws for hands. He drew near the girl with a single claw outstretched toward her. With wide, frightened eyes, the girl squirmed and tried to scream from behind the gag.

The movie ended, and Billy's sight returned to the gym. Mr. Ravenwood was pretending to examine the tear in the jersey, but he was really studying Billy.

"What is it, boy?" the man asked. "You look like you ate something that didn't agree with you."

"No, I *saw* something that didn't agree with me," Billy replied, taking a step away from the teacher. "I saw you threatening a girl who was tied up. You were about to do something bad to her."

A look of shock spread over the Birdman's face. He threw Billy's jersey on the floor and took a quick step toward him.

"I knew there was something wrong with you the minute I laid eyes on you," the angry man barked. "You're not normal. In fact, you're quite *abnormal.* Something should be done to keep you away from other people."

The teacher quickly stepped into his office and picked up the phone.

"Mr. Sixkiller, this is Ravenwood in the gym," he said into the phone. "The Buckhorn boy is acting strange and needs to be severely disciplined immediately. Probably expelled from school!"

The Birdman listened through the receiver for a moment.

"I'll bring him directly to the office so you can hear the full story." He slammed down the phone and yelled at Billy. "Come with me, weirdo. You're about to find out what the wrath of Ravenwood can do."

Grabbing Billy's shoulder, the teacher pushed the boy toward the principal's office. Again, a movie started running in Billy's head. This time it was in color. He saw Ravenwood opening the trunk of a car. Inside was a dark-skinned teenage Native girl who had been tied up. She was gagged and blindfolded.

Ravenwood picked her up in both arms and carried her toward an abandoned building that seemed familiar to Billy. The girl kicked and struggled and managed to get free of her captor. She fell to the ground but couldn't get up because her feet were tied. The gym teacher reached into his back pocket, pulled out a handgun, and hit the girl in the head with it. She passed out from the blow.

Then the movie stopped. Billy saw that he was now inside the principal's office. The movie had played in his head while they were walking to Mr. Sixkiller's office. The principal rose from his desk.

"I overheard this boy talking to his buddy," Ravenwood said. "He confessed to cutting the brake line on the school bus. It was part of a bigger plan."

"What? That's impossible!" the principal said.

"That's a lie!" Billy responded. "Mr. Ravenwood is a bad man. He's done bad things to kids."

"Whoa, wait a minute," Mr. Sixkiller protested. "This man came highly recommended. He's got a flawless employment record."

"I think the lightning scrambled the boy's brain," the gym teacher said. "Billy said he made a small cut in the line so the fluid would drain out slowly and not be noticed right away. Then he jumped on the bus and pretended to save them so he could be called a hero."

"Is this true, Billy?" the principal asked. "I remember that Lieutenant Swimmer said some people in the police force thought you'd cut the line to become more famous."

"No, I didn't mess with the bus at all," Billy reaffirmed. "I told you how I found out about the brakes. The same way I just found out what this man has been doing. You have to believe me."

"That's just too far-fetched for me," Mr. Sixkiller replied as he reached for his phone. "And this is too difficult for me to figure out. I'm going to let the police sort it out."

Mr. Sixkiller called Lieutenant Swimmer and explained the situation. Then he dismissed the teacher from his office, telling him to make himself available to the police if needed. He told Billy to sit down and wait for the lieutenant to arrive. In the meantime, the principal also called Billy's father to tell him of the latest incident.

Billy was very worried that if no one believed him, he'd be spending the night in jail, and the Birdman would harm another child. The boy didn't realize he'd have a chance very soon to convince others he was telling the truth.

"I really want to believe you," Lieutenant Swimmer said as he put Billy in the back seat of his police car. "But your story is pretty wild. You can't go around slandering an upright member of the community that way."

"There has to be some way I can prove it to you," Billy said from the back seat as they headed for the police station. "I am completely innocent, and I believe Mr. Ravenwood is completely guilty. He's probably going to hurt another girl in the very near future."

"And you say you saw this when he touched you?" the lieutenant asked. "Does this supposedly happen whenever you touch someone?"

"Only if that person has been involved in a situation where someone was hurt or in danger," Billy answered. "Or if they're about to be involved in that type of event. At least that seems to be the way it works. I'm still trying to figure it out."

They arrived at the police station, and the lieutenant escorted Billy inside. Surprisingly, Little Wolf was lurking in a corner of the waiting room. One of the other officers there, Sergeant Bowers, showed Billy to the conference room.

"Your father is on his way," the sergeant told Billy. "He'll be present when we talk to you."

As the officer left to get Billy a soda, the little Indian managed to scurry into the room before the door closed.

"What are you doing here?" Billy asked in a whisper.

"Wesley sent me to find you to see if you were all right," Little Wolf said. "He had a vibe that there might be something wrong."

Little Wolf quickly put a finger to his lips to signal Billy to keep quiet. In a few minutes Sergeant Bowers returned with a canned soda and Billy's father.

"Is Billy under arrest?" Mr. Buckhorn asked the officer.

"No," Bowers replied. "We're just trying to get a handle on what's really going on. Can I get you anything, Mr. Buckhorn?"

"No, just please move this along as quickly as possible," he replied.

Bowers handed Billy the soda, and both of their hands touched the can briefly. A black-and-white movie began to run in Billy's head. In it the officer was squatted down beside his police car. Someone from inside a nearby old house was shooting at him. When the firing paused, Bowers stood and fired off three quick shots. A scream of pain came from inside the house, and the shooting stopped. The movie ended.

"Were you just involved in a shootout?" Billy asked the officer. "With someone inside an old house?"

"Yes, I was," the policeman said. "But that hasn't been made public. How did you know about it?"

"Yeah, how did you know?" Billy's dad echoed the question.

"I tried telling you the other day, Pops," Billy answered with frustration. "But you were too fixated on some guy in some historical archive." He turned to Bowers and said, "I just saw a black-and-white movie of it when you handed me the soda can."

"Hold on," Bowers said. "Let me call the lieutenant. He'll want to hear this straight from you."

"I'm sorry I didn't pay more attention," Billy's father said when they were alone. "I didn't think you were serious."

Just then the sergeant returned with Lieutenant Swimmer. Billy described the movie he'd just seen in his head.

"Wait here," the lieutenant said.

The two policemen left the father and son again. What the Buckhorns didn't know was that Swimmer was checking with the others in the station to see if anyone had spoken to the newspaper or radio station about the shootout. No one had. That meant that Billy couldn't have read or heard the story in the news media.

Swimmer and Bowers stepped back into the conference room. Two other uniformed officers came in with them, a man and a woman.

"I'd like to introduce Officer Frank Barnes and Officer Laney Williams," Swimmer said. "Billy, I want you to shake hands with both of them and tell me if you see anything."

Officer Barnes, a white man in his forties, stepped closer to Billy. They shook hands.

Right away, a black-and-white mental movie began. Barnes was up in a tree hanging on to a branch. Farther out on the branch was a meowing cat. Barnes looked down at an elderly woman on the ground below him. The cat belonged to her.

Then Barnes reached for the cat and lost his balance. Losing his grip, he fell off the branch. In a panic, the officer grabbed for a lower branch and held on. The movie ended.

"It was kind of funny," Billy said, with a confident smile. "This man almost fell out of a tree trying to save an elderly woman's cat."

Officer Barnes's jaw dropped. He was in shock.

"That's exactly right," he said. "I nearly broke my leg because of that cat."

Officer Williams, a Native American woman in her thirties, then extended her hand. Billy shook it. This time a color movie played. Williams was leaving a bar at the edge of town called Shooter's Music Tavern. She wasn't in uniform but wore jeans and a Western-style shirt.

Coming from behind a parked car, a very drunk man grabbed Williams. He turned her around and tried to kiss her but missed. In a rapid series of moves, the officer twisted the man's arm and threw him to the ground. Seeing that he was knocked out cold, the woman continued on. The movie stopped.

Billy described the scene and said this event would probably take place sometime in the next few days.

"I was planning on visiting Shooter's tomorrow night," Williams said. "I go a couple of times a month to unwind. I think I'll skip it this time."

"Okay, I've seen enough," Lieutenant Swimmer said. "I don't usually go in for psychics or omens and such, but I believe you're the real thing."

"Boy, am I glad to hear that," Billy said with a sigh.

"I'm speechless," Billy's father admitted. "I didn't believe such things were real."

Little Wolf stepped out from under the conference table and gave Billy a thumbs-up signal. Of course, no one but Billy could see him. The little man left the room to go report Billy's progress to Wesley.

"I think this means your vision of Ravenwood is correct too," Swimmer continued. "He sounds like he's up to no good. But we don't have any real proof to go on." He paused to think for a moment. "We'll start doing a background check on Ravenwood and begin an investigation. I can't go around arresting people based on visions. I have to have solid evidence. Do you understand?"

"Yeah, I get it," Billy replied.

"Of course," Mr. Buckhorn said.

"Billy, you're free to go," Swimmer said. "But don't be surprised if we contact you again very soon."

"Sure thing."

"In the meantime, we don't want to tip off Ravenwood that he's being investigated. I'll tell the principal that Billy is in the clear but ask him not to say anything to the gym teacher."

Billy and his dad agreed with the plan.

"I'm late for a meeting at the college I'm in charge of," Mr. Buckhorn said, turning to his son. "Can one of the officers take you back to school to get your truck?"

"I can run him back," Officer Williams said.

"Thanks," Mr. Buckhorn replied. "Billy, I'm sorry for not paying more attention to what you're going through. We can talk some more about it later. Okay?"

"Sure thing, Pops."

Mr. Buckhorn patted his son on the back and left the station.

After Williams dropped off Billy at the high school, the boy drove out to Grandpa's house. As he moved through the countryside, he thought about what had been going on. It all seemed too strange to be true. How could such things happen to a backwoods Cherokee teenager? He really wanted no part of it. But he also wanted to talk to somebody about it.

At his grandpa's, Billy found a note stuck to the front door. *Gone to the woods to gather medicine,* the note read. *Won't be back for a few hours.*

Then Billy drove home to see if his mother had gotten back from work. He found a note from her stuck on the refrigerator door that read, *Running errands—fix yourself a snack. Be back in time for dinner.*

He decided to call his dad to find out when he'd be home. "I'm in meetings until at least eight o'clock tonight," his voicemail message said. "Leave a message." Billy hung up without saying anything.

Why couldn't he find someone when he needed to talk? When he needed to vent? Billy even looked around to see if Little Wolf was lurking anywhere, but there was no sign of the little man. He had probably joined Wesley in the woods after leaving the police station.

Should I call Abramson again? he thought. *Better not. He'll probably certify me as insane.*

Billy realized that the mini-jolts and the movies in his head had drained him of energy. He decided to take a nap. Flopping down on his bed, he soon fell asleep.

But it was not a peaceful sleep. In a vivid dream he saw a girl being tied up by a man inside a darkened cabin. In the background, he saw two other girls. They had already been tied and gagged. They looked drugged or dazed.

At first, he couldn't see who the man was. Within the dream, he forced himself to look up to see the man's face. He began getting a headache, and the images started to fade. But somehow Billy willed the dream to continue. He willed it to show him what he needed to see.

With great effort he was able to tilt his view far enough upward to see the back of the man's head. At that moment the man became aware that Billy was looking at him. The man turned his face away from the girl, and his angry eyes met Billy's. It was Ravenwood! Rage filled the man's face, and his human face changed into the disfigured face of a black-feathered raven with dark, piercing eyes!

Then the gym teacher's whole body transformed into a large, ill-shaped raven. He became an enraged bird that flew toward Billy, squawking and flapping and clawing at him. The shock of the image jolted Billy out of the dream and back into his room. He sat upright in bed, feeling hot and sweaty but at the same time cold and clammy.

This seemed like more than a dream, more than a nightmare. It felt like his very soul had crossed over into another place. Somewhere between the land of the living and the land of the dead. Was this a real event happening now, or was it something that might happen in the future? Did Ravenwood actually see Billy during the dream? These were questions with no answers.

And this wasn't something he could tell anyone, except maybe Grandpa. No one would believe it. He wasn't sure he believed it himself. He had learned from Grandpa that some powerful medicine men, both good and evil, could transform themselves into animals. Birds or dogs usually. They did this so they could travel without being recognized. The good ones did it to check up on their own patients. And the bad ones did it to spy on people they wanted to harm.

But Ravenwood is a white man, Billy remembered. *How did he learn these secret Cherokee medicine skills?*

Billy checked his pocket watch and saw that it was time for school to let out. He decided to go visit Chigger to see what, if anything, had happened there the rest of the day. Chigger and his family lived in a trailer home parked at the end of a long gravel driveway northeast of town.

"My parents told me I can't hang out with you anymore," Chigger said when he answered his front door. "The gossip around town has gone viral. People are making all kinds of strange claims against you."

Chigger stepped out on the porch so his mother wouldn't see that it was Billy he was talking to. He closed the door behind him quietly.

"It's like Bigfoot sightings," the boy continued. "People are saying they've seen you doing all kinds of shady things all over the place. It's not even possible for one person to be in all those places at the same time." That statement caused Chigger to begin wondering. "Is it?" he added.

"How long have we been friends?" Billy asked, disturbed that his own friend was doubting him. "How long have your parents known me?" He pulled at the ends of his hair, his go-to stress move.

"I know, I know," Chigger replied. "It's totally bogus. But what can I do? My father rules the family with an iron hand. And Mom's too scared of him to argue or disagree. So here I sit like a rabbit in a trap."

Feelings of hurt, betrayal, and anger grew inside Billy. He paced back and forth on Chigger's porch. He spoke more to himself than to Chigger. "A few days ago everyone wanted to meet the boy who saved the kids on the bus. Now people think I'm some kind of dangerous freak. What's going on?"

"Keep your voice down or my parents will hear you," Chigger said.

Billy stopped pacing and faced Chigger with hurt, angry eyes.

"Of all people, I thought I could at least count on you, Chigger!" he yelled and turned away.

Storming off the porch, Billy ran back to his truck. He put the gear in reverse and sped backward out of the gravel driveway. Bits of gravel flew up from the spinning tires and pelted Chigger in the face and arms. Knowing that he'd let down his best friend, Chigger watched as Billy disappeared down the road.

How will I ever fix this? Chigger wondered.

CHAPTER 5

Turning Point

When he got home, Billy started pulling out his camping gear from his closet. *It's time to head for the woods,* he thought. *Time to surround myself with earth and sky and trees and nature. Maybe they can help now.*

It was his turn to leave behind notes and messages for others to find. He left one note on the refrigerator to his mother. *Gone to the woods to be alone,* it read. *I won't be back in time for dinner.* He left another note on his dad's desk upstairs. *Gone to connect with the real me,* this one read. *I can't be the person others want me to be.*

With gear and food in the truck, he hitched up his boat trailer and headed south. Down State Highway 82 he went, toward one of his favorite places on earth, Lake Tenkiller. The huge body of water had more than one hundred miles of shoreline. Plenty of room to get away.

He threw his camping equipment and some food into the skiff and backed it into the water at a public boat area he'd used many times before. After parking his truck in the nearby lot, he pointed the boat toward an island that he and Chigger had discovered a while back. At the time, they thought it might even be the island where the Thunders had sent Fire down to earth.

79

Shaped like an arrowhead, the tree-covered chunk of land was not much bigger than a football field. But it was surrounded by acres and acres of lake. It was isolated from the camping and fishing sites used by normal people.

But he wasn't normal, was he? He had been declared abnormal. And for some reason, that was how people had come to think of him. *So be it,* he thought. *I'll just see what being abnormal is all about.*

In no rush, the teen took his time crossing the lake. He remembered that his world had been turned upside down the last time he navigated these waters. Thankfully, this afternoon the sky was free of clouds, the Thunders safe at rest.

Soon the flat-bottomed boat touched the island's rocky shore. Grabbing his gear, Billy stepped out and into the shallow water. A few tugs had the boat up on dry land. He tied the bow rope to a tree stump and hiked inland.

Locating a small, flat hill near the middle of the island, he dropped his gear on the ground. He decided he'd tour his temporary home to make sure it didn't hold any surprises. He didn't want to be visited by a wildcat or black bear that might be living there.

Once that had been done, he set up camp and built a fire. And as darkness settled in, he was feeling right at home. He cooked the ideal outdoor dinner for himself over the fire. It was a campfire creation his grandpa called "cowboy stew." All that was required was a can of beef stew and a can of ranch beans. Pour them both into a cast-iron kettle and set it into the coals. A few minutes later, you had the heartiest meal west of the Mississippi. And a few minutes after that, you only had one pot and one spoon to clean. To do that job, Billy used water from the five-gallon jug he'd brought.

Once again, a star-filled sky floated overhead. Billy rolled out his sleeping bag next to the fire and slipped into it. Above him were spread out the animal star groups, the constellations,

CHAPTER 5

known to the Cherokee. And splayed out diagonally across the black velvet like a multicolored splatter of paint drops glowed the Path of Souls, what most people called the Milky Way. The stars were the spirit campfires of the Star People, according to traditional tribal lore, and the spirit homes of all the ancestors who'd passed away.

One star group, the Pleiades, was also believed by some Indian peoples to be their origin point, where they'd come to earth from another dimension through a hole in the sky.

Whoever or whatever they are, they'll keep me company this night, he thought.

Just then a shooting star raced across the sky above him. It was a sign of a coming change—at least that was what Grandpa said. The teen knew it was really only a meteorite, a chunk of space rock entering earth's atmosphere. But Billy was beginning to question everything, like those quaint old Cherokee ideas about how things worked in the world. Maybe those were just the fantasies of old men and little boys. That was what floated through Billy's mind as he drifted off to sleep.

He slipped into a deep, peaceful slumber. It was like his coma in the hospital after the lightning strike. Blurry images and stories swirled around him in the night. At one point, Billy seemed to be flying over the land, looking down. He passed over the nearby plant nursery, with its greenhouses and rows of dead plants. It had been closed down for years. And later he saw a whole group of Little People singing and dancing around a fire.

When he awoke the following morning, he took a moment to remember the dream images from the night before. As he got up, he somehow felt lighter, and his head felt clearer than when he'd gone to bed. The feelings of betrayal and anger had diminished. A new sense of comfort had settled over him in his sleep, but he didn't know where it had come from.

That was because he didn't know that Wesley had spent the entire night doctoring him from afar with Cherokee songs and prayers. When Billy's mom and dad discovered the notes he'd left for them, they'd called Wesley and asked for his help. And for the first time in a long time, Wesley had turned to Little Wolf and the other Little People for their very special help.

Together they'd held an all-night stomp dance in the field behind Wesley's house to conjure the power and vision that Billy would need in the days ahead. For they sensed that a battle between the Dark and the Light was brewing in the Cherokee Nation.

Back on the island, just after sunrise, Billy prayed to the seven directions. He was truly grateful that the bad feelings he had felt the day before had left him. His thankfulness was part of this morning's message to the rising sun.

Afterward, he packed up his gear and cleaned up his camp-site. Carrying his trash with him, he shoved his skiff from the shore and cranked up the engine. He'd decided it was time for him to firmly take the next step on that ladder. The ladder he'd seen in his vision at the stomp dance was making more sense to him now.

He drove back home as quickly as he could and unhitched the boat. Walking toward his house, he was surprised to find his father sitting on the front porch with Lieutenant Swimmer. Billy's dad had usually headed for his teaching job at the college by this time of morning. He and the lieutenant were talking quietly and seriously while looking at an open file folder.

"Is everything okay?" Billy's father asked, rising from his chair. "You had us worried sick."

"Everything's fine," Billy replied, hugging his dad. "More than fine. And I'm sorry I worried you. I just needed some time to sort out a few issues." Looking at Lieutenant Swimmer, he asked, "What's going on?"

"Yesterday, after you left our office, we began trying to gather information on Ravenwood," Swimmer said. "We went back to the high school to interview him, but he'd left. We looked for him at the address the school had for him, but he wasn't there either."

"Maybe he was just out running errands or something," Billy's dad offered.

"The odd thing is that there was just a boarded-up old house at that address," the lieutenant replied. "It looked like it hadn't been lived in for years. Ravenwood seems to have disappeared." He handed the open file folder to Billy. "And so has this girl." He pointed to a photo of a teenage girl clipped to the inside of the folder. "Her mother called us and said she didn't come home after school yesterday."

Billy looked at the photo and realized that the girl looked familiar. She was a dark-skinned Native girl with short cropped hair. Did he know her from one of his classes?

"Her name is Sara Cornsilk," Swimmer continued. "She's a student at your school."

"I guess I've seen her around," Billy said. Then he remembered where he'd seen her. "Wait. I saw her yesterday afternoon in a weird, scary dream I had," he said with excitement as he recalled the images. "The gym teacher was taking her out of the trunk of a car and carrying her into an old empty building."

"You saw this yesterday?" Swimmer asked.

"Yes, and it was in color," Billy confirmed. "That means it hadn't happened yet." He thought about it for another moment and then added, "But it could have happened later in the day."

"Can you tell me more about the building you saw in your vision?" the lieutenant inquired.

Billy searched his memory. "Not really. That wasn't clear in my dream. But it did seem like it was an old warehouse or office building. And it was vaguely familiar, like I'd seen it or maybe even been there—but I'm not sure."

"So we've got two people we need to find and fast," Swimmer said. "I hope you're wrong about this, Billy. But I'm afraid you might not be."

With that, the officer hurried back to his police car and sped away.

"I'll call your mother and let her know you're back," Mr. Buckhorn said. "Are you going to school today?"

"I don't think so," Billy replied. "I need to do something to help find Ravenwood before he does anything to that girl."

"It sounds too dangerous," his father said. "Why don't you let the police handle it?"

"Because I feel like it's my duty somehow," Billy answered. "It seems like it's time for me to step up and begin to follow in Grandpa's footsteps."

With those words, Mr. Buckhorn fell silent. He'd known that someday his son would say those words. He'd known that someday the seeds of ancient stories, beliefs, and practices would sprout in the fertile soil of his soul. These seeds had been planted by Billy's grandmother and grandfather. But Billy's father just hadn't thought this day would arrive so soon.

"It's not an easy path, you know," Mr. Buckhorn said.

"I know."

"But if you feel the calling, I won't prevent you from following that path," Billy's father said. He paused and looked into his son's eyes. They seemed deep and mature for a sixteen-year-old. "What's next then?"

"What else?" Billy said. "Go see Grandpa. You know he's the best in three counties at finding lost people and things."

"What about school?" his father asked.

"I've got more important things to tend to right now," Billy said.

"Good luck—and stay safe," his father said, rubbing the hair on the top of his son's head. "As always, I've got to get back to the college."

As he walked to his car, Billy's dad was worried. Was his son destined to get caught up in the strange world of Cherokee medicine? It was a world filled with mysterious events and unexplainable happenings. For the first time, he was beginning to realize it could also be dangerous.

As Billy walked to his truck, he wished Chigger was with him. Billy had always been a bit more adventurous than his friend. But it was really part of an act. Pretending to be braver than Chigger was what had often given Billy the courage to embark on an adventure in the first place.

Billy drove to Wesley's house as fast as he could. He had a lot to tell the old man and a lot to ask of him. When he arrived, he found his grandfather's truck parked in the front yard. The front door to the house was open, and Billy stepped inside.

"Grandpa," he called several times as he searched inside the house. No reply came. He stepped into the backyard and called again. Still no reply. And a quick search didn't locate Little Wolf either.

What's going on? Billy thought. *Why are people disappearing?*

Then he heard a moan coming from a row of sunflowers growing in the back of Wesley's garden. Billy ran toward the sound. There he found his grandfather sprawled on the ground. His head was bloody and seemed to be covered with shallow stab wounds.

"Grandpa, what happened?" the panicked boy cried.

Wesley struggled to speak. His words were weak.

"I was attacked by a raven, a large one," the wounded elder said between breaths.

"Don't try to talk," Billy cautioned. "Save your strength."

"No, this is important!" Wesley said, gathering all his energy. "It's a Shape-Changer, Billy, a Raven Stalker. He must be stopped, no matter what."

The elder then passed out. Billy ran inside to call his mother at the hospital.

"We'll send out an ambulance," she said. "Wait right there."

"No, I'm bringing him in myself," Billy protested. "It'll take too long for an ambulance to get here. Just have everything ready." He hung up before she could say no.

Billy drove his truck around the side of Wesley's house and into the back. He knocked a hole in the garden fence and backed the pickup close to his grandfather. From inside the house, he brought out some blankets and spread them in the bed of the truck. Somehow, with a burst of superhuman strength, he lifted the wounded elder up and into the truck. With the bungee cords he used to tie down cargo, Billy strapped Wesley in so he wouldn't bounce around.

Breaking every speeding law in the Cherokee Nation, he raced to the hospital. Thankfully, his mother had emergency room staff standing by. They wheeled Billy's grandpa into the ER and began working on him. Billy had to stay out in the waiting room.

About a half hour later, Billy's dad joined him. Billy told him how he'd found Wesley in the garden with his head and hands covered in blood and stab wounds.

"That's the strangest thing I've ever heard," Mr. Buckhorn said. "How did something like that even happen?"

"Grandpa said it was a Shape-Changer, a kind of witch known as a Raven Stalker," Billy answered. "I think the bird stabbed Grandpa with his beak over and over again."

Mr. Buckhorn sat speechless. He knew his father was a medicine man, a healer. His mother had been one too. But he'd never believed that anything dangerous would ever come of it. And Billy wanted to follow in his grandparents' footsteps. That was sounding more and more like a very bad idea.

A doctor who was removing his surgical face mask and gloves came out of the operating room. He walked toward Billy and his father.

"It's not as bad as it looks," the man reported. "Head wounds sometimes bleed more heavily than similar wounds in other parts of the body."

"Can we see him?" Mr. Buckhorn asked.

"Yes, very briefly. But he specially asked to see his grandson first," the doctor said. "He said he needs to talk with him about things that concern a medicine man and his apprentice."

"Sorry, Pops," Billy said as he followed the doctor down the hall. "I'll try to make it quick."

The doctor led Billy to his grandfather's room and left him to enter alone. The boy opened the door to the room and found his grandfather lying in bed with tubes attached to him. Wesley's head was wrapped in gauze bandages, and so were his hands.

"Grandpa, what's going on? You told me Raven Stalkers were a thing of the past. Now you say one just attacked you."

"It was the dark, shriveled soul of Benjamin Blacksnake," Wesley said with great weariness. "He lived among the Eastern Cherokees in North Carolina. He died in 1964."

Billy blinked a few times. He didn't understand.

"He was a well-known Raven Stalker in his day," Grandpa continued. "Bad medicine through and through. Raven Stalkers would sometimes visit sick people who were near death and drain them of their last bit of life. The person would die, but the Raven Stalker would be strengthened and able to add years to his own life."

"Why is he here now?"

"I think Blacksnake's evil spirit took possession of your Mr. Ravenwood," Wesley answered. "He's living here in our world through your gym teacher's body. He probably took over the teacher's life back in North Carolina before coming here."

"How do you know all this?"

"He identified himself to me just before he attacked," Grandpa replied. "He'd become aware that I was getting close to discovering the source of the evil your grandma warned us about. Using his remote-viewing powers, he found me and made his move. He seemed proud that he'd outsmarted me."

The doctor stepped back into the room and said, "That's enough for now. He needs to rest."

Reluctantly, Billy stood to leave. "One more thing," he said loud enough for the doctor to hear. Then he leaned in close to his grandfather and whispered, "If an evil dead medicine man is controlling Ravenwood and using him to kidnap kids . . . how do we stop him?"

Grandpa let out a big, mournful sigh and looked up at Billy. "That's beyond my skills, I'm sorry to say," he said.

Billy gently touched his grandfather's arm.

"Then I'll take it from here," he told Wesley. "You get well." He turned and left the room before his grandfather could say anything else.

Of course, Billy couldn't tell anybody what Wesley had told him. It sounded like the delusions of a crazy old man, not to be taken seriously. Billy drove directly to the police station to talk to Lieutenant Swimmer. He had to convince the man that Ravenwood was definitely dangerous and able to hurt anyone who got in his way. And he had to do it without saying anything about Raven Stalkers or dead medicine men.

The receptionist at the police station, Mrs. Atwood, said that the lieutenant and most of the officers were in the field searching for the missing girl.

"You have to tell Lieutenant Swimmer that he needs to focus on finding Ravenwood," Billy said. "He's got the girl somewhere, and he's more dangerous than anyone realizes."

Mrs. Atwood assured him that she would give Swimmer that message, but Billy wasn't sure she would follow through.

Then he drove to the high school to find the principal, Mr. Sixkiller.

"Mr. Ravenwood is *not* the upstanding member of the community you think he is," Billy told him. "Someone from his last job must have lied when they endorsed him for the gym teacher job."

"Why aren't you in class, young man?" the principal said, ignoring Billy's statement. "You were reported absent from school this morning."

"Didn't Lieutenant Swimmer call you yesterday?" Billy asked impatiently.

"Why, yes, he did, but—"

"And didn't he tell you that Ravenwood is now under investigation?"

"Yes, but I don't see—"

"And didn't he tell you that I'm in the clear?"

"Yes. Yes, he did."

"So I don't have time to play games," Billy said, his impatience growing. "I'm helping the police track down Ravenwood. He's a dangerous man who does bad things to kids."

"Do you have proof?"

"Yes, and you can talk to Lieutenant Swimmer if you don't believe me," Billy replied with authority. "Now, who did Ravenwood's recommendation come from?"

"Well, our own gym teacher, Mr. Wildcat, recommended Ravenwood after he got sick," the principal answered. "I didn't speak to him, but Mr. Wildcat sent me an email just before Labor Day. It said he was very sick and would not be able to teach this semester."

"Please give me Mr. Wildcat's home address and phone number so the police can talk to him," Billy requested. "He may have some clues about who Ravenwood really is."

Sixkiller hesitated for a moment. He was not sure that a sixteen-year-old should be involved in a police matter. Billy could see that the principal had his doubts.

"I'm not comfortable sharing this information with a student," the principal said.

"Look, Mr. Sixkiller, my grandpa is laid up in the hospital with severe stab wounds," the boy said. "He says Ravenwood was his attacker. The police are searching for him and a missing student as we speak. Any delays could mean injury or death for that girl."

That shook Sixkiller to the bone.

"I hope I don't regret doing this later," the principal said.

He opened a nearby filing cabinet and looked through the folders. He found Mr. Wildcat's file and took it to his desk. Grabbing a piece of paper from a drawer, he quickly scribbled an address and phone number.

"I hope you're wrong about this," Mr. Sixkiller said as he handed the paper to Billy. "But if you're right, I'll be the first to back you up. Go get him, son."

Billy took the paper and left.

CHAPTER 6

Shape-Changer

Billy decided *not* to go to the police station with Mr. Wildcat's address and phone number. He thought it would take too long for the police to check it out. Relying on his own instincts and feeling a real sense of urgency, he drove to the address himself.

The house at that address was a two-story log home similar to his own. But Mr. Wildcat's yard had been neglected for a while. The grass was tall, and the front flower bed was overgrown with weeds. Mail overflowed from the front porch mailbox too.

Billy rang the doorbell and waited. No one stirred. He knocked loudly on the door and again waited. Still no response. He peeked into the house through a front window. The house was dark. Nothing moved.

He decided to take a look at the back of the house and called out several times as he walked, "Mr. Wildcat, are you here? Hello, is anyone home?"

He reached the back door and found it slightly open. He looked around outside to make sure no one was watching and stepped inside. He found himself in the kitchen, surrounded by the foul odor of stale and rotting food. It was dark, so he flipped on a light switch. No lights came on.

Moving through the room, Billy discovered half-empty containers of take-out food scattered around. On the kitchen table and on the counters sat pizza boxes, burger bags, and sacks from three or four other local fast-food restaurants.

"Mr. Wildcat are you here?" he called out again. Still no answer. Moving out of the kitchen and into the living room, he noticed a partially opened side door. *It might take me to a basement,* he thought. He flipped on a light switch located on the wall just inside the door. The basement light came on, and right away he heard what sounded like a person moaning loudly.

Cautiously he made his way down the creaky wooden stairs that led to the basement, but he wasn't prepared for the sight that greeted him at the bottom. A blindfolded man lay strapped to a hospital gurney. He was trying to scream through the gag that had been tied over his mouth. And he was trying urgently to break free of his restraints.

Billy ran to the man, slipped off the blindfold, and pulled down the gag. It was Mr. Wildcat. He was alive, but his eyes were hollow and sunken. His body was nothing but skin and bones. He could barely speak.

"Thank God someone finally came," he said weakly. "I don't think I could've held on much longer."

"Mr. Wildcat, who did this to you?" Billy asked as he removed the straps.

"That whacked-out monster Ravenwood," he replied as he tried to sit up. "He showed up on my doorstep Labor Day weekend. He tied me up and put me down here. He sent an email to Mr. Sixkiller pretending to be me. It said that I was too sick to teach this semester. He even lied about knowing me and gave himself a reference for the job under my name."

"I wondered how he pulled that off," Billy said. "Let's get you to the hospital right away."

He grabbed the man to help him stand. Before they could take a step together, a black-and-white movie began to run in Billy's head. He saw the gym teacher tied to this gurney here in the basement. Ravenwood entered and began chanting a strange song. It sounded like an ancient form of the Cherokee language. He drank a dark liquid from a glass that sat on a nearby shelf. In a moment, he began to change into a raven—a huge, oversized version of a very ugly raven. Then the movie stopped.

"Grandpa was right," Billy said, more to himself than to Mr. Wildcat.

"What?" the gym teacher asked.

"Nothing," Billy replied.

He helped the man get outside and into his truck's extended cab. The teacher lay down in the back seat, using a blanket for a pillow. During the drive to the hospital, Mr. Wildcat revealed more details about his ordeal.

"You'll probably think I'm nuts, but I swear I saw Ravenwood transform into a bird—a big, weird raven," Mr. Wildcat said. He watched Billy and waited for a response.

"You don't have to convince me," Billy replied. "Just now I saw a movie in my head of him in the middle of his shape-change. The man's been possessed by the evil spirit of a dead medicine man."

That response surprised and shocked the teacher, who was familiar with normal, everyday reality, not the workings of the supernatural.

"What else happened?" Billy asked.

"One day I was tied down to the gurney, and he flew up above me," the teacher said. "He flapped his huge wings and then landed on my chest. I was so scared that he was going to eat me or something."

"He's what my grandfather calls a Raven Stalker," Billy told him. "They feed on your life force, not your flesh."

"That explains it," Mr. Wildcat said, thinking about what had happened to him. "He seemed to be strengthened by my fear. A shiver passed through him as he soaked it up. Then he stuck his beak in my mouth and began sucking. The more he sucked, the weaker I felt. He'd return every few days for another feeding. Then he'd give me just enough food and water to keep me alive."

"Did he say where else he was going besides the high school?"

"Not really," the weakening teacher answered. "He said he came to eastern Oklahoma to be where everything is green. He liked to be away from town at a place where water, earth, plants, and sky all came together." His voice trickled off to a whisper near the end of his sentence. Billy knew he'd better step on it to get the man to a doctor before it was too late.

"Keep this up and we'll have to give you a job as an ambulance driver," the receiving nurse in the emergency room said. "Who have you got this time?"

"This is Mr. Wildcat, the high school gym teacher," Billy said. "And he may need the help of a medicine man in addition to what you can do for him. He's been under the spell of what you'd call a witch. Now I've got to report this to the police and visit my grandpa, who's on another floor."

Using the phone at the nurses' station, Billy called the police station and got Mrs. Atwood again.

"Did you give Lieutenant Swimmer my message?" Billy asked. He could tell she was filing her fingernails.

"Well, he's been kinda busy, and there's other stuff goin' on here, so—"

"Look, lady," Billy interrupted. "You need to quit focusing on your cosmetic concerns and put me through to Swimmer!" Before she could respond, he added, "I found Mr. Wildcat, the gym teacher, and he was nearly dead."

"I thought Ravenwood was the gym teacher," the woman replied, putting down the fingernail file. "And you'd better watch yourself, mister. That's no way to talk to law enforcement personnel."

Billy contained his anger as best he could. "Please get Lieutenant Swimmer on the radio, ma'am, or patch me through to him. Whatever you have to do. Because he needs to hear what Mr. Wildcat, the real gym teacher, had to say."

Reluctantly the receptionist called the lieutenant on her police radio. When he came on the line, she connected Billy to his radio. He quickly gave his report about the attack on Wesley and the discovery of Mr. Wildcat in the basement.

"That's good work, young man," the lieutenant said. "Keep this up and we'll have to put you on the police force."

"No thanks. I've already been offered a job driving ambulances today. Have you got any ideas about where this maniac is hiding out?"

"We've begun searching for abandoned properties, since that's the only clue we have so far. We've called in the county sheriff's department to help us out. The area we need to cover is huge."

"Please let me know if you come up with anything," Billy said. "I'm going back to visit my grandpa."

They ended the call, and Billy took the elevator up to Wesley's room.

"He's not finished with me," Grandpa Wesley said, sitting up in his bed. "I can feel Blacksnake or Ravenwood or whatever you want to call him." He spoke between bites of chocolate pudding that came from a lunch tray beside his bed. "He's out there somewhere. I can't see him, but I feel like he's . . . sort of circling overhead."

Billy looked out the window and scanned the sky, but he didn't see any signs of an oversized, deformed raven.

"I'll keep an eye out for him," Billy said. "The police are searching empty buildings outside town, but there are so many. It'll be tough to find the right one."

"You can find him," Wesley said with confidence. "You have the power, but it just hasn't been developed yet. It takes practice and time."

Billy gave his grandpa a gentle pat on the arm and said, "I'll do my best."

After taking the elevator down to the main floor, he walked out to his truck parked in the hospital's lot. He thought more about what his grandfather had told him. *You can find him. You have the power.*

Just then a shadow passed over Billy's face. He looked up and spied a rather large black bird flying overhead.

"Ravenwood!" Billy said out loud with excitement. "Flying around in broad daylight!"

He continued watching the bird as it headed south. Billy jumped in his truck and sped off in the same direction. He tried to keep sight of the bird as he drove. Sometimes it was through the front windshield. Other times he had to poke his head out the rolled-down driver's-side window. The bird flew straight, but Billy had to zigzag down the streets to follow it.

Before long he was out of town and heading south on State Highway 82. *That's the road to Lake Tenkiller,* Billy thought.

He drove down the highway with one eye on the road and the other eye on the raven. After about fifteen minutes, the bird started losing altitude. Billy saw it come in for a landing ahead of him, not too far from the western shore of the lake.

"So he's been hiding out at the old abandoned plant nursery all this time," Billy said out loud. "Why couldn't I see that before?"

He turned his truck off the highway and into the back entrance to the nursery. There was usually a padlocked chain across that entrance, but it had been cut. Driving slowly through the grounds, Billy scanned the rows of dead plants and shrubs. He looked for any movement but saw nothing.

The empty buildings, run-down equipment, decaying plants, and dead trees gave the place an eerie feeling. *What a perfect place for the dried-up soul of an evil medicine man to hide out,* he thought.

In a few minutes he came to the nursery's main building, located in the center of the property. A car was parked near the front door of that building. Billy recognized the car. It was the one he'd seen in his nightmare vision when Ravenwood took Sara Cornsilk out of his trunk.

Billy then flashed back to memories of the place when he and Chigger used to play there as young kids. Chigger's dad had supervised the workers who took care of the plants. Sometimes on a Saturday, he and Chigger had gone to work with his dad, where they'd played hide-and-seek among the greenhouses and rows of plants.

I wish you were with me now, Chigger, Billy thought.

He knew that Sara was in danger, so he needed to take action as quickly as possible. Again he decided there wasn't time to call in the police. He'd have to check it out himself.

Moving as quietly as he could, Billy parked his truck and stepped inside the building's main entrance. It was dimly lit inside, and he had to wait for his eyes to adjust. The front area had been a reception area, but it was now empty. Behind the reception space was the first of many warehouse growing rooms.

Billy took two quiet steps into the first warehouse room and suddenly felt a cool spray of mist cover his face. For a moment he smelled the sweet fragrance of flowers. The room began spinning, and then the teen passed out and fell to the floor.

Billy didn't know how long he'd been out. He was just waking up when he heard a raspy voice say, "You're not as clever as you think you are, Lightning Boy."

Billy opened his eyes to find that he was tied securely to an office chair that had little wheels. He was in a darkened warehouse that smelled of manure and rotting plants. He blinked several times, trying to become accustomed to the dim lighting.

"I was the one who spread those nasty rumors about you," the raspy voice continued. "Small-town people are so gullible when it comes to gossip."

Ravenwood stepped into Billy's line of sight. Or *was* it Ravenwood? As Billy watched, the outline of the figure seemed to blur and shift. One moment he looked like Ravenwood. The next moment he looked like someone else, a shriveled old Native American man. Mixed in there was also the fuzzy image of a large ugly bird with beady black eyes.

"And now you've stepped right into my trap," the Birdman said. "You've arrived just in time to witness the entire glorious process. I've been saving the girl until you showed up, and I'm sure you'll enjoy the show."

The constantly changing *thing* stepped back into the darkness. A moment later there came a loud click from behind Billy. Lights came on in another area of the warehouse. In the middle of the lighted space was a worktable that had Sara strapped to it. Her head was covered with a cloth sack.

Ravenwood wheeled Billy's chair across the floor until he was within a few feet of Sara. Then the Birdman stepped over to the girl and removed the sack. Sara's mouth was taped shut. She jerked and tugged and tried in vain to break free of her bonds.

"The first step is to spark fear into your subject's heart," the Birdman said. "You've heard the saying that we have nothing to fear but fear itself. Well, in this case, it's very true. Fear is such a delicious energy. I like to start a soul meal with fear as the appetizer."

The Birdman picked up a large knife from a table close to the gurney. He licked the blade as though it held the juice of a tasty piece of food. He turned the blade back and forth to catch the light and reflect it onto Sara's face.

Billy saw Sara's eyes fly wide open in fear. That was the reaction Ravenwood was after. He bent his face down near hers and took in a deep breath.

Billy's vision had somehow been enhanced. Maybe the mist sprayed into his face had done this. Or maybe his own psychic abilities allowed it. Whatever the cause, he could actually see the fear energy glowing out from Sara. Then, when the Birdman breathed in, he could see that cloud of fear get sucked into his nostrils.

It was easy to see that Ravenwood gained strength from Sara's fear. He stood tall and erect and then turned an angry gaze toward Billy. This time when he spoke, there was no sign of the raspy voice.

"When you meddled in my affairs and warned that bus driver about the dangerous bus, you robbed me of a glorious feast!" The Birdman closed his eyes and thought about what he'd missed out on that day. "The fear I would have tasted that day could have fed me for weeks."

He opened his angry eyes and vented his fury at Billy. "But you had to go and spoil everything! You've interfered with my plans once too often!"

As the anger bubbled up from inside Ravenwood, he began a transformation. His shifting outline took the form of the old Indian medicine man. Billy guessed that this was the true form of Benjamin Blacksnake, the entity responsible for all of this.

"Your grandpa got what was coming to him," Blacksnake barked. The raspy voice had returned. "And after I'm finished with the girl here, you'll get what's coming to you."

Blacksnake began chanting the summons he'd used on Mr. Wildcat. Another step in the transformation began as the old man shape-shifted into an oversized raven. When the change was complete, he spread his wings and rose up into the overhead space near the warehouse rafters.

He then swooped down, landing on Sara's chest. Sticking his beak into her open, screaming mouth, the bird began sucking the life force from her.

Billy struggled to free himself of the rope that kept him tied to his chair. When that didn't work, he realized he could scoot the chair across the floor on its wheels. While the Raven Stalker was focused on Sara, Billy pushed himself off a support post and hurled himself backward toward the table.

He slammed into the table with the back of the chair and succeeded in knocking the bird off Sara and onto the floor. This enraged the Shape-Changer, and he directed his wrath toward Billy.

Having seen what the Raven Stalker could do with a person's fear, Billy controlled himself enough to keep the terror he felt from rising up in him. Instead, he channeled that energy into anger. He needed to fight the Birdman's anger with his own.

"Come and get me, Birdman," Billy screamed in a guttural voice. "I'm not afraid of you."

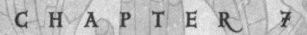

CHAPTER 7

Abnormally Bizarre

Chigger really missed hanging out with his best friend. They'd known each other since first grade. And now he was forbidden to see Billy because of some silly rumors. That was all they were. Rumors that said Billy cut the school bus brake lines. Rumors that said Billy was just trying to get publicity and become famous. Rumors that said Billy was having delusions, that he imagined he could see people's past or future.

Chigger felt he needed to get away and clear his head. He decided to borrow his dad's car to take a drive. He wanted to go visit one of the places where he and Billy had played as kids. The Greenhouse Plant and Tree Nursery had been a very active business once upon a time. His father had supervised the workers then. He remembered that the nursery went out of business years ago when the economy was bad.

Driving south through the wooded hills on State Highway 82, Chigger arrived at the back gate to the nursery in a short twenty minutes. He and Billy had sometimes come in through this gate after the place had been shut down. No one really watched this entrance.

Chigger turned his dad's car off the main road near the gate. He'd expected the entrance to have a chain across it to keep people out. But the chain had been cut and was lying in the dirt.

He drove down the narrow back road that led to the middle of the property. As he looked at the rows of dead plants and empty greenhouses, he thought of the days when he and Billy had free run through the place. Catching bugs, running foot races, and playing hide-and-seek were the games of those days. They'd even played cowboys and Indians, but Billy always got to be the Indian.

As he reached the center of the property, he saw Billy's pickup truck parked in front of the main building. Another car was parked beside it. *Why is Billy's truck way out here?* he wondered.

Chigger thought hard for a minute. He knew the police were on a manhunt for Mr. Ravenwood. He'd heard that Billy's grandpa had been hurt in some weird attack. He knew that Wesley was teaching Billy the medicine ways of the Cherokee, things that were over Chigger's head. Then a thought struck him. *Could this be where Ravenwood is hiding out? And could Billy have discovered that?*

He looked more closely at the car parked beside Billy's truck. It had a sticker on the back windshield that said *Tahlequah High School Faculty.* That meant it was definitely a teacher's car. He peered into the back seat through a side window. The inside of the car was littered with food wrappers, gym clothes, and file boxes.

Chigger tried the back-door handle and found it unlocked. Opening the door, he reached into the nearest file box and pulled out what looked like a very old book. It had a worn leather cover and was bound with leather strips. He opened it and flipped through it.

Page after page and line after line were handwritten in the Cherokee language. Chigger knew from his class in tribal history that this language had been invented by Sequoyah in the 1800s. Along with the words were crude drawings that showed plants and healing methods. With the little knowledge he had of the subject, Chigger realized that this was one of the ancient books of Cherokee formulas and spells. It was something a medicine man like Wesley might use. And he also realized that what he had stumbled into was probably dangerous and beyond his understanding. It was time to call the police or the sheriff or *somebody*.

Dropping the old book back into the box, he closed the car door, jumped in his dad's car, and sped away. He knew that just up the road was a gas station that had a phone.

Chigger didn't have a cell phone. Neither did Billy. A few years back, Billy's teenage cousin on his dad's side, Jason, was in a serious car wreck. The accident left him paralyzed from the waist down. He had been using his cell phone while driving. Ever since then, Mr. Buckhorn had forbidden Billy to have a cell phone until he turned eighteen. Chigger's parents liked the idea and did the same with him. The boys regularly used the few public pay phones still left in the area.

In a matter of minutes he was on the phone and dialing the police station, a phone number his father made him memorize in case of emergencies.

As usual, Mrs. Atwood answered, but she had been scolded by her boss. She now understood that anything having to do with Billy Buckhorn had top priority. When Chigger mentioned where he'd found Billy's truck, the woman shifted into high gear and alerted Lieutenant Swimmer to the situation. The lieutenant, in turn, blasted a message to all law officers in the area with a "code red."

Chigger drove back to the nursery to wait. Within minutes, sheriff's deputies and local policemen surrounded the greenhouse location. Not sure what they would find inside the warehouse, they had arrived without sirens. Stealth mode.

On foot, the officers split up, with a few silently sneaking in the front door. The rest moved in through the back of the place. Chigger anxiously waited outside by Billy's pickup.

With guns drawn, Lieutenant Swimmer and Officer Williams stepped into the front of the warehouse room along with Sergeant Bowers and Frank Barnes. The remaining force, including men from the sheriff's office, stepped in from the back. They all arrived inside in time to hear Billy scream, "Come and get me, Birdman. I'm not afraid of you."

What the officers saw they couldn't comprehend at first. Billy was tied to an office chair. Sara Cornsilk was strapped down on a worktable. And a very large, menacing black bird was on the floor next to the table. The bird flapped its huge wings and rose up off the floor.

The policemen thought the bird had been startled by their arrival and was flying away. But instead, when it had almost reached the rafters, the bird emitted an ear-splitting screech. It dived downward with great speed and was about to attack. It was headed straight for Billy!

It was Officer Laney Williams who got off the first shot. Then, as if startled out of a nightmarish daydream, the others fired at the diving raven. A volley of shots rang out. Several bullets tore through the bird's body. The ugly beast released a shrill, tormented squeal as it tumbled downward. Seconds later the bird's corpse hit the concrete floor with a loud thud.

Lieutenant Swimmer ran to the raven to make sure it was dead. Officer Williams took care of Sara, undoing the straps and making sure she was okay. Sergeant Bowers untied Billy from the chair.

"Are you hurt, young man?" Bowers asked him.

Before Billy could answer, Lieutenant Swimmer yelled, "Get over here. You've got to see this!"

Everyone circled the lieutenant and the dead bird. The bird's body was twisting and convulsing as it lay on the floor. Its feathers shriveled and turned into powder. Its wings morphed into human arms. For a brief moment they saw Ravenwood, the gym teacher, lying before them.

But the process wasn't complete. Ravenwood's face and hands began aging before their eyes. Seconds later they saw the shriveled body of a very old American Indian man. In an instant the old man's eyes popped wide open. There was a look of horror and panic in them, as if he'd just realized the harsh reality of his situation.

His body jerked and stiffened as it quickly began to decay. A ghostly green mist flew up out of that body and floated above them. The mist shortly formed into the shape of a man, an evil man with an evil grin. Then the form shot upward and disappeared.

The whole thing was enough to make your head spin with confusion and disbelief. Then everyone looked back down at the floor. Mr. Ravenwood's dead body was lying where the bird and the old Indian had been.

"What the hell just happened?" Swimmer asked, looking at Billy. "Do you know what's going on here?"

"Yeah, sort of," Billy said, still in awe. "But you wouldn't believe it."

Just then they heard a voice call, "Billy? Billy, are you okay?"

They looked around to see Chigger coming into the warehouse.

"Chigger!" Billy exclaimed with excitement. "Boy, am I glad to see you!"

The two old friends hugged and left the warehouse together. Lieutenant Swimmer never got a real answer to his question.

A few days later, Grandpa Wesley was released from the hospital. He and the rest of the Buckhorn family were invited to a little celebration at the police station. Chigger and his parents were also invited, as were Sara and her family. Of course, Lieutenant Swimmer also asked a couple of newspaper reporters to come so the local police department could get some good publicity.

During the event, Billy and Chigger were given citations for bravery in honor of their actions in the case. They'd help stop a dangerous child predator before he had a chance to seriously hurt any children in their area.

A more in-depth background check had revealed that Ravenwood had harmed several children among the Eastern Cherokees in North Carolina. But then he was using the name Raulingwood instead of Ravenwood, so there was no record of the man as he was known in Oklahoma. As an athletic coach in that eastern state, he'd kidnapped and tortured several students.

Sara, who was an attractive sixteen-year-old Cherokee girl, was especially grateful to Billy for his heroism. She approached him near the punch bowl as he chatted with Chigger.

"Billy, I want to thank you for saving me," she said in a low, sweet voice. "If you hadn't rammed your chair into that evil bird thing, there's no telling what it might have done."

"Ah, it was nothing," Billy replied, a little flustered by the attention from the girl.

"Oh, no," Sara protested. "It was definitely something."

Chigger just watched with amusement as the conversation continued.

"As a matter of fact, my parents and I would like to invite you over for dinner," she said. "We'd like to spend some time with you to get to know you better."

"Well, uh, I guess that'd be all right," Billy replied with a stutter.

Then, unexpectedly, she raised her index finger to her lips and kissed it. She touched the kissed finger to Billy's neck right on top of the spiderweb scar. Using her other hand, she slipped a piece of paper into his hand. She gave him a big smile and trotted back to her parents. Billy flushed with embarrassment. Chigger took full advantage of the moment.

"Billy's got a girlfriend," he said in a low, mocking tone.

"Oh, shut up, Chigger," Billy said as he opened the folded piece of paper.

"What does it say? What does it say?" Chigger asked excitedly.

"It's her address and phone number," Billy answered, looking toward Sara, who stood across the room. She winked at him, and again he blushed.

After that, Chigger's parents came over and stood next to Chigger.

"Billy, I want to apologize for listening to those rumors and not trusting you," Chigger's dad said. "We should've known better." He reached out his hand to Billy, and they shook.

Chigger's mom gave him a hug and added, "You're welcome at our house anytime."

Then Chigger chimed in. "And I still want to manage your career when the reality TV offers come pouring in," he said with a laugh.

Billy punched his friend in the arm and knew that everything was back to normal. Well, almost everything.

The next day a newspaper story reported a few details about the kidnapping of Sara and the death of Mr. Ravenwood. The story reminded readers of Billy Buckhorn's brush with lightning. Then it went on to explain how he'd amazingly prevented the injury of a busload of students. Finally, it praised him for his other accomplishments in saving Mr. Wildcat, his own grandfather, and Sara Cornsilk. The story even mentioned how Chigger had helped by stumbling onto Ravenwood's hideout.

But there was no mention of the strange events that had taken place in the plant nursery warehouse or eyewitness accounts of the Raven Stalker's supernatural actions against Sara, the gym teacher, or Billy's grandfather. However, rumors about those hidden details ran rampant through the community, the state, and even the nation. That's how the legend of Billy Buckhorn got started and then blew up on social media.

It wasn't long before letters from newspaper readers, social media consumers, and Internet enthusiasts started arriving at the Buckhorn house. One woman wanted Billy to come and touch her car to see if she was going to have an accident. Another woman wanted Billy's help in locating a lost wedding ring. A man asked Billy to help him find his twin brother, who'd gone missing several years ago. An elderly Cherokee lady said she'd pay him to come to her house and rid her of a ghost that haunted the place.

On and on the requests came in. Billy and his dad talked about what should be done with all these requests. They decided it would be best to ask Wesley about that. Wesley was at home healing from his wounds, so Billy and his dad drove to the elder Buckhorn's house.

Three generations of Buckhorns sat down at Grandpa's kitchen table to drink coffee and talk. Billy showed the stack of letters to Wesley.

"That's how it begins," the elder said. "People hear about your abilities. Maybe they hear about how you helped someone they know. Pretty soon they're lined up outside your house, waiting for you to perform the miracle they need."

"What am I supposed to do?" Billy said. "I can't help these people. I don't even know where to begin."

"I do," Wesley said with a smile. "Your grandma taught me before she died. And you've already begun your training. You've already experienced the power of the dark side of the medicine, so you know what you may be up against."

Billy let that thought sink in for a moment before he spoke again. "In my vision at the stomp dance, I saw a ladder with thirteen rungs. Why thirteen? I thought that number was bad luck."

"Good question," Wesley replied. "I bet your dad knows the answer to that."

"As a matter of fact, I do," Billy's dad said. "The number thirteen came to mean bad luck among European Christians a long time ago. Gatherings of witches, known as covens, numbered thirteen. Friday the thirteenth became unlucky after the Catholic pope had several of his enemies arrested or killed on that day a thousand years ago."

"It's a European myth?" Billy asked.

"Yep," Billy's dad replied. "But if you think about it, Jesus and his disciples numbered thirteen, so it really doesn't make sense."

"Among us Cherokees and several other tribes, the number thirteen is actually a good thing," Wesley added. "Our old lunar calendar has thirteen months because there are thirteen full moons within a year. And, as you saw in your vision, there are thirteen steps on the ladder of Cherokee spiritual growth. When you reach the top of the ladder, you become a true human being, according to the old ways."

"Okay, I'm beginning to get it," Billy said thoughtfully. "I have a lot to learn. Like how did Ravenwood get mixed up with the dead medicine man Blacksnake?"

"I'll tell you exactly how that happened," Grandpa said.

He stepped into his bedroom and returned toting a large, old book. It was the book Chigger had discovered in Ravenwood's car at the nursery. Wesley placed the book on the kitchen table in front of Billy. Its cover was held closed by a leather strap and metal clasp.

"Go ahead and take a look," the elder instructed.

Billy undid the metal clasp and opened the book's worn leather cover. Unexpectedly, a palpable force was released from the books pages that hit the teen squarely in the chest.

"What was that?" Billy said, grabbing his chest. "Something hit me."

"That, literally, is the power of the spells," Wesley explained. "Most people wouldn't feel that, but you did. That's the sign that tells me you're ready to proceed with the training."

Billy's father sat silently observing the other two Buckhorns as they took another step together into the supernatural realm.

"This is *the* oldest copy of the Cherokee book of spells I've ever seen," Wesley said. "It is an original, more complete version of the copied pages I inherited from your great-grandfather."

"This should be kept in a rare book collection in a university," Billy's father said as he looked over Billy's shoulder in awe. "It should be studied and catalogued."

"And made available to other people with bad intentions?" Wesley asked. "No. This copy belonged to Benjamin Blacksnake and is potentially very dangerous. It was found among Ravenwood's personal belongings, and I'm hanging on to it. It will eventually become Billy's."

"How did you get it?" James asked his father.

"Lieutenant Swimmer gave it to me," Grandpa replied. "He said the case was closed, and it wouldn't be needed as evidence. Especially since they're pretending they didn't see what they saw in the warehouse."

"How did Ravenwood get hold of it?" Billy asked.

"That's something else the police shared with me," Grandpa answered. "Swimmer said Raulingwood lived in an old house where Blacksnake had once lived on the Eastern Cherokee reservation. I guess Blacksnake's ghost lingered around the house, waiting for some unsuspecting victim to find his book of spells hidden there."

"So it really wasn't Raulingwood, or Ravenwood, who was harming those kids," Billy observed. "Blacksnake had taken over his body and his life."

"That's right. Ravenwood was really a victim too."

"This is all so bizarre," Billy said. "It's hard to believe it's real."

"Oh, it's real, all right," Wesley said. "And it's just the beginning for you, young man. When I was in the hospital, you stepped up and did what needed to be done. You took the next brave step on the ladder in your vision. On the ladder of your life. The things you'll see and the things you'll do in the future would boggle a normal person's mind."

"Ravenwood called me abnormal," Billy said. "He meant it as an insult."

"You seem to come from a long line of abnormal people," Billy's dad said with a smile.

Wesley picked up his cup of coffee and proposed a toast. "Here's to being abnormal," he said. "And, Billy, may you have a long, abnormal life."

Three generations of Buckhorns clinked their cups together in celebration.

"What's next on Billy's medicine man training agenda?" James asked his father.

"Billy needs to spend more time learning to read and write the Cherokee language using Sequoyah's syllabary and helping me treat people with Cherokee herbs and formulas," the elder answered. "It can take up a lot of time."

"If I'm going to do this right, I probably should drop out of school so I can focus on the healing," Billy offered.

"Not so fast, young man," his father countered. "Graduating from high school has got to have top priority."

"There's always the GED," Wesley interjected.

"What's that?" Billy said.

"General Educational Development," James replied, giving his father a disapproving look. "It's essentially a set of tests you take to demonstrate your knowledge of certain subjects. If you pass the tests, you get the equivalent of a high school diploma."

"That works for me," Billy said enthusiastically. "I bet there's a book you can use to study for the tests." After a pause, he continued with "*GED for Dummies* or *CliffsNotes* or . . . something!"

"That's not an option for you," his father said. "You need to get a proper diploma, because you are going to college."

"Maybe I will and maybe I won't," the teen said, rising from his seat. "Not everyone is geared toward sitting in classrooms, listening to boring lectures, and writing useless essays!" He took a few steps away from the kitchen table but turned back. "I'll be attending the Wesley Buckhorn College of Supernatural Knowledge. That's way more exclusive than any Ivy League institution!"

The teen turned once again and stomped away, leaving his father and grandfather staring at each other.

"To be continued," James said as he left his father's kitchen to follow his son out of the house.

CHAPTER 8

The Intertribal
Medicine Council

After receiving the long-awaited message from the ancestor spirits on the day of the Full Green Corn Moon in August, Osage elder Cecil Lookout and his family had spread word of the spiritual warning to the members of the Intertribal Medicine Council, or ITMC. Then, coming from all parts of North America, this group of elders gathered on the first day of autumn, September 22, in St. Louis, Missouri, on the ancient Native American mound next to Cecil's home.

Participation in the Medicine Council was unlike participation in most organizations. There were no annual dues, no formal bylaws, no rules of order, and no political posturing. Required qualities for membership included a powerful intuition, dedication to service, scrupulous morals, an impeccable reputation within your own tribal community, and familiarity with one's own traditional tribal medicine practices.

It was during that autumn meeting that Cecil's archaeologist son, Ethan, reported several important but disturbing facts to the council. Ethan was one of the few Native American diggers in the country, and his primary focus was on ancient Native American Mound Builder cultures and sites. North America was home to thousands of village locations where Indigenous peoples had constructed earthen mounds as part of cultural and religious communities from about AD 800 to AD 1500.

"By now you've heard of the passing of council member Elmore Proctor," Ethan announced to those gathered for the autumn meeting. "When I heard of his death, I immediately traveled to visit his family, and I've already conveyed a message of sympathy on your behalf," he said.

It was essential to maintain the participation of the full thirteen members of the council to keep the group's energy and power in place, so the remaining twelve members voted to immediately look for Proctor's replacement.

And since Proctor was also one of the five Keepers of the ancient Sky Stone, his piece had to be recovered and reassigned to another member for protection and preservation as soon as possible.

The Sky Stone, constructed a thousand years ago, consisted of four ring-shaped pieces that fit together tightly when inserted into the slots cut into the round center piece. By themselves, these five pieces made for a unique sculptural creation, but they became something much more when the hexagonal hole in the middle was fitted with the six-sided quartz piece known as the Fire Crystal.

According to prophecy and legend, the reassembly of all five pieces, plus the crystal center, activated this device, transforming it into a supernatural portal connecting the Middleworld and the Upperworld and connecting humans and the Sky People. A mysterious and powerful medicine man had fashioned this magical object from a single meteorite that fell to earth the day twin sons were born to the first divine ruler of Solstice City. Reactivation of the Sky Stone could only happen at the right moment in time by the Chosen One as part of the fulfillment of the ancient prophecy.

"A more serious issue is that no one in Elmore's family knows the whereabouts of the keys to the bank deposit box where his section of the Sky Stone has been stored," Ethan continued. "I was allowed to search among a few of his private things and could not locate it."

A palpable gasp spread through the meeting.

"I'll be heading back down to Choctaw Country in a few days to continue the search," said Ethan, "so don't start worrying yet. There are a couple more relatives to check with who may know about that key."

"But you have some good news for us, don't you, son?" Cecil said.

"Yes, I do," the archaeologist replied. "We've long known the cape and staff belonging to the Son of the Sun were buried with his body at Spiral Mounds in southeastern Oklahoma. As his direct descendant, several years ago I submitted a claim of ownership to the Spiral Mounds director for his remains and funerary objects. For a long time, we never received a response from Director Langford, because there's no precedent for such a claim. He basically didn't know what to do or how to respond, but he left me a phone message saying there's been a change in the case."

"At least we're secure in the idea that the staff containing the Fire Crystal remains buried at that location, right?" Cecil said.

"Right," Ethan replied. "In addition to contacting Director Langford, I'm going to reach out to an archaeologist friend in the area, Dr. Augustus Stevens, to see if he can help us out with this. I'll report back when I know anything."

That ended Ethan's report to the group. His father continued the announcements.

"We also must seriously begin our search for the Chosen One," Cecil informed this unique collection of Native American healers, prophets, and spiritual leaders. "In August the Ancient

Ones said the Thunder Beings were about to make their choice, so here we are in late September, and by now this person's miraculous abilities *must* have been witnessed by people in their community. It's time to reach out to everyone you know in Indian Country so we can locate this very important person. Our very future here in the Middleworld depends on it."

After the group concluded their business, an honor dance was held for Elmore Proctor to remember his years of service to the council and to assist him in his spirit world journey.

When the ITMC had finished its business, Cecil met with his son to discuss the problem of the missing key to the bank deposit box. The elder felt there was more to the story.

"We suspect foul play in Elmore's death," Ethan told his father in a private meeting. "I will return to Elmore's home community to gather more detailed information, because dark medicine from a not-so-upstanding medicine man nearby may be the ultimate cause of his death. It could be the work of the Owl Clan."

"We should go together," Cecil said, and his son agreed.

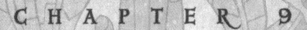

CHAPTER 9

Pumpkin Pie
and the Crystal Cave

s autumn progressed, Billy and his father continued to argue about whether or not Billy had to attend high school or take the GED tests. Billy's mother, of course, agreed with her husband on the matter, so the teen was outnumbered, and he kept going to school.

Billy's relationship with Sara provided a convenient means of escape from the argument, at least at first. A couple of afternoons a week, he drove to her house after school to do homework together. But those eventually evolved into make-out sessions in Sara's bedroom, because both her parents worked and didn't get home until after five o'clock. The teens made sure Billy was long gone before then.

And another couple of afternoons a week, Billy spent time at Wesley's house trying to read and write Cherokee, but that was too much like schoolwork for Billy's taste. He knew this was an important part of the training, but he had trouble applying himself to anything associated with books or studying or practicing.

So the time spent with Sara combined with the time spent with Grandpa left little time to spend with Chigger. And Chigger resented it.

"It's part of life," Chigger's mother had explained when he'd complained to her. "Things change. People change. You can't expect friendships to always remain the same. Why don't you take up a new hobby, other than reading comic books, or think of some other activity to take your mind off Billy?"

Although he really didn't like the idea, the boy decided to give his mother's advice a try. There were clubs at school he could join. What about theater? He'd always felt he had a flair for performance and drama. Who knows—he might meet a cute girl and end up with a girlfriend of his own. He vowed to look into it.

Within a couple of months after the Raven Stalker episode, Billy's life had settled into what seemed like a more normal pattern. The mini movies in his head mostly ceased, and he'd gotten used to writing the syllabary in his composition notebook on a regular basis.

But by early November, one thing that had begun to bother Billy about Sara was the amount of time she spent on social media. He was convinced she was addicted. More specifically, what *really* bothered him were the increasing number of posts that included details about him, his activities, his appearance, and his interactions with her.

"The details of my life are not intended as content for your online media life," he told her in a rather blunt way. "Kids at school I don't even know are talking about the places you and I have been and the things we have done."

"Ah, that's just part of being famous," she replied dismissively. "You'll get used to it. You'll see."

That was the day Billy began finding less and less available time to spend with Sara and more and more available time to do almost anything else.

When the Thanksgiving break arrived, he knew it was time to get away from his daily routine and try to mend fences with his longtime best friend. It hadn't been all that hard for the boys to convince their parents to let them go on a camping trip instead of staying home for the holiday.

Billy's dad was usually carrying on about the "myth of the first Thanksgiving." He said the Pilgrims never really invited the Indians over for dinner to thank them for helping them survive, so the Buckhorn family often didn't do much that day. Sometimes Billy's mom worked at the hospital during the holiday to earn extra money for the family. That's what she'd be doing today.

Chigger's parents, Sam and Molly Muskrat, needed to spend most of the four days fixing several leaks in the roof of their aging mobile home. The last storm that blew into Cherokee country had ripped loose several roof sections. The next storm would bring damaging rains that would ruin carpets and furniture unless those leaks were sealed. Luckily Chigger was able to escape those home repair duties.

Eastern Oklahoma's crisp autumn air always reminded Billy of his grandma Awinita. The Cherokee medicine woman had usually served hot apple cider and warm pumpkin pie whenever he went to visit her and Grandpa Wesley in the autumn months. Sadly, she'd passed away when Billy was only six years old. But he continued to smell the sweet smell of apple cider and pumpkin pie at odd times and places during the season.

Like this morning when he woke up inside his tent on the bank of the Arkansas River. He and Chigger were on a canoeing and camping trip. It would take them along this wide, winding river for the four-day Thanksgiving holiday. Chigger lay in his sleeping bag on the other side of the tent a few feet from Billy—snoring.

The smells that Billy had expected to smell in that tent that morning included Billy's stinky feet, sweaty camping clothes, stale potato chips, and decaying fallen leaves that lay near their camp. Not apple cider and pumpkin pie.

Then Billy realized it was probably just his mind playing tricks on him. After all, it was Thanksgiving Day. Many families would be starting to prepare the day's big meal. That could include baking pumpkin pies in the oven and warming up apple cider on the stove. So his own memories of Thanksgiving Days gone by might have produced the strong smells in his brain.

Billy unzipped his sleeping bag and checked the portable thermometer hanging from the tent's center support pole. It read thirty-two degrees. That was warmer than the TV weatherman had predicted. Grabbing his camouflage coat, the brown-skinned boy crawled out of the tent to greet the frozen morning. He already had on his clothes because he'd worn them to bed the night before.

Rays of sunlight fell on his face, and he smiled.

"Good morning, Grandfather Sun," he said in English. Then he repeated the greeting in newly learned Cherokee. He could see the fog of his warm breath in the chilly air as he spoke.

Picking up a few dried twigs and dead leaves from the pile they'd collected yesterday, he set about the task of building a fire. He started by arranging the kindling in the shape of a little tipi in their fire pit. He struck a match and touched the flame to the base of the small leaf-and-twig construction to get a fire going.

His grandpa Wesley liked to joke that traditional Cherokees used only "traditional Cherokee matches" to light fires, like their ancestors had done in the old days. Of course, there was no such thing as a traditional Cherokee match. And traditional Cherokees often used the best and easiest method they could find to do things, as did most Natives.

After adding a few larger pieces of wood to the fire, Billy performed the seven-directions ceremony Grandpa Wesley had taught him. He hadn't missed a morning since his dangerous clash with the Raven Stalker.

He honored the four directions—east, south, west, and north—for the wisdom and strength each brought to him. Then he honored Father Sky above him and Mother Earth beneath him for their life-giving energies. Finally, he honored his own heart, his own being—a gift given by Creator, who was the source of it all.

When he'd finished, he could still smell the apple cider and pumpkin pie. It was a comforting smell, so he decided to stop questioning it. He just accepted it. After all, it *was* better than smelling those other odors he'd thought of.

Then he decided to play a little trick on his friend. Moving quietly toward the tent, where Chigger still lay sleeping, Billy roared like a bear and pawed at the sides. Inside, Chigger abruptly sat up and yelled at the top of his lungs. He feared for his very life. At that point Billy howled with laughter at his friend's frightened response.

Chigger sighed at once again being pranked by his old friend.

"You got me good, Billy Buckhorn," Chigger said as he stumbled out of the tent. He was pulling on his own army-surplus coat. "And I was having this great dream about hot apple cider and warm pumpkin pie."

That took Billy by complete surprise.

"That's weird, because I've been smelling those very things since I woke up," Billy said. "But I just thought my mind was playing tricks on me."

"Speaking of pie and cider, what's for breakfast?" Chigger asked, though he already knew the answer.

"Whatever we can shoot or catch," Billy said. "Would you rather go hunting or fishing this morning?"

"How about a quick trip to McDonalds?" Chigger joked. "Do they have a paddle-through window?"

"Out here all you could get is an order of flies and a chocolate snake," Billy said as he joined in the joke.

As the boys chuckled at their own brand of humor, Billy grabbed the coffee pot and bag of ground coffee.

"I'll start some coffee," Billy said. "You look like you could use a cup."

Chigger ducked back inside the tent briefly. When he came back out, he was holding two large protein bars wrapped in shiny foil packages.

"Or we could just chow down on these," he said.

He handed one of the bars to Billy. He was proud that he'd brought something Billy hadn't.

"I thought we were going all natural on this outing," Billy said as he tore open the wrapping on his bar. He took a bite.

"That was your big idea," Chigger said, taking a bite out of his own bar. "I never agreed to any such thing."

"At least you didn't bring your comic books on this trip," Billy said. "You didn't, did you?"

"No, I figured you'd probably just burn them in the campfire or throw them overboard, so I left them all at home."

"Good!" Billy said sternly and then smiled.

The two friends squatted by the fire. Warming themselves and watching the coffee boil, they chewed on their breakfast.

"Chigger, I'm sorry I haven't had more time to spend with you lately," Billy said between bites. "It's just that—"

"I know, I know," Chigger interrupted. "Since you hooked up with Sara, you don't have time for anything or anyone else. That's the problem!"

"I didn't realize that girlfriends demanded so much time and attention," Billy said in his own defense. "It's a new experience for me. And I do enjoy being with her."

"More than doing things with me, I guess," Chigger replied.

Rather than answer, Billy poured them both a cup of the freshly brewed black coffee.

"Don't make this a 'you against her' thing," Billy said. Handing his friend a cup, he added, "I've only known her for two months now. You and I have been pals all our lives. And as far as I'm concerned, we always will be."

Chigger sipped and chewed quietly for a long moment. Billy's vow of lifelong friendship had begun to sooth his hurt feelings.

"Okay, I accept your apology," Chigger finally said, standing up. "But don't think this little trip completely makes up for ignoring me." He turned and headed for the tent.

"I swear, Charles Checotah Muskrat, you sound more like my girlfriend than my girlfriend!" Billy called out.

Chigger stopped dead in his tracks, turned, and made a running dive at Billy. He hit his mark, and the two boys wrestled and rolled not far from the fire.

"Hey, hey, hey," Billy protested as he wrestled. "You'll get us both burned!"

Chigger released his hold and fell on his back. The boys broke out laughing. That felt good to them both. The tension that had been hanging over them had dissolved. Soon they became totally focused on the day's adventure.

The sun was still low in the sky as they broke down camp and cleaned up the site. Quickly their gear was packed away and stowed. After one last check of the campsite, the pair stepped into their canoe and shoved offshore.

They moved easily downstream. Because they were following the flow of the river, they really didn't have to work that hard. This river flowed south and east through Oklahoma. Then it passed through Arkansas and spilled into the Mississippi River. All that water was headed for the Gulf of Mexico.

But the boys weren't going that far. They were only going as far as the state line—if they felt like it. There was really no set place to get to. This trip was more about the journey itself— exploring for the sake of exploring.

As the day moved along, so did the river. It took them through several changes in landscape and scenery. Plowed fields, jagged bluffs, majestic oaks, and sandy shorelines cruised by. The sun rose in a cloudless sky, warming the air to a pleasant sixty degrees. That was what Billy's thermometer read. At midday they fished from the canoe as it floated along. Chigger used a cane pole he'd brought. Billy tried his hand at gigging.

A gig is a long pole tipped with a forklike spear. Billy learned from Grandpa Wesley that the Cherokees had used them a lot in the old days. Gigs were good for harvesting fish, frogs, and lizards to eat. Billy was almost as good with a gig as he was with a blowgun. Chigger remembered that his friend had won first prize in the blowgun contest during the Cherokee National Holiday in September.

Billy successfully speared three fish, and Chigger pulled in two. Soon they stopped at a curve in the river to cook their meal. Finding a sandy shore, they built a small fire using dried driftwood. To the main course, the boys added dried fruit and nuts they'd brought from home.

Just as the pair finished eating, the ground beneath their feet began to shake. Chigger, who was squatting at the edge of the river washing his hands, lost his balance and fell into the water. Billy, repacking supplies in their canoe at the time, managed to keep the craft from floating off down the river. Both of the boys stayed low to the ground until the shaking ended.

"I always wondered what an earthquake felt like," Billy said.

"I didn't know we had earthquakes in Oklahoma," Chigger said.

They remained quiet and still for a few minutes more, not sure if more shaking was to come. When it seemed safe, the teens stood and looked around. Nothing nearby seemed to have fallen or broken or caved in. No gaping holes had apparently opened up in their area.

"Maybe Mother Earth was trying to tell you to take a bath," Billy said. "You are beginning to smell a little ripe."

"Ha ha," Chigger replied as he stepped into the canoe. "Very funny."

Before shoving off again, the pair checked the map to see what might be coming up ahead. Billy's dad, the college professor, had told him of ancient Native burial grounds near Spiral, Oklahoma. The site had once been home to the original peoples of the area, known as Mound Builders. They had created cities a thousand years ago that were larger than cities in Europe at the time. This was long before the Cherokees were forced by the US government to move from their homelands to eastern Oklahoma.

Billy found Spiral Mounds State Park on the map. It seemed to be a little farther downriver than the boys wanted to go. Chigger spotted a section of the river that looked interesting. From what he could tell on the map, it was closer to them and seemed to be away from farmlands, homes, or towns. That was just what they were looking for. They decided to shoot for that spot before nightfall.

The afternoon shadows grew long as the sun set in the west. The boys had to do some real paddling to keep on schedule. It would be no fun trying to set up camp in the dark.

Before long they arrived at the stretch of river they were looking for. A rugged rocky shore rose straight up from the water's edge for about one hundred yards, creating a sheer cliff face. Piles of rocks of various sizes lay at the foot of the cliff, partially blocking that part of the river. Billy thought the rock pile might have been the result of the earthquake.

Just as he finished that thought, another round of ground shaking began. This time the boys were in the canoe floating on the water. Waves coming from both riverbanks crashed into them, tossing their little boat back and forth, up and down. Luckily, they'd strapped all their gear to the canoe's interior crossbars, so nothing fell overboard.

But, as the quake continued, slabs of the cliff face began to break free and plummet into the water below. The teens were far enough away not to be in the line of fire of the falling boulders, but whole new sets of waves were generated each time a slab slapped the river's surface. Each wave tossed the canoe to and fro, making Chigger feel seasick.

After what seemed an eternity, the quaking ceased, and the wave action ended. Billy surveyed their surroundings. A shelf of flat land jutted out from a section of the cliff nearest them. It looked to be just large enough for a campsite with room for a fire pit, the tent, and a parking place for the canoe.

The boys quickly paddled to the shore, stepped carefully out of the canoe, and tested the ground to make sure it was solid.

"Hope that's the end of the quaking and shaking," Chigger said nervously. "I'd hate to wake up flat as a pancake in the morning under a bunch of boulders."

"This is so unusual," Billy said. "I think my dad said there haven't been any earthquakes around here since the 1800s."

The boys really didn't have time to discuss the history of Oklahoma earthquakes. It was rapidly growing dark in their overnight river canyon home. The two quickly set about the task of unloading the canoe and making a camp. Because they'd done this so many times over the years, it didn't take them long to get set up.

By the time night fell, they had food cooking over the open fire they'd built. This time the food came from freeze-dried food packs furnished by Chigger. They weren't as tasty as wild rabbit or fresh fish, but they didn't require catching or skinning. Chigger was once again proud that he'd thought of bringing something Billy hadn't thought of.

After they'd eaten their freeze-dried chicken-fried steaks and mashed potatoes, Billy launched into a different history lesson he'd learned.

"What do you know about the Mound Builder Indians, Chig?" he began.

"Not much," Chigger replied. "We had a couple of pages on them in my American history class last year. In the part about prehistoric America. But I don't remember school stuff when I'm not in school. Heck, I hardly remember it when I'm *in* school."

"*Mound Builders* is the name archaeologists have given to large groups of Indians who lived in villages near rivers about a thousand years ago," Billy told him. "They had big permanent towns that often covered huge areas of land. There were hundreds of these communities spread all across America. Over time those Natives became the tribes we know today."

"How do you keep this stuff in your head? Is it part of what your dad taught you?"

"Yeah, but I'm kind of into learning where things came from. What was around before we came along, you know?"

"Sure," Chigger said with a "whatever" attitude. He wasn't big on lectures about some old piece of historic trivia.

"Anyway," Billy resumed, "they're called Mound Builders because of the large earthen mounds they constructed. These were places where the chiefs and priests lived. The chiefs ruled over thousands of people. The priests led large numbers of religious followers who believed that the Milky Way was the path of the souls of the dead."

Chigger yawned a big, loud yawn meant to shut down Billy's lecture before it went any further. But Billy kept on.

"One of the Mound Builder religious centers was located just down the river from where we are now, at Spiral," he continued.

Chigger began snoring loudly as if he'd fallen asleep.

"Okay, okay," Billy said. "I get the message. But you're missing a little-known bit of Native American history."

Chigger made big, loud gestures of moaning, smacking his lips, and scratching his head to prevent Billy from saying another word. Chigger's dramatic actions achieved their purpose. Billy agreed to call it quits for the night.

They remembered to do one last thing before curling up in their sleeping bags. That was to check the battery on the satellite phone they'd brought. They kept this special piece of high-tech gear in a waterproof bag. That way it wouldn't get wet if their canoe tipped over.

The Cherokee Nation Marshal Service had loaned the device to Billy and Chigger after the boys helped rescue Sara from the Raven Stalker in September. That was when the tribe learned that neither Billy nor Chigger owned cell phones.

Deputy Marshal Travis Youngblood had offered to make the boys honorary youth marshals, which included a crash course in emergency preparedness. He'd worked with the boys, and they'd become friends in a short time. Deputy Youngblood had loaned them the phone, known as a sat phone, as sort of an award for bravery in the face of danger.

What was great about sat phones was that they worked in places cell phones didn't. All you needed was to be out in the open. The phone worked by sending and receiving signals to a satellite circling thousands of miles above the earth. And Deputy Marshal Youngblood had already programmed his phone number in, along with several other area emergency service numbers. "Call me anytime, day or night," Youngblood had said.

Chigger pulled their phone out of its container and turned it on. He could read both the battery level and signal strength on the unit's LED screen.

"They're both at full strength," he reported. "Sure hope we don't have to use this thing," he added as he shut it off and stuffed it back in the waterproof bag. "I bet we're the only kids in the Cherokee Nation with a satellite phone. Too bad we can't play video games on it out here in the dark."

"I *could* call Sara on it to say good night," Billy said.

"I think I'm gonna be sick," Chigger replied with great drama. "All that smoochy talk between you two makes me wanna barf."

He made a grand gesture of gagging by the light of the camp lantern. Then the boys fell silent. Though they'd forgotten about it earlier, the campers could still smell the aroma of pie and cider floating on the air.

The night was mostly quiet. The only sound to be heard was river water flowing nearby. The calming noise quickly put the fearless explorers to sleep.

Billy awoke the following morning with a start. He lay in his sleeping bag and listened to his surroundings. He heard nothing but the sound of the gently flowing river. He looked across the tent. Chigger's sleeping bag was empty. He was already up and gone.

Billy stepped outside the tent. The morning air felt warmer than it had the previous morning. But there was no sign of his friend anywhere in the campsite. This was unusual. Chigger rarely ventured into unknown places without Billy.

But ever since the Raven Stalker incident, Billy's friend had become a little more adventurous. He hadn't been as fearful of doing things alone at night. He hadn't looked to Billy to always take the lead. Maybe this was because Chigger had been forced to do many things alone since the era of Sara began. Or maybe he had grown more courageous. After all, Chigger had played a role in saving Billy's life in the nick of time.

"Chigger!" Billy called out. "Where are you?"

No answer.

He searched the camp area for clues to his friend's location. That was when he noticed a piece of yellow cloth. It was tied to a cluster of vines growing up the face of the jagged cliff behind the campsite. He recognized the cloth as part of the trail kit they'd brought with them. The yellow flags could be used to mark a trail in the woods by tying them to trees or shrubs.

Within a few steps, Billy was close enough to the cloth to reach out and touch it. That was when he first noticed a hollowed-out indentation in the cliff rock next to the cloth. Just above that indentation was another one. And then another one above that. Stepping back and looking up, Billy realized that these were man-made steps cut into the side of the cliff. And they seemed to run up about thirty or forty feet to a ledge that jutted out from the cliff face.

"Chigger, are you up there?"

Again, no answer.

"All right, here I come," he said loudly, half expecting Chigger to jump out from behind a rock or something. But there was nothing for Chigger to hide behind. So up the carved-out staircase Billy went.

When he got to the top step, it was an easy sideways move to reach the ledge he'd seen from below. The ledge stuck out from the cliff far enough for him to safely stand upright. A pattern of crumbled rocks lay scattered around the ledge, looking as though they'd once formed a stone wall.

More earthquake damage? he thought.

Looking up from the fallen stones, Billy gazed westward across the river, discovering undulating rows of tree-covered hills disappearing into the distance.

Upstream to his right was the highway bridge they'd paddled under yesterday. Downstream to the left a few miles were the ancient Indian mounds at Spiral.

Turning back to the ledge, he saw Chigger's bootprints between the rocks in the layer of dust that covered the ledge. Those prints led directly to an opening in the side of the cliff. It was a cave! And Chigger had entered it by himself! Billy was shocked. His timid friend had gone in there alone.

He stood at the mouth of the cave and called in. "Chigger, are you in there?"

To his relief, there was a reply from within the darkness.

"Billy, you gotta see this!" Chigger's excited voice rang out. "It's stupendous!"

"I don't have a flashlight," Billy said. "How can you see where you're going?"

"Hang on," Chigger replied. "I'll bring the light to you."

In a few moments Billy saw the bouncing beam of a high-powered flashlight coming toward him through the darkness. In another few moments Chigger's form emerged from that darkness.

"Look at you," Billy said when his friend reached him. "Exploring a deep, dark cavern all by yourself."

"Different, huh?" Chigger said with a big grin. "Wait till you see what I found. This way."

He turned the light back toward the darkness. He walked down a narrow path that led deep into the cliff. Billy followed. As the pair moved inward, the light from outside faded behind them. Soon they were engulfed in a black velvet blanket pierced only by the light in Chigger's hand.

Strange shapes and alien forms surrounded the teens. These were revealed as the flashlight's beam glanced over the cave's inner surfaces. Stalactites hung from the cave's ceiling. Stalagmites grew upward from the uneven floor. These mineral structures looked like pairs of frozen arms reaching toward each other.

Ahead, Chigger and his light came to a stop.

"This is what I wanted you to see," Chigger called out.

Billy caught up to his friend a moment later. Chigger's light pointed to a place where the path split in two. To the right, the flashlight showed a path leading downward into the darkness. And to the left there was a path leading upward. Right in the middle where they stood was the edge of a cave wall that separated the two.

"Now look closer," Chigger said, pointing the light at a spot on the dividing wall. Billy stepped closer to the bright spot to see what Chigger was talking about. After his eyes adjusted, a panel of markings and etched drawings came into focus.

"What did I tell you?" Chigger asked proudly. "Is that stupendous or what?"

Billy remained silent as he examined the markings more closely. These were cut into the stone, carved by some sharp object. On the left side of the panel was a crude drawing of what looked like a half man, half bird standing next to some sort of pedestal or altar.

On the right side was another drawing. This time there was a creature that looked like a big snake with antlers floating underwater. Billy reached out to touch the markings and realized that there was a layer of dust partly covering them. Brushing the dust away revealed two more shallow symbols.

On the right near the serpent, an arrow pointed to the downward path. Below the arrow was a large X. On the left near the half-man, half-bird figure, an arrow pointed upward. It also had an image that looked like a sun coming up over the horizon.

"Well, what are we waiting for?" Billy asked. "Up or down? Which way?"

"I'll let you pick," Chigger replied. "I'm not ready for that kind of pressure."

Billy gave his friend a funny look. "What are you talking about, Chigger? This is your discovery. You get to choose."

That seemed to make Chigger nervous. "Okay, let me think about it for a minute."

He stood there with a pained look on his face. Billy thought this was ridiculous. He grabbed the light from Chigger's hand, pointed it along the upward path, and headed out.

"Wait for me!" Chigger yelled when he realized he was being left behind.

Within about fifty feet, the boys rounded a corner in their upward climb and came upon an amazing view. The cave opened up into a large space filled with hundreds if not thousands of whitish-clear quartz crystals. Some came up from the floor. Others grew out of the walls and the ceiling. These gems jutted this way and that. As Billy moved the flashlight's beam across the crystals, countless numbers of smaller light beams were reflected and refracted in every direction. The resulting light show was dazzling.

"WOW" was all Chigger could say.

"Double WOW" was all Billy could say.

They continued on the upward path through the crystal-encased room. The path eventually curved again and ended in a smaller crystal room. Searching the space with their light beam, they found a raised multisided platform in the middle of the space. It was about four feet tall and looked like the pedestal they'd seen in the markings at the beginning of the path.

Standing upright in the top middle of the pedestal was a large, perfectly shaped six-sided quartz crystal. When the light fell on it, smaller beams of light shot out from it in several directions. These refracted beams lit up more drawings on the curved walls surrounding the pedestal. Chigger held the flashlight in place while Billy went to investigate the images.

A closer look at the etched images revealed what seemed to be a scene showing the half man, half bird surrounded by a group of people.

"What do you think that bird-man image is there?" Chigger asked. "Another evil Shape-Changer?"

"I don't think so," Billy replied. "This whole space has a good feeling to it. I think it's a symbol for something else, something people like."

The drawings of people fell into two groups. The outlines of half of the people were clearly drawn. The outlines of the other half of the people were kind of fuzzy, like they were out of focus or something. Or they might have been ghosts.

"I wonder who made these markings," Billy said.

"And how old they are," Chigger added.

"We need a petroglyph expert or someone who can decode what these drawings mean," Billy remarked. "This whole thing is beyond belief."

"We should bring your dad in here," Chigger suggested. "He might know what they mean or at least know somebody who knows."

Billy walked back to the room's central pedestal to examine it more closely.

Taking the flashlight from Chigger, he pointed its beam straight down on top of the center crystal. When he did, the single beam was split into six individual shafts of light, refracted through the gem's six sides. Those six beams of light shone on six small glass panels embedded in the walls of the room. Neither of the boys had noticed those panels before.

At that moment a soft, dim light began to pulsate from within the crystal-covered walls of the room. It felt almost like the cave was alive and breathing, or its heart had begun softly beating.

"Billy, I think we should move on," Chigger said with a quiver in his voice. "This place is haunted."

He began inching his way out of the room.

"Maybe it is, but I don't think anything here will harm us," Billy replied. "I get nothing but good vibes from the place."

Chigger continued to move back down the path.

"Let's go back down near the cave entrance where we started and see where the other path leads," Billy said finally. "No telling what's down there."

"I don't think that's a good idea," Chigger replied. "There was a big X near the arrow for that path. I think it means don't go there."

"Don't be such a coward," Billy replied as he moved past Chigger and started back down the path. "It might mean X marks the spot where treasure is hidden."

"I hadn't thought of that," Chigger said. "I guess it wouldn't hurt to check it out."

The boys quickly made their way back to the fork in the path and took the one on the right side of the divide. As they moved downward, the cave formations became more gnarled and misshapen. The outcroppings looked a little like melted people of different sizes.

Within a few minutes the boys came to a section of the path that had become partially blocked by large boulders. The huge rocks looked like they might've fallen from the cave's roof.

"More results from yesterday's earthquakes," Billy suggested.

"Or something is warning us that danger lurks below," Chigger said with a nervous laugh, "and we should turn back."

"C'mon, Chig, don't be such a party pooper." Billy chuckled as he picked his way over the fallen boulders and through the narrow opening.

The path took them in a wide downward spiral along the outer edge of another, lower cavern. This space was shaped like a large barrel lined with beautiful dark purplish crystals. However, the flashlight's beam was not reflected or refracted by these crystals. Instead it seemed that the light was fully trapped and absorbed by them.

After a few more rounds of the spiral, the boys reached the bottom of the cavern. The path ended at a little flat open area. It was a dead end. Or was it? They realized that the wall they faced was actually a door, a large door made of a flat stone.

"The cavern floor must be on the other side of this door," Billy observed. "I wonder if it can be opened."

The boys began examining the door and its surroundings more closely. Etched into the surface of the door was another set of symbols, along with a drawing of the same snake with antlers they'd seen earlier. Next to the door stood a pedestal like the one they'd seen in the upper clear-crystal room. But the crystal resting on top of this pedestal was a dark purplish color. And it was much smaller—small enough to fit in your hand. It gave off a dim, eerie purplish glow.

Chigger's curiosity led him to reach out and touch the dark crystal. The glow grew brighter with his touch. Withdrawing his hand, he took a quick backward step.

"What was that about?" Chigger said.

"Beats me," Billy responded. "Do it again, but this time leave your hand on the crystal."

Slowly Chigger reached out, put his hand on the gemstone, and left it there. The crystal began to once again grow brighter. The longer Chigger's hand remained in place, the brighter it glowed. And it grew warmer the longer he touched it. After a few long seconds, he pulled back from it.

"This is creepin' me out," the boy said, stepping away. As he stepped back, he lost his footing in the loose dirt beneath his boots. To keep from falling, he reached to grab hold of something that would support him. His flailing hand found the dark crystal and pulled on it. Rather than keeping him from falling, the crystal came loose from the pedestal. Chigger clutched it tightly as he fell to the ground.

Once the crystal left its base, a seal of some sort around the stone door was released. The boys heard a *psssst* and felt a rush of cold, stale air coming from the edges of the door. It moved open a few inches. Waiting to see if anything else was going to happen, the pair remained still and quiet for a long moment.

As Chigger stood up, Billy moved toward the open door. Gently at first, he pushed on the door. Realizing that the heavy stone would need a bigger push, he motioned for Chigger to help him. Together the boys managed to push the stone door fully open.

Billy shined the flashlight through the opening. He saw that the stone path they stood on extended beyond the door a few feet. Beyond that, his light fell on what he assumed to be the cavern's floor. It appeared to be made of smooth dark glass.

He cautiously took a few steps through the doorway into the enclosed chamber, followed by Chigger. Feeling a little brave, Chigger started to step out onto the glassy floor, but Billy suddenly thrust out his arm to block him.

"Wait," Billy instructed.

"Why?" Chigger asked.

Without answering, Billy squatted down at the edge of the glass and reached out his hand. When he touched the dark surface, his fingers sank into it.

"Because it's not a solid floor," Billy said, lifting his fingers out again. "It's some sort of liquid." The flashlight revealed dark drops of the fluid dripping from his fingers.

"What the—?" was all Chigger could get out.

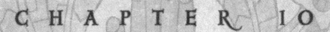

CHAPTER 10

Tunnel Vision

"**O**kay, I've seen enough," Chigger said in a loud whisper as he backed away from the dark liquid at the bottom of the cavern. "This place is totally creepy. We got to get outta here before I completely lose it."

Billy was still pointing the light across the liquid floor when he thought he saw a ripple in the fluid. Chigger saw it too and gasped.

"Man, I'm tellin' ya, I don't like what I'm seein'!" the boy whispered loudly.

He grabbed the flashlight out of Billy's hand and intended to head back up the path. The flashlight's beam quickly swept across the ceiling of the cavern. Chigger saw a wave of movement ripple over the surface.

"The ceiling just moved," he whispered loudly again. "What's with this place? The ceiling moves. The floor that's not a floor moves. And I think I might've just peed my pants."

Billy grabbed the flashlight back from his terrified friend and pointed it upward. He didn't like what he saw there either.

"The ceiling moved because it's covered with bats," he reported to Chigger. "Let's move up the path as quickly and quietly as we can."

The pair proceeded up the spiral path, trying to be as invisible as possible. Billy focused the flashlight on the walkway in front of them. Partway up, he noticed that Chigger was still clutching the glowing purple crystal tightly in his hand.

"Are you keeping that thing as a souvenir?" Billy asked.

Chigger was fixated on the colony of bats and the moving liquid. He had forgotten he still had the gem.

"That's a good idea," he replied as he stuck it in the pocket of his pants.

At that moment, the boys heard a gurgling, bubbling sound coming from the lake below them. And that was it. That was the moment that sent them over the edge.

"Run!" Billy shouted.

The shout started a very surprising chain reaction that began with the bats. Startled by the shout, the flying creatures spread their wings one by one. Dropping from their ceiling perches, they took to flight.

Meanwhile, Billy and Chigger were struggling to get up the spiral path. It was covered with loose dirt, causing their feet to slip and slide beneath them. This made their progress very slow.

Overhead the bats began to swarm, circling the barrellike cavern in growing numbers. Their movement created a whirl-wind of dank air.

The boys were reaching the fallen boulders that partially blocked the path. Just then the whirling bats broke from their circling pattern. The sound of their flapping wings was deafening. And just as the boys started through the narrow opening, the bats headed for that same narrow opening. Billy was in the lead.

Chigger heard the bats coming from behind him. He managed to duck down and lie flat on the path below the opening. The creatures flew above him. Billy had just stepped through the opening when the bats arrived in full force. He was hit by a barrage of bats. Their talons and teeth tore into his flesh as they passed by him. They weren't trying to harm him. They were merely in a rush to escape the cave, just as the boys were.

To make matters worse, Billy couldn't drop to the ground to get out of their way. The sheer force of their numbers kept pushing him along the path. He was forced to take step after step until he reached the mouth of the cave. Beaten and bloodied by the bats, he stumbled out onto the cave's ledge.

Back down the cave path, the last of the bat swarm flew past Chigger, so he was finally free to stand up. He ran up the path as fast as the loose dirt would let him.

"Billy are you all right?" he yelled. "Billy!?"

There was no answer, only the sound of hundreds of bats flying out of the cave. Then a fearful yell came from Billy. But that sound faded quickly away.

When Chigger reached the mouth of the cave, there was no sign of Billy, only droplets of blood on the floor of the ledge. The panicked boy peered over the edge of the ledge toward the ground. There, thirty or so feet below, lay Billy in a bloody heap—not moving.

"Billy, Billy!" Chigger screamed. He scurried down the cliff steps as fast as he could. Reaching his wounded friend, the boy yelled again. "Billy!"

He tried to revive his friend but couldn't. He put his ear to Billy's chest to see if he could hear a heartbeat. Thankfully, he could—a very weak one. What should he do now? He stood and looked around, trying to make his panicked mind work. Then a thought came to him.

What would Billy do?

An answer immediately flashed in his mind, and he ran to the canoe parked near their tent. Pawing through one of the backpacks, he came up with the sat phone.

"Hang in there, Billy," Chigger said as he turned the phone on. Thankfully, all the important phone numbers had already been programmed in. He hit the quick-dial number for Travis Youngblood back in Tahlequah. The deputy marshal answered before the third ring. Chigger launched into a high-speed account of where he was, what had happened, and what condition Billy was in.

"You've got to hurry and get some medical help over here," the boy said. "Billy looks bad."

"Okay," Travis said. "Stay calm and keep the sat phone on. The rescue team can use the phone's GPS signal to find you."

"Hurry!" Chigger yelled as Travis hung up.

Within minutes, the deputy marshal made a top-priority emergency call to a nearby medical helicopter ambulance service. These air ambulances performed what they called a medevac service—short for medical evacuation. Within another few minutes, a life-saving team had lifted off from Fort Smith, Arkansas, the base for the closest medevac copter.

As he waited, Chigger gripped the sat phone like it was the only thing keeping him sane. After a few long minutes, the phone in his hand rang. It made him jump.

"A medevac copter is on its way," Travis reported. "It could be there in fifteen minutes, Chigger. Just hold on."

While Chigger waited for help to arrive, he dug out the first aid kit and some clean cloth. He set about the task of cleaning Billy's wounds and applying pressure to the deeper ones. This he'd learned to do during the marshal's emergency-training program. Though his friend had passed out, Chigger talked to him as he worked on him.

"Billy, I'm so sorry this happened to you. It's all my fault. I'm the one who foolishly went into the cave to begin with. I never should've done that. Will you ever forgive me?"

After what seemed like an eternity, Chigger heard the sound of helicopter rotors off in the distance. He looked up to see a white helicopter moving into position above him. The words

Flight-Life were printed in large letters across the bottom, along with a big red cross.

Soon two ropes dropped from the craft. Two men quickly slid down those ropes. They were followed by a stretcher in a harness. Stepping back, Chigger let the men get to Billy as quickly as possible.

"Deputy Youngblood told us to medevac him to the Indian hospital in Tahlequah," one of the medics told Chigger. "But there's no room for you. Sorry."

This was crushing news. Chigger didn't know how he was going to survive not knowing what condition his friend was in. All he could do was watch as the paramedics loaded Billy into the copter. Quickly it zoomed away.

He was left with a lonely silence. Now what was he supposed to do? Thinking it through, he realized he needed to get back home. His father had already planned to pick them up at the nearby highway overpass tomorrow. He'd need his ride a day early.

He called his own home phone number and explained to his dad what was going on. Without delay, his father jumped in his truck and headed for Chigger's location.

Meanwhile, the Flight-Life copter rushed toward Tahlequah with its human cargo. All the while, the paramedics on board watched their patient and kept track of his vital signs. They also called ahead to the hospital to prepare them for their arrival.

When Billy had been struck by lightning during Labor Day weekend, his mother, the nurse, was on duty at the hospital. This time she wasn't on duty, so an ER nurse called her at home. She and Billy's father rushed to the ER as quickly as they could. Grandpa Wesley arrived soon afterward.

In a surprisingly short time, the medevac copter touched down on the hospital's helipad. Quickly, the ER personnel rushed to the craft to retrieve their patient. Because Billy had become a local celebrity, they all knew him there at the hospital. The ER doctor in charge of Billy's case, Dr. Jenkins, was a friend of Billy's mom.

Mrs. Buckhorn quickly changed into her nurse's uniform so she could assist in the ER. Billy's father and grandfather were forced to stay out in the waiting room, left to worry about what was going on in the operating room.

Once inside that room, Billy was attached to all kinds of tubes and machines designed to keep him alive and track his vital signs. Dr. Jenkins and his staff quickly moved into high gear, further cleaning the teen's wounds, stitching up his gashes, and pumping him full of medications.

But even though they worked as hard as they could, Billy began slipping away. His heart rate slowed and got weaker. His brain activity decreased. Dr. Jenkins couldn't understand why this was happening. Billy had suffered a few broken ribs in the fall. But there was really nothing life-threatening about his wounds.

When Billy's heartbeat stopped, the *beep-beep-beep* sound on the monitor went flat. Then the doctor and his staff switched from high gear to super high gear. Billy's mother grabbed the paddles that would send electric current into Billy's chest. Dr. Jenkins waited for the AED machine to charge up.

When it was fully charged, he yelled, "Clear!" so all the other staff would stand back.

Then he applied the paddles to the boy's chest. The paddles, made to shock the heart back into action, zapped electricity into Billy's chest. But Billy's heart did not respond—maybe because his body had already been shocked by a direct lightning strike, Dr. Jenkins thought.

The doctor repeated the process two more times, again with no response. Sadly, they had to declare Billy Buckhorn dead at 11:45 a.m. on the day after Thanksgiving.

Billy's mother burst into tears.

No one but Billy knew of the remarkable things he'd experienced since he and Chigger had attempted to escape from that cave . . .

When the colony of bats had swept through the narrow opening, their wings had beat on him furiously as they passed. He threw up his arms and hands to cover his head and face, but their talons and teeth tore into him dozens and dozens of times. The pain Billy experienced grew until it became unbearable.

The bats' collective force against his body pushed him ever upward along the path and out onto the cave's ledge. Unable to see where he was, he stumbled off the ledge. His own scream was the last thing he remembered hearing. Just before he passed out from hitting the ground, he thought he smelled apple cider and pumpkin pie one last time.

In the darkness, he felt no pain. But he was aware of things around him. Not his earthly surroundings like the camp, the river, or Chigger. Not those things. There was something else in the darkness with him. Something comforting. And that soothing smell of pie and cider.

Suddenly he heard a ripping sound—like two pieces of Velcro being separated. The next thing he realized was that he could see again. And what he saw shocked him. It was like he was hovering a few feet off the ground. Below him was a bloodied body, and that body didn't look like it was in very good condition.

Wait a minute, he thought. That was his own body! Lying down on the ground. Not moving.

But for some reason, seeing his own body down there didn't bother him. It really seemed like someone else's body. Then the physical body and the ground below him seemed to move farther away. He floated upward past the ledge and the mouth of the cave. He literally reached the sky.

That was when he was suddenly pulled at lightning speed away from the river. Soon the view of the land and the sky faded from sight. He began to zoom through a dark tunnel. Up ahead, at the end of the tunnel, he could see a very bright light. As he got closer to the light, he slowed down.

But the light was more than just light. It was full of good feelings. There was a sense of no worries—like whatever you'd done during your life was not that important. And the smell of pie and cider grew stronger than ever.

Even though he didn't have physical eyes, Billy had to squint in that bright light. He could see the outline of someone nearby. In a few moments, though, he got used to the brightness, or someone dimmed the light. Finally, he could see who was there in the light with him.

"Grandma Awinita?" Billy said. "Is that you?"

"Indeed it is, Grandson," she said. Somehow there was a warm, comforting love coming from her. Billy could actually feel it flow through him. He'd never felt anything like it.

"Where am I?" he asked.

"Somewhere between the land of the living and the land of the dead," she replied. "But you have to understand that the dead aren't really dead. They've left their physical life and simply gone on to another life. A better life. Just like I did when you were six years old."

Billy was confused. He'd always thought that ghosts were the spirits of the dead, and Cherokees stayed away from ghosts at all costs. The ones he'd heard about weren't very nice. How could that be a better life? These were thoughts he had in his mind but didn't speak.

"I understand your confusion," Awinita replied, having heard his unspoken thoughts.

For the first time, Billy realized that she wasn't using her mouth to speak to him. He could read her mind.

"Ghosts *are* the spirits of people who were once alive on earth," she continued. "But they got very attached to something or someone. They can't let go and move on into their new life. They are trapped and sometimes get angry and confused, so they act out."

"Where does that leave me?" Billy asked.

"You're at a crossroads," the elder replied. Showing Billy an area behind her, she said, "Over there is the border. Cross that barrier and you can't return to your life on earth. That's why I'm here, to help you decide what to do."

"You mean I have a choice?" Billy asked.

"Your entire existence is made up of choices. This just happens to be a big one."

Billy waited to hear more.

"You have an unfolding gift that will allow you to do things on earth you never dreamed possible," Awinita went on. "As your powers increase, you will be able to help people and heal them. And I will give you guidance from this side. I know I don't have to worry that you'll ever misuse those powers. I know you won't do things like Benjamin Blacksnake has done."

Hearing that evil name came as a shock to Billy. Everything had been so warm and loving, and then *BAM!* It felt like he'd been hit with an electrical shock. Billy suddenly felt off-balance, like the ground beneath him was about to give way.

"What's it going to be?" his grandma asked. "Willing to go back and fulfill your destiny? Or do you want to end your life on earth and cross over?"

The area behind Awinita glowed with welcoming love and care. And Billy thought he saw a familiar figure step out from the barrier. Was that his great-grandfather, the one called Bullseye Buckhorn? Yes, it was. Billy recognized him from old family photos.

Then he thought of Chigger and Grandpa Wesley back on earth. He wasn't ready to leave them. He was only sixteen years old, after all. He still had a lot of life to live.

"I want to go back," he finally said. No sooner had he thought that thought than he felt another hard-hitting electric shock. *BAM!* While recovering from this second one, he began to move away from his grandma and back down the tunnel.

"You made a good choice, Billy," his grandma said with a heartwarming glow. "From now on you and I will be connected. I will be your helper from this side when you need me. The cider and pie you've been smelling—that's how you know I'm around. Do you understand?"

He was nodding his answer when he came out of the tunnel and found himself hovering once again over his own physical body. But it was in a different place. He looked around, trying to figure out where he was. Finally, he saw his mother in her nurse's uniform and realized he was in the Indian hospital.

As Billy watched from above, the doctor placed two large electrical paddles on his physical chest below.

"Clear!" the doctor yelled.

BAM! Billy felt the electric shock in his spirit body for a third time. He was starting to fade out again, drifting back into the blackness.

"Time of death is 11:45 a.m. on November 29," he heard the doctor declare just before he faded into the silent darkness.

The next thing Billy knew he was gasping for air. It felt like someone was sitting on his chest. He began flailing his arms— his physical arms! Then he opened his eyes, his physical eyes! Dr. Jenkins grabbed one of Billy's arms, and his mother grabbed the other. Realizing he was back in his physical body, Billy stopped jerking and gasping.

His eyes came to focus on his mother's face. It was wet with tears that had flowed freely just a few moments ago.

"My boy's alive," she said with great excitement. "It's a miracle!" She hugged him tightly until he complained.

"I can't breathe, Mom," Billy said. "Give me some air!"

She released her grip on her son as the boy looked around the room. In a moment, he spotted the person he was looking for.

"Dr. Jenkins, why did you declare me dead?"

This question stunned everyone in the room. They all fell silent. The doctor stepped closer to his patient.

"How did you know I declared you dead?" the doctor asked. "You were . . . well . . . dead."

"I heard you say it plain as day," Billy replied. "I was floating over the room at that moment. I watched everything that happened."

The doctor didn't know how to respond to that information. He did not believe this was even possible.

"You had no pulse or heartbeat," he said. "We tried to revive you three times with no success." Then the puzzled look on his face faded. "But we're all glad you pulled through, young man," he said with a smile. "Your mother was right. It *is* a miracle. We couldn't bring you back, but somehow you did it yourself."

With their patient revived, the hospital staff scurried around preparing for the next steps of his medical treatment. He was, after all, covered with scrapes, bites, and cuts from head to foot.

And once again, the boy who'd survived a lightning strike, saved a busload of kids, and almost single-handedly brought down a child abuser was about to begin another chapter in his remarkable life.

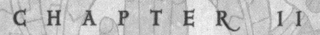

CHAPTER 11

Talking to the Dead

Billy began recovering nicely from his bat wounds and was allowed to go home three days after he'd been declared dead. His girlfriend, Sara, was among the first to welcome him home.

"I thought I'd lost you forever," she said tearfully as she held on to his bandaged hand. "I don't know what I would've done without my Billy."

What Billy didn't know was that Chigger was standing just outside his room. He heard every word. Billy's mother had met him at the front door and told him he could visit briefly with Billy when Sara left. She was about to leave Chigger at Billy's bedroom door but noticed something odd about the boy.

"You don't look good, young man," she said.

She grabbed his chin and held his face up toward the light. He had dark circles under his eyes. His skin was pale, especially for a full-blood Cherokee.

"I'm just a little tired," Chigger replied. "I've been feeling this way since the day Billy got hurt. I'm sure I'll get over it."

She left him and returned to the kitchen. There she picked up a tray of food and a local newspaper. In a few moments she came back and said, "I'll have Sara out of there in no time."

She moved past Chigger, opened Billy's door, and entered.

"Here's your lunch," she said. "I want you to eat all of it too." Then she turned her attention to Sara. "Sara, honey, I don't want Billy to get too tired seeing a lot of visitors today. Would you mind coming back tomorrow? You could have another short visit then."

"All right, Mrs. Buckhorn," the girl said. "I need to go home and get on the Internet. I have to update all my online friends about Billy's recovery. You wouldn't believe how many new friends are following me since Billy's hospital miracle!"

Billy, who had never been a fan of publicity or social media, cringed. It bothered him more and more that his girlfriend seemed to be so hooked on it, but he didn't say anything this time. And Billy's mother really wasn't a fan of Sara's either. But she also didn't say anything.

To Billy, Sara said softly, "I'll see you tomorrow, my sweet."

Before leaving, she kissed the tip of her own finger and held it up to the lightning scar on the side of Billy's neck, the same thing she'd done back when she first thanked him for saving her life.

Sara was very surprised to find Chigger waiting in the hall, especially since Mrs. Buckhorn had just said she didn't want Billy to have a lot of visitors. It was then that Sara realized that Billy's mother might not be on her side in her battle for Billy's attention.

Sara had originally thought Chigger might be a little bit of a threat to her. Now she was sure of it. But she was also sure Billy would choose her over this scraggly boy.

Sara moved past Chigger without speaking.

"Hello, Sara," Chigger said sweetly with a smile. He knew that he was the winner of this round in the contest.

"You have two minutes with Billy today," Mrs. Buckhorn announced to Chigger as she left Billy's room.

"Yes, ma'am," Chigger answered.

Stepping into the room, he found Billy studying the newspaper Mrs. Buckhorn had just brought in.

"I thought I'd lost you forever," Chigger said with a mocking sweetness as he batted his eyelashes. "I don't know what I would've done without my Billy." He tilted his head and gave a girlish smile.

"Ha ha, very funny," Billy said as he looked up from the newspaper. That was when he, too, noticed Chigger's sickly appearance. "Are you all right, buddy? You don't look good at all."

"I'll be fine," his friend replied. "Probably got the flu or something. What's in the newspaper?"

Billy folded the paper over to the story he was reading and handed it to Chigger.

"I managed to get written up in the newspaper again," he said. "You know I hate publicity. Especially this overblown flashy stuff. They make it sound like I can walk on water."

Chigger took the paper and scanned it. The headline read "Lightning Boy Returns from the Dead." The photo under the headline showed the weblike scars on Billy's neck from the lightning strike back in September. The story reminded readers of the whole lightning ordeal. And it told of how Billy had used psychic "gifts" to save the busload of children.

What the article didn't report was that those gifts had faded a little over time. He no longer saw flashes of scenes from people's lives when he shook their hands. However, when he met someone, he could "read" them, sort of feel their intentions. This told him if they were up to no good or not.

Thankfully, though, he was still able to learn a whole school lesson by sleeping on a textbook overnight. He'd used that technique to begin learning the Cherokee syllabary and a few of the phrases in his grandfather's medicine book. It was about time he repeated that process. *When I recover,* Billy thought.

"My offer still stands," Chigger said with a smile. "I'll be your agent any day. I'm sure I can get you a reality show and everything."

Chigger stopped smiling when he saw that Billy wasn't smiling.

"Sara's fascination with her online friends has started to wear thin," Billy said. "And so have your jokes about reality TV."

Chigger tried not to smile upon hearing the news regarding Sara. "Okay, I get it," he said.

A half smile came to Billy's face. "But I don't think I ever thanked you for saving my bacon once again. If it wasn't for you, I would've died. And I mean *really* died. For good."

Chigger hadn't expected this at all. "It was nothin'," he said. "All I did was make another phone call, just like when I found Ravenwood's hideout."

"What you did was use *all* the skills and tools we learned from the Marshal Service," Billy insisted. "The ER staff told me what a good job you did in cleaning up my wounds down on the river. That's *not* nothing."

"Okay, time's up," Billy's mother announced as she stepped into the room. "Visiting hours are over for today."

Chigger did a gentle fist bump against Billy's bandaged hand and said, "Thanks, bro."

"Chigger looks kind of sickly," Billy's mom said after the boy had left. "I'm a little worried about him."

"So am I," Billy agreed.

"He said he started feeling weak the same day as your accident," she added. "Maybe you can convince him to see a doctor. Or pay a visit to Wesley."

"Grandpa is the one person I haven't seen much of since I got home from the hospital," Billy complained. "Can you call him for me? I do need to talk to him."

"Okay, I will," Mrs. Buckhorn said. "But right now you need to get some rest. Remember, your uncle John is coming by this evening to bring a get-well message from my side of the family."

An alarmed look clouded Billy's face.

"Don't worry," she said calmly. "He promised not to preach this time."

"But, Mom, do I have to?"

"Billy, he's family. He's my brother. Please do it for me."

"Okay—for you," he said in a defeated voice.

"It's like pulling a painful tooth," his mother advised. "Best to just get it over."

With that, she turned out his light and closed the door.

During his afternoon nap, Billy had a nightmare about bats coming at him. Big bats. They grabbed his legs and arms and were about to tear him limb from limb. But then his grandma Awinita appeared nearby. He could smell the apple cider and pumpkin pie. It was like someone turned on a bright light that hurt the bats' eyes. They fled and left him alone with his grandmother.

"Something came out of that cave with you and Chigger," Awinita said within the dream. "Something that's infecting the people of the Cherokee Nation."

Billy awoke with a start. He blinked his eyes and looked around his room. Had his grandma just been there? She must've been. He could still smell a hint of cider and pie. Maybe she was still nearby.

Then he heard his bedroom door creak open a bit. He looked over and saw his mom peeking in. When she saw that he was awake, she opened the door the rest of the way.

"Your uncle is here," she said. "Can he come in?"

"Yeah, I guess so," Billy answered glumly as he sat up in bed.

His mother turned and motioned down the hallway for her brother, the preacher, to come ahead. In a few moments the man, with his slicked-back jet-black hair and tan suit, stepped into the room.

"Don't excite him," Mrs. Buckhorn told her brother. "It's not good for his health."

"Of course not, Rebecca," he replied. "Of course not."

He waited a moment to see if his sister was going to leave the two of them alone. He saw she wasn't, so he stepped closer to Billy's bed. As he did, the aroma of cider and pie floated into Billy's mind.

"Ah, Billy, it's such a blessing to see you doing so well," John began. "To see you brought back from the brink of the grave. It was the hand of the Lord. Hallelujah, child! Praise God! Like Lazarus, whom Jesus called forth from the tomb!"

John continued with his message, but Billy became distracted. He began hearing a buzzing sound in his ears. Within that buzzing came a voice. It was weak at first, but as Billy tuned in to it more, it grew stronger. Soon he could tell it was Awinita's voice.

"There's someone over here with me who wants to speak to you," she said. "I'm right here, so you don't need to be afraid of it."

Billy nodded in reply to his grandma's statement. Uncle John took that to mean he could keep going with his message. Billy's mother continued to watch to see if her brother's preachy get-well message was upsetting Billy. Her son seemed surprisingly calm and relaxed.

But Billy hardly noticed his preacher uncle's presence as a barely visible scene began to unfold in Billy's bedroom behind the man. It was faint at first, but, like Awinita's voice, it grew stronger as Billy focused on it.

A glowing hole opened in the bedroom wall, and a glowing image of Awinita stepped through that hole. With her was a softly glowing American Indian man. Billy understood him to be the spirit of a person once alive on earth. Behind his grandma and this man was something else: a cluster of other translucent glowing people who seemed to be waiting for something.

Billy looked to see if his mother or uncle was aware of this golden vision. They didn't seem to be. Then Awinita and the man moved in closer.

"This is your mother's brother Luther," she said. "That, of course, makes him your uncle too."

Billy had never heard of an uncle named Luther. The spirit man stepped forward.

"He has a message for his brother and sister at this time," Awinita said.

Billy listened, straining to hear what the spirit man was saying. But Luther wasn't as practiced at speaking with the world of the living as Awinita was. She had been appearing to Billy's grandpa Wesley for years during the Live Oak stomp ground's annual ceremonial dance, so she knew how to do it.

At first Luther's message was no louder than a weak whisper. Awinita's spirit glowed brighter than before, which helped to amplify the strength of his message. Billy could finally hear the man clearly. The boy listened carefully for a brief time. Then Billy relayed the message to his uncle John and his mother, whose name was Rebecca.

"John, your brother Luther has given me a message for you," Billy blurted out, interrupting the preacher's speech.

At the mention of Luther's name, both John and Rebecca jerked like they'd been slapped in the face.

"What did you just say?" John demanded.

"Luther says you have a lot of nerve preaching to other people about their sins and shortcomings," Billy continued. "He says his life ended because you were arrogant and reckless. Those are his words, not mine."

"How dare you mention that name!" John roared. Then another thought struck him. "How do you even know of him?" he asked. "He died more than twenty-five years ago, and no one in our family has spoken of him since."

"You know Billy speaks the truth," Rebecca said, drawing her brother's attention toward her. "I've never said a word to anyone in all these years, but the truth has been spoken today."

"Answer me, boy," the preacher demanded. He turned his attention back to Billy and stepped closer to him. "What devilry is this?"

"Luther is here now, speaking to me," Billy said calmly, pointing with his lips. "His spirit stands behind you, alongside my grandmother Awinita."

Both Rebecca and John looked in the direction Billy had pointed. They saw nothing.

"Now I understand," John thundered as he turned back toward his nephew. "This is coming from that devil-worshipping Wesley Buckhorn and his demonic ghost wife!" He moved ever closer to Billy, his rage building.

Rebecca thrust herself in front of her brother.

"You self-righteous, pompous pretender!" she screamed in his face. Without turning away from John, she spoke to her son. "Billy, what else did Luther tell you?"

"He said John was in an alcoholic stupor when he got behind the wheel of your father's car. And then he backed over your younger brother, Luther, who was playing at the end of the driveway."

John sharply gasped in a breath of air. So did Rebecca. Together they turned to look at the teenager sitting in his bed. His face glowed with calm peacefulness.

"Then he blamed the accident on a neighbor he didn't like," Billy continued. This completed Luther's message.

John's body grew stiff, and his face turned red. Looking as though he might burst, he ran from the room in a state of panic. Billy's mother stood motionless and watched him flee. Moments later, they heard John's car start and speed out of their gravel driveway. Mrs. Buckhorn turned to look at her son, who remained calm.

"There are others here with me," Awinita told Billy. "They are waiting for a chance to connect with their loved ones on earth." She indicated the cluster of waiting souls. "There's no hurry," she added. "But when you are well, you can carry out this work with

Grandpa's help. But only if you want to. Only if you think you can handle it."

Awinita glowed brightly for an instant, smiled, and then faded away. The host of spirits with her faded away too.

Rebecca stared at her son in awe as she came close to him. She had a million questions and not a clue of how to ask the first one. She lay down quietly on the bed next to him.

"Please tell me what just happened," she softly said at last. "Explain it so I can understand."

"I died and lived to tell about it," her son answered. "And this is part of the reason I came back. To help people connect with their loved ones. To help people with their problems."

And then, for the first time, he told someone the details of what had happened in that cave and what had happened while he was dead. He had told no one because he feared that people would think he was crazy.

But his mother, the medical-minded nurse, did not think he was crazy. From that day forward, Billy began to rapidly heal from his many wounds. It was another mystery to Billy's mom and dad. How did he recover so quickly? At the same time, however, Chigger's health was rapidly deteriorating.

On Saturday, Billy persuaded his mother to allow him to visit both Chigger and Grandpa Wesley. Not wanting him to venture out on his own yet, she agreed to the outing only if she drove. The still-bandaged Billy had to agree.

His mother first drove him to Chigger's mobile home a few miles away, where Chigger's mother greeted them at her door with a very worried look.

"Today he just won't get out of bed," Mrs. Muskrat told them. "His skin is sickly pale, and he won't eat. And he's in a really bad mood all the time. I've begged him to let me take him to a doctor, but he just sort of growls at me."

"That doesn't sound like Chigger at all," Billy said.

"Where's Chigger's father?" Mrs. Buckhorn asked.

"Sam is working a temporary job over in Arkansas," Chigger's mom replied. "He won't be back for a couple of days."

"Can we come in?" Billy asked. "I need to see what's going on with Chigger for myself."

Mrs. Muskrat opened her door and allowed them in. Almost immediately a heavy feeling settled over Billy. He felt tied up, and simply walking became a chore. And the inside of the home seemed dark even though the drapes were open and the sun shone brightly outside.

"Do you feel that heaviness?" he asked, looking from his mother to Mrs. Muskrat.

Both women shook their heads. They weren't aware of anything like that.

"Please wait out here," Billy said. "I want to see Chigger alone."

As Billy stepped into Chigger's room, the heavy feeling increased. It felt like trying to walk through syrup. And there was a strange odor hanging in the air. Billy couldn't quite place it, but it was kind of sour.

Chigger's comic book collection was scattered about the room, and several copies lay open on the bed around the boy. It seemed to Billy that his friend had become obsessed with them, and Chigger was thumbing through the pages of one now, as if he'd become a speed reader.

As Billy moved closer to the bed, Chigger turned his head toward his visitor, although his hands still thumbed through a comic. The ill boy slowly refocused his vision to see who was there in his room. Chigger's bloodshot yellow eyes revealed just how serious the teen's trouble was.

"Hey, Chig," Billy said in a cheery voice. "I've come to see how you're doing."

"I'm surprised Sara let you out of her sight," Chigger said with a weak, gruff voice. "She's got it in for me, you know."

"I'm here now," Billy replied. "What's going on with you?"

"What's going on is that I'm tired of playing second fiddle to you," Chigger said angrily. "The famous Lightning Boy is adored by everyone. Able to leap tall buildings and come back from the dead."

"You know none of that matters to me," Billy said, taking a few more steps.

"Save that phony-baloney crap for someone else," Chigger answered sharply. "Fame and glory *are* what you're really all about. In no time you'll be the most famous Cherokee that ever lived."

As Chigger spoke, his strength grew. His voice took on a deeper, raspier tone, and the yellow in his eyes shifted toward the color purple. Billy hardly recognized the figure who now lay in Chigger's bed. His voice and words sounded nothing like the friend Billy had known for more than ten years.

"I can tell you're not yourself today," Billy said. "I'll leave you alone. Maybe you'll feel better tomorrow."

"Don't let the doorknob hit you in the butt on your way out," the raspy voice said. "And tell that woman who calls herself my mother to leave me alone."

Billy left the room as Chigger began a series of deep dry coughs.

"Mrs. Muskrat, I think you need to call your husband and get him back here as soon as possible," Billy said once he was back in the living room. "Chigger's illness might make him hard to handle. I mean physically."

Mrs. Muskrat didn't move as she tried to understand what Billy was saying.

"And we need to get Grandpa Wesley over here as soon as possible," he added, turning to his own mother. "Chigger isn't just ill. It feels like something's in there with him. Something bad has taken control of his mind."

Neither of the two mothers could utter a single word in reply. What Billy was saying didn't seem real. Chigger's mother finally moved to the phone to call her husband.

"We'll be back with my grandpa as soon as we can," Billy said to Mrs. Muskrat while she waited on the phone.

When Billy and his mother got back in the car, she asked, "What was that all about?"

"I don't know for sure," Billy answered. "Something evil has taken hold of Chigger and is dragging him down."

His mother blinked. "You're beginning to sound like my brother John," she observed and looked at her watch. "I have to start my shift at the hospital soon. Why don't I leave you at your grandpa's house? He can bring you back here later."

Billy agreed, and they drove to Wesley's house, located in a remote wooded area north of Tahlequah.

Grandpa Wesley had practiced Cherokee doctoring with Awinita since they were a young married couple. There had been healers in earlier generations of both Wesley's and Awinita's families. Wesley had carried on the medicine work after his wife passed away, thanks to the medicine book his father, Bullseye, had left him. A few years later, he'd begun teaching Billy about Cherokee healing and traditions.

When Billy arrived at his grandfather's house, there was a line of Native people waiting on the old medicine man's front porch and in the front yard. Billy had never seen so many people there. *What was going on?*

When the waiting crowd saw the bandaged Billy, a murmur of awe spread among them. They knew of this boy's return from death's door. They also knew of the busload of children he'd saved and the girl he had rescued.

A few of the gathered folks reached out to touch him as he passed. They hoped that he might bless them somehow.

"*Didanawisgi,*" someone said, calling him a medicine man in the Cherokee language.

"*Usquanigodi,*" someone else said. "Miracle."

Billy did not like this development at all, but he just smiled politely and kept heading for his grandpa's front door. He found Wesley sitting at the kitchen table with mortar and pestle in hand. He was grinding the dried leaves of a medicine plant into small pieces. He looked up from his task.

"What are you doing here, Grandson?" the elder asked. He got up and gave Billy a hug. "Shouldn't you be home getting well?"

"What's going on out there, Grandpa?" Billy replied with a question of his own. "Why are there so many people needing help?"

"It's been like this for days," Wesley said. He offered his grandson a place to sit and resumed his task. "They all seem to be suffering from similar problems. They're tired and depressed and angry for no reason. And they've all seen bats near their homes."

That last sentence caught Billy's attention.

"Bats?" he said. "They've seen bats?"

"We hardly ever have bats around here in cooler months," Wesley said. He poured the ground-up herb into a plastic bag. "Now they're everywhere. I don't get it."

"I do," Billy said. "Bats are one of the things we found in that cave. And bats are what gave me these wounds and nearly ended my life. On top of that, Grandma said that something came out of that cave with me and Chigger. Something that was infecting the Cherokee people."

Wesley stopped what he was doing. "You've seen Awinita again? Even since your near-death experience?"

Billy told him about the bat dream and the visitation from his grandma the previous day.

"That helps to explain why my traditional remedies aren't working as well as they should," Wesley said. He got up and left the room.

Soon he returned with the ancient Cherokee book of formulas and spells that had been recovered from Ravenwood's car in September, the book that had once belonged to Benjamin Blacksnake. Even though that man had used the book's pages for evil, it also contained much of the tribe's oldest and best healing knowledge.

Wesley placed the book on the kitchen table and began flipping through its pages. Billy recognized more of the words handwritten there than before. He hadn't quite gotten around to memorizing or practicing the syllabary as much as he'd hoped. But Wesley could read and understand it all.

"What are you looking for?" Billy asked, looking over the elder's shoulder.

"I sort of remember seeing something about the deeper meaning of bat sightings," Wesley said. "But I don't remember where it is written or what it said."

Near the back of the book, Wesley came to a cluster of pages that contained writing in very unfamiliar characters.

"I haven't figured out what this part of Blacksnake's book is about," Wesley noted. "This writing and these characters are definitely not part of Sequoyah's syllabary."

Billy looked closer at the odd markings. "I'd almost swear that's the same kind of markings Chigger and I found on the door at the bottom of the cave," he said. "But we really didn't have time to study them."

Wesley flipped through a few more pages until he came to a couple containing several crude drawings.

"Wait!" Billy said just as the elder was about to turn the page. There, in the lower righthand corner, was an image he'd seen before.

"That's the same picture we saw in the cave," Billy exclaimed. "It was scratched into the rock wall next to the path that led down into the dark cavern."

"Are you sure, boy?" Wesley asked.

"Positive," Billy replied. "What is it and why is it in this book?"

"That's the symbol for the ancient Horned Serpent," Wesley said in a somber tone. "It is known to the Cherokees as the Uktena. These creatures are said to live underwater, in the Underworld, and have a bright diamondlike gem on their foreheads. That stone could supposedly impart great powers to any man who could take it. But all who tried to steal it from the beast died in the process. And the beast's scales are considered to be powerful warrior medicine."

"In your teachings about tribal legends, why haven't you told me of this beast before?" Billy asked, still looking at the drawing.

"It's part of the oldest Cherokee beliefs about the three worlds," the elder explained. "The physical earth where we live is the Middleworld. Above us, the Upperworld, is where Grandfather Sun, the Thunders, and other spirit beings live. Below us is the Underworld, where creatures such as the Horned Serpent, the Water Panther, and many other dangerous creatures from tribal legends exist."

"Oh, right," Billy said. "Pops mentioned that a while back. He said the three worlds are connected at their centers with a kind of axis pole or something and that many tribal cultures share that belief. Deep pools of water and caves are pathways to the Underworld."

"So to answer your question, I didn't mention the Uktena because no one has actually seen one for decades, maybe centuries," Wesley said. "Many Cherokee medicine people think it has gone extinct or possibly was just a cultural symbol for terrifying, evil things."

Then Billy realized something.

"I think I saw one," he said and sat down hard on one of Wesley's wooden kitchen chairs. "At least, I may have seen its back. Something slithered in the liquid at the bottom of the cave."

He explained how the floor had turned out to be some sort of dark liquid instead of a floor. And he told of the ripple of movement he and Chigger had seen in that liquid.

Billy finished by saying, "But I thought those cave drawings were done by people of the older Mound Builder culture, not Cherokees. At least that's what Pops seemed to think."

Billy's father was considered the expert in the histories and cultures of Native people of the region. He taught several college classes in these subjects and, at times, shared his knowledge with Billy.

"Then we'd better sit down with your dad and put our heads together on this as soon as possible," Wesley said. "Your father doesn't really believe in the teachings of tribal cultures, but, intellectually speaking, he knows more about them than anyone else around here."

Wesley stuck a piece of folded paper in the big book to mark the page where the Uktena drawing could be found. Then Billy remembered something else.

"I just remembered why I came here," Billy said as his grandpa closed the book. "It's Chigger. He's worse off than any of these people waiting to see you. Can you come with me back to his house?"

"Of course," Wesley replied. "Just let me get my medicine bag, and we'll go."

Wesley closed and locked his front door. He explained to those waiting that he had to make an emergency house call to treat someone who was in really bad shape. Being patient people, these Cherokees didn't usually mind an extra wait. They often brought beadwork, decks of cards, or other things to occupy their time.

But today was different. Today they were all suffering from some unknown ailment that made them cranky and impatient. Several of them complained loudly as grandfather and grandson left the house.

Wesley suddenly stopped and turned back toward the crowd. He raised his hands and closed his eyes. Loudly he spoke a paragraph of formal Cherokee in a forceful voice. The sound of his voice speaking those ancient words caused everyone to fall silent.

Wesley finished his words and opened his eyes. He gave the line of waiting people a stern look. Everyone in the crowd seemed to realize how childish they'd been acting and became embarrassed. Silently they turned their eyes toward the ground.

Satisfied that he'd achieved his goal, Wesley walked to his truck. He and Billy drove away.

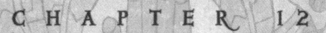

CHAPTER 12

Heavy Darkness

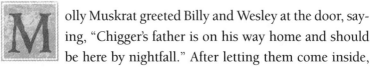

Molly Muskrat greeted Billy and Wesley at the door, saying, "Chigger's father is on his way home and should be here by nightfall." After letting them come inside, she added, "Mr. Buckhorn, I hope you can help my son. I've never seen him like this. Billy was right. He's not himself."

She waited in the living room as Wesley and Billy entered Chigger's room, where they found the boy asleep in bed. Shockingly, bits and pieces of shredded comic books lay scattered across the bed covers and on the nearby floor. A Chigger in his right mind would never do such a thing to his precious stockpile of pop culture superhero classics.

"Tell me what you're picking up in here," Wesley whispered to his grandson. This would be an opportunity for the medicine man to see how much the student had learned. "What does your intuition tell you?" he added.

"There's a heavy darkness all around Chigger. I felt it when I visited a while ago with Mom. Walking feels like trying to move through molasses. The air has a sour smell too."

"What else?" the elder asked as he moved closer to the boy's bed.

"I feel like something is controlling Chigger from the outside," Billy answered. "It's almost like he's a puppet connected with strings."

"Good read," Wesley said. "There is something more than just a physical illness going on with this young man. He might be under the spell of a Night-Goer. I'll have to use my quartz vision crystal to help me see deeper into what's really going on."

Wesley and other medicine men had dealt with Night-Goers before. This was a type of Cherokee witch that usually attacked someone who was already sick. The Night-Goer tried to make the person sicker and sicker to the point of death. The witch wanted to collect the person's internal organs at the time of death, because those fresh organs were a potent source of power.

Wesley took a chair from Chigger's desk in the corner of the room and placed it near the bed. Then he opened his leather medicine satchel. From it he removed a thin clear quartz crystal. He sometimes used the crystal to help him focus. It improved his ability to "see" into his patients.

He set the crystal down on his knee and pulled a smaller medicine bag out of the satchel. The little bag contained a mixture of doctored herbs that also improved Wesley's effectiveness. Using the leather strap attached to it, he put the little bag around his neck.

Suddenly Chigger awakened and sat up in bed. His eyes opened wide with anger.

"What is the meaning of this intrusion?" he demanded. The raspy voice was back. "Leave at once."

It seemed as though Chigger didn't know them at all. The sickly boy squinted and seemed to exert some kind of energy toward the pair. Billy then began to feel an unseen force pushing against him. Wesley felt it too and almost tipped over in his chair. Getting to his feet, he stumbled backward.

"What is that?" Billy asked. "It's becoming very hard to breathe in here."

"Chigger has developed some new forceful power," Wesley said. "Or, more likely, someone is channeling power through him against us."

Billy worried that the pressure might harm his grandfather. He moved sideways so he could stand in front of the elder. Chigger focused his force in Billy's direction. Immediately the younger Buckhorn felt a hard unseen wall come between him and his grandpa.

Billy resisted and pushed back against the force, so Chigger quickly thrust his head toward Billy. This movement increased the pressure and pushed the teen to the floor.

"Ow!" Billy yelled as he landed on his wounded arm. The sound of Billy's yell seemed to disrupt the wall. This allowed Wesley to rush to his grandson.

"Are you all right?" the elder asked.

"I think I opened up a few stitches in my arm," Billy said as a red spot of blood spread across one of his bandages.

"This is more than a Night-Goer," Wesley said as he helped Billy to his feet. "We'll have to retreat and try to figure out what's at work here. Come on, let's get your arm looked after."

As Billy backed away from the bed, Wesley quickly grabbed his crystal from the floor where it had fallen. The two Buckhorns rushed from the room and closed the door.

After the intruders left his room, Chigger reached under his pillow. He found what he was looking for, the wonderful purple crystal he'd taken from the cave. It glowed as he stroked it. He'd grown very fond of it. It seemed to speak to him in a low whisper. It was more than a beautiful object. To him it was alive.

As he looked into the heart of the gem's center, he could somehow see for miles and miles. There was something there. Or someone. Chigger wasn't sure. But he felt a presence that had bonded with him. It was a stronger bond than friendship or family. It was an ancient being that called to him. Holding the crystal tightly, he lay down. He pulled the covers over himself and the crystal so they could be together in the purple darkness. The boy drew his legs up close to his chest. He felt safe—like a baby in his mother's womb.

Out in the living room, Wesley and Billy tried to breathe in deeply. The pressure in Chigger's room seemed to have cut off their oxygen for a while. After a few minutes, their breathing returned to normal.

"Is there a relative or a friend you can call to come stay with you until your husband arrives?" Wesley asked Mrs. Muskrat. "I don't think you should be here alone."

"Why?" Chigger's mother asked. "What's going on?"

"I can't explain it all just yet," Wesley replied. "But we'll be back when we know more about what we're dealing with. In the meantime, get someone to stay with you, and don't allow your son to leave this house."

Wesley knew Chigger's mother was frightened and worried, but there was nothing he or Billy could do for her at the moment. The best thing for them to do next was figure out what had been let loose in the Cherokee Nation. That was the only way they'd be able to stop it.

They drove to the college where Billy's dad taught, hoping he'd be in his office rather than in the classroom. Billy had already told his father about the markings he'd seen in the cave. The professor had been fascinated by his son's description. "Fascinating" seemed to be Professor James Buckhorn's favorite word.

What was happening now, though, had moved way beyond fascinating. What Billy, Wesley, Chigger, and the whole tribal Nation were facing was a supernatural event beyond anyone's wildest nightmare. Billy and Wesley just had to convince the professor of this.

The professor's father and son arrived just as the professor was returning to his office from teaching a class. It was the first time ever that both of them had shown up at his office at the same time.

"To what do I owe this unique visit?" he asked. The professor carried a large stack of student papers. "Wait a minute, young man," he said to Billy as he put the stack down on a chair near the door. "What are you doing out of bed?"

"We're here on urgent business," Wesley told his son. "And Billy is an important part of that business. You need to stop whatever it is you're doing and listen to what we have to say."

"Sounds serious," James said as he unlocked his office door. "Come in."

He opened the door, picked up the stack of papers, and went inside. The two visitors followed him in.

Billy always enjoyed going to his dad's office. One wall was lined from floor to ceiling with books on Native American topics. Another wall was covered with maps that showed where all the Indian tribes of North America lived. On a third wall hung a display of Cherokee masks, Plains Indian war shields, and other artifacts from Native tribes. It was a whole intertribal museum crammed into one small room.

Billy's father pushed an intercom button on his desk phone, and a secretary answered.

"Yes, Professor Buckhorn," the woman's voice said.

"Please hold all my calls and move my student meetings to tomorrow," he said.

"Yes, sir," she replied and ended the call.

The professor's son and father began telling him what had been going on. The words came tumbling out of them like pieces of a jigsaw puzzle pouring out of a spilled puzzle box.

"Whoa, whoa, whoa," James said. "Slow down and put this story in some kind of order."

Wesley explained about the large number of people who'd been coming to see him for help. He told about the bats they'd seen. Billy described Chigger's situation and what he had done to them. Wesley showed his son the drawing of the Uktena in the Cherokee medicine book, and Billy revealed what he'd seen in that liquid at the bottom of the cavern.

"If I didn't already know and love you two, I'd think I was listening to a couple of kooks," the professor said when they'd finished their tale. He then opened a drawer in his desk and pulled out a stack of opened books and computer printouts. He plopped the pile down on his desk. "But, Billy, I listened when you first told me about that cave. The drawings and markings you found made me curious. I began doing some research."

He spread the books and papers out on the desk. Wesley and Billy leaned in to take a closer look at them. What they saw was a group of photos, drawings, and charts. These displayed aspects of the ancient Mound Builder cultures, buildings, and locations.

"Billy, I believe you and Chigger stumbled on the greatest archaeological discovery in modern times," the professor said with a serious tone. "You know I'm not one to believe much in religious myths, but the things that have been happening to you got me thinking. What if there really is a core truth at the heart of tribal legends? What if some sort of ancient force has been let loose here in our state?"

A shockwave washed over Billy as those words sank in. Could this be his own father saying these things? The man believed only in what could be seen or touched. He had faith only in fact and science.

Billy and his grandpa had always assumed tribal legends and cultures had some truth to them at their roots. But now his father seemed to think these ancient stories could contain a kernel of truth—or even were factually true.

"This is a welcome change of attitude," Wesley said in surprise.

"What do we do now?" Billy asked.

"Son, I think you and I should return to the cave," his father answered. "We'll bring the college archaeology professor with us. We need to document the markings and drawings as soon as we can. Our Dr. Stevens is known the world over as the best digger in this state."

"Digger?" Billy asked. "What's a digger?"

"That's a nickname for an archaeologist," the professor replied, standing up. "They hate being called that, but everyone does it anyway." He began restacking the papers and books as he spoke. "Wesley, I suggest you call all the medicine people and stomp dance leaders together. They should be informed of what's going on. They need to know what they're up against. And maybe they can help you figure out how to help Chigger."

All three were silent for a moment as they realized what was happening and how crazy it all seemed.

"Time for the Buckhorns to swing into action," Wesley said finally.

CHAPTER 13

The Beast

Unknown to Billy, Wesley, or James, mysterious things had been happening in the area around that cave along the Arkansas River. Awinita was right. Something had come out of the cave with Billy and Chigger. And it wasn't just the bats.

After the helicopter had flown the wounded Billy to the hospital, and after a stranded Chigger had been picked up by his father, in the dark of night, the last remaining creature of its species had risen out of that murky liquid at the bottom of the cavern. The last surviving Horned Serpent, known to the Cherokees as Uktena, had slithered up that spiral pathway and out of its underground prison.

But Uktena wasn't the species' original name. Other tribes at other times had known of the beast and called it other things. Tie-Snake, Crawfish Snake, and Great Snake were just a few. Each tribe had a name for it spoken in their language. Ancient stories of the creature and its strange powers had passed from father to son. Passed from tribe to tribe. All the way down south to Central and South America. All had been warned of its dangers. But those warnings were mostly long forgotten.

And now, for the first time in centuries, the creature's nostrils breathed in fresh air. His antlers felt the warming rays of the sun. For the first time in ages, his shimmering scales were able to feel fresh water. And for the first time in centuries, the muscles of his scaly body were able to stretch out to full length.

His scales were rejuvenated. His mind refreshed. His entire being set free.

He flowed leisurely downstream, down the Arkansas. He wasn't concerned in the least that every living thing in his wake began to wither a little. They didn't die. They just became weakened. Every fish, lizard, plant, or mammal that came within twenty feet of him. What was actually happening was that a few years were being robbed from the ends of their lives, and those years were added to the life of the Uktena. This power was the very thing that Cherokee witches longed for. According to legend, the Raven Stalkers, Night-Goers, and Night-Seers originally learned their dark magic from the Horned Serpent and passed it on to evildoers like Benjamin Blacksnake. It all started in ancient times when humans and animals could talk to one another.

And every creature that happened to gaze into the Uktena's eyes became dazed. Those dazed animals were unaware that the beast would soon devour them. Easy meals.

But the creature was missing his most prized possessions. The very things that provided his ultimate power were not in their places. The brilliant and mysterious gem that once was fixed to his forehead had been stolen. And the dark crystal attached to the tip of his tail—it, too, had been removed. When the gems were returned to their rightful places, though, the beast would be fully restored.

The very rare gem from the beast's forehead was known as a Fire Crystal, and once upon a time it had blazed forth with a brilliant, blinding light. The very sight of it could paralyze or kill a two-legged one. And the dark crystal from its tail contained loose pieces inside that rattled a warning whenever someone approached from behind. No one and no thing could catch him unawares.

The beast only had two weaknesses, and, ages ago, the two-legged priests had learned one of them. They'd tricked him and lured him into a trap. They had spoken the powerful magic words that had cast a paralyzing spell on him. His mind had been conscious, but his body had been unable to move, unable to fight back. That was when the crystal was removed from the tip of his tail.

Then the priests removed the crystal from his forehead. They must've known of its great power. That was why they kept it for themselves. The one called the Sun Priest fixed it to the tip of his long staff. And the other two-leggeds worshipped him because he'd tamed the so-called evil beast. Why was it that, for those two-legged humans, everything was either good or evil, black or white—opposites. Their minds were so petty.

Finally, while the beast was still paralyzed, they had transported him to the cave and sealed the doorway to his liquid prison. The two-leggeds knew the beast would remain close to the dark crystal, and the potion within the lake made sure of it. So they placed the gem on the pedestal with a warning sign to keep other humans away.

But the power of the potion had weakened over time, and at long last, just a few days ago, the door had opened with a *psssst* sound. The creature had waited until the two-legged intruders had left. He'd waited until the winged night-flyers had flown. With that prison door open, he was free to roam the countryside once again.

Of course, he was still connected to those two gemstones, the forehead gem and the dark tail crystal. He could feel their presence in the world. Especially the purple one. It was connected to him by an unseen force, connected to his mind through invisible strings.

So when the two-legged intruders had fled from the cave, the beast had felt the crystal leaving as well. He'd realized that the two-legged ones must've taken it with them. Oh, the anger and pain he'd suffered when he left the dark liquid, when he found the pedestal empty and the crystal gone.

With his eyes closed and his mind focused, he'd felt it moving farther and farther from him, until it came to rest a mere sixty miles to the north. The map in his mind told him where the crystal now resided. He didn't know the intruders called the place it was near Tahlequah. He'd never heard of the Cherokee Nation.

But he'd been able to mentally reconnect with the crystal and reattach those unseen strings. Whoever had it now would hold it only for a short while, for he would retrieve it in due time. All in due time.

For now, he was content to float in the river headed for a landmark he knew very well. It was a place the two-legged beings had built long ago. A place near the water with mounds that held the bones of their dead. A place that held the bones of a powerful two-legged one.

This one had been worshipped by tens of thousands as more than a mere man. They'd said he was part man and part god. Ceremonially dressed in a cape made from the feathers of the hawk and appearing as half bird, half man, he'd left the center of his kingdom at Solstice City to come to the cultural and religious outpost at Spiral Mounds.

The man who'd found out how to trick the beast and imprison him in that cave was none other than the Son of the Sun, such a lofty title. It was said that he'd held the keys to the Upperworld, that through his performance of the annual death ceremony at Spiral Mounds, he'd controlled the fate of souls in the afterlife.

He had certainly controlled the fate of the Snake Priest, whose magnificent reign had ended so tragically. Memories of that golden era flooded the beast's mind. Hundreds—no, thousands—of people had worshipped the Horned Serpent from the base of the serpent's temple pyramid located in the eastern woodlands.

With the aid of the secretive members of the Owl Clan, whose powers had come from the Underworld, the Snake Priest had risen to glorious heights. Those practitioners of the dark medicine had bound the Snake Priest and Horned Serpent together. The intertwining of their energies was what had attracted so many worshippers—lost, forgotten souls searching for meaning, longing to belong to something bigger than themselves.

The Snake Priest had mistakenly believed he was invincible, that his army was all powerful. His enormous ego caused him to make mistakes, mistakes like attacking Solstice City during the winter solstice ceremony. But the spies sent by the Son of the Sun knew they were coming, knew the hour of the attack.

The Snake Priest's followers were slaughtered like cattle. The sun demigod personally beheaded his own twin brother, the Snake Priest, in a spectacle event witnessed by thousands.

These twins—Shakuru, meaning "Sun," and Monkata, meaning "He of the Earth"—had been born on the very day the Upperworld had birthed a new star with such grandeur and power it was seen the world over. That same day, fiery pieces of the Upperworld had rained down on the Middleworld, crashing to the earth. It had been another reminder of the power of the Thunders and their companion, the Thunderbird.

That midsummer day more than a thousand years ago had witnessed the parallel births in the heavens and on the earth. What tragic outcomes those births eventually brought, at least in the eyes of the beast.

What a glorious day it would be when the beast located that sun god's burial site. When he found those bones and scattered them to the four winds. What a glorious day when, at long last, the stolen gem was once again fixed to the Horned Serpent's forehead.

That would be a day the world would remember—and regret.

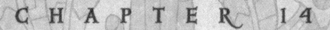

CHAPTER 14

The Gathering

Back at the college, Billy's father was able to organize a trip to explore the cave on short notice. It wasn't hard to convince the head of the college to give Professor Buckhorn and Professor Stevens time off for the project. Finding and exploring an unknown archaeological site used by the Mound Builders would bring good publicity to the college. Professor Stevens got permission to bring along a young man named Doug as well. Doug was a graduate student studying the ancient Native Americans of Oklahoma.

Two days later, the team of four headed south from the college. They drove a well-equipped college van and towed a boat trailer behind them. After driving for a while, they decided to stop. A convenience store on the side of the road gave them a good place to go to the bathroom and buy snacks.

As he was paying for their goodies, Billy's dad saw the front page of a local newspaper. The headline read "Parts of Ancient Mounds Destroyed by Unknown Vandal." Picking up the paper, he looked closely at the photo under the headline.

It showed that large holes had been dug into one of the mounds at Spiral Mounds park. These were ragged openings, not anything made with proper tools. And there was a strange path of withered plant life. It led from the river to the site.

"After exploring the cave, we'll have to check this out," James said. He handed the paper to Dr. Stevens as they headed back to the van.

They arrived at their destination about an hour later. It was a park area with a boat ramp on the Arkansas River. They put their gear in the boat and then put the boat in the river. After doing a final check to make sure they had everything they needed, the team got in the boat and headed south downriver. They followed the same route Billy and Chigger had traveled.

"Here it is," Billy soon announced as they rounded a turn and came to the campsite used by the boys. Pointing upward, he added, "And there's the cave."

Quickly they unloaded the boat and made ready for their first cave entrance. Lights, cameras, tape measurers, pick hammers, and logbooks were items they placed in their backpacks.

The two professors and the graduate student were excited about what lay ahead. To them this was a chance to learn new information about the ancient peoples of the area. It could also make them celebrities in the world of diggers. That meant they could write books about their find and have their pictures published in magazines.

To Billy, however, this expedition meant much more. It was a journey into the deeper mysteries of life, an expedition to the supernatural side. A trip to an ancient time.

"Awinita, I need you to be with us today," he whispered while looking up at the cave. "Help us learn what we need to know for the good of our people and for Chigger." He gave a little nod to send his request on its way.

Awinita hadn't really told him what he needed to do to ask for her help, so he just did the best he could. No aroma of pie or cider reached his nose now.

Once inside the cave, each member of the team started performing his duty. Billy led the way with a powerful flashlight. The graduate student shot video as they went. Dr. Stevens took still pictures and jotted down notes. Billy's dad spoke into a small tape recorder, describing what they saw and experienced.

The group reached the wall where the path separated into two. They examined and documented the markings and drawings etched into the stone.

"The half-bird, half-man figure is clearly a priest of the early Mound Builder culture," Billy's father said. "He would've led the people in ceremonies. He probably ruled their society. And this creature on the right looks like the mythological Horned Serpent featured in several ancient tribal cultures."

Then, as Billy and Chigger had done, the team first took the upward path. They were amazed by the beautiful crystal room that Billy took them to. And more amazed by the upper white-crystal room. No one knew what the scenes on the walls were. Their meanings had been lost in the mists of time.

But their expedition continued. They photographed every step and every space within the upper and lower regions of the cave. When they finally made their way to the door at the bottom of the cavern, Dr. Stevens closely studied the markings on it.

"My grandpa Wesley has a very old medicine book that has the same kind of markings on a few pages, but he doesn't know what they mean or where they came from."

"Fascinating," Stevens said, just as Billy's father often did.

Then Billy showed them the pedestal where the dark crystal had resided and explained what happened when Chigger touched it. Peering through the open stone door, they examined the pool of dark liquid. They filled a test tube with a sample of the fluid. There were no signs of ripples or movement of any kind there.

And no signs of bats either. The cave had been totally vacated.

"We need to find a language key," Dr. Stevens said, still thinking about the markings on the stone door. "That will allow us to decode the meaning of the markings. They must be the symbols of an unknown language."

"That's fantastic," Billy's dad said. "Maybe they're part of an alphabet that could be the oldest written Native language. This came way before Sequoyah invented the Cherokee system of writing in the early 1800s."

"Fascinating," Billy and the graduate student said together, mocking the older men. The younger two laughed, but the two professors didn't understand what was so funny.

"Well, we should wrap things up here and head to a motel for the night," Professor Buckhorn said. "Tomorrow we can get an early start to see what happened at the mound site."

That evening, Professor Stevens used the motel's Wi-Fi network and navigated to a research website used by colleges all over the country. The system's main computer memory was so large it could find the smallest bits of information on a specific topic, information stored within huge database collections at college libraries.

He pulled together the most recent discoveries of other archaeologists. People had been digging up ancient Native American sites for decades. Sometimes these excavations had been done with respect for ancient Indigenous cultures and peoples. Other times, not so much.

What the professor found was, of course, fascinating. It was also very relevant to what his team had found in the cave that day.

"Two other archaeologists have recently found symbols that look like the ones we found," Dr. Stevens said. "These seem to appear only in the most secret of chambers. But there's one archaeologist we definitely want to talk to, one of the few Native Americans in the field, an Osage named Ethan Lookout."

"Why do you want to talk to him?" Billy asked.

"His specialty is Mound Builder cultures, and he claims to have a special connection to artifacts buried at Spiral Mounds. He's excavated at all the major mound sites and published several unique papers in anthropology journals."

"It does sound like we do need to connect with him," Billy agreed and then let out a big yawn. "I just realized how tired I am. I'm going to hit the hay."

While the two professors carried on their discussion, Billy went to bed. That night, as he slept in the motel room, he began to dream. At first, he was high atop a large earthen mound. A building with a thatched roof stood on the mound's flat top. He looked out across the grassy meadow below the mound. There he saw hundreds of people looking up at him. He saw that these were American Indian people wearing simple clothing made of animal skins and natural materials.

The sound of their voices began to rise up to his ears. They were singing the haunting chant of a beautiful song. Then he looked down at his own body within the dream. He noticed he held a long carved wooden staff. Images of plants and vines seemed to grow up to the top of the staff. A large pink diamond-like gem was attached to the very top. It shone brilliantly in the noonday sun, almost like a flame.

He walked to the edge of the mound top and held up the staff. That was when he saw he was wearing a cape made of hawk or eagle feathers. The crowd below cheered. They seemed to adore him. He put the staff down, and from the mound's edge, he leaped outward. Much to his surprise, he did not fall to the ground. He drifted out over the crowd.

Then he floated over them as they continued to cheer. Then the mound scene faded away, but Billy began to fly across a changing landscape. The sun was setting in the west, and it created a beautiful sight filled with billowy orange clouds. Soon his altitude dropped, and he gently glided to the ground near a river. As he landed, he saw Grandma Awinita coming out of an old log cabin that stood in the midst of a cluster of trees. Her thoughts reached his mind.

"Welcome, Grandson. Welcome to my home in the spirit world. This is where you can find me whenever you need me."

Billy looked around at the beautiful setting. The sounds of the running water and singing birds were very peaceful. But his mind was a jumble of worry and concern.

"I need you now," he said to her with his thoughts. "Chigger's in trouble. The Cherokee people are in trouble. And some sort of monster is on the loose."

"I know, I know," she said in a comforting tone. "With your help, all will be set right."

She led him to a tree stump near the river, where he sat down. With her glowing energy and her thoughts, she calmed his mind and quieted his concerns. He was then able to enjoy that peaceful place.

"Tell Wesley that the purple crystal is the cause of Chigger's problems," she said. "The first thing that must be done is to get that object away from your friend. You'll call your grandpa as soon as you can to let him know."

She also revealed other things to him. But she said he would forget when he woke up from this dream. The memory of these things would come back into his mind as he needed them.

"Is this a dream or is it really happening?" he asked when she'd finished.

"Both," she replied. "Sometimes that's just how this dimension works."

Meanwhile, back on the ground, Wesley had called together all the upstanding medicine men and women he knew. None of the medicine people with questionable reputations were invited. Those mercenary wizards, witches, sorcerers, and conjurers were known to take money for their services, usually hired to do harm to a rival or enemy.

A meeting such as this had not been held in the Cherokee Nation in over fifty years. Not since the 1960s, when non-Native outsiders began using Native ceremonies for their own purposes. "New Age" believers began borrowing Native American ceremonies and cultural items for their own uses while fake medicine men advertised healing services and charged fees to an unaware public. Native people called some of them "plastic medicine men."

Now the Cherokee healers gathered at Live Oak stomp grounds, the place Billy and Wesley went for all-night ceremonies a couple of times a year. The people who came to Wesley's meeting this day were mostly elders like him. There were a few younger ones scattered among them, but, sadly, there were fewer healers among the people than ever before.

After everyone had been cleansed in a traditional way, they sat in the seven arbors facing the central square. This was where everyone normally danced during the all-night stomp dance in a spiral around the central fire.

Wesley sat in his traditional place in the arbor of the Red Paint Clan, the Cherokee clan of medicine people, the clan of healers. The elder stepped out into the square to speak.

"I'll get right to the reason for this gathering," he said, speaking in the Cherokee language. "How many of you are treating more people than you normally do?"

Almost everyone raised their hands. A murmur of chatters spread through the crowd.

"And how many of those people have been seeing bats near their homes?" he asked.

Again, almost everyone raised their hands. The chatter became louder as the healers realized they all faced similar problems.

"And are these folks getting better after your treatments?" Wesley asked. "Are they being healed by traditional methods?"

One very loud "No" after another rang out from the group. The chatter among the healers burst loudly across the dance grounds.

"All right, all right," Wesley said in English, trying to calm everyone down. He waited for them to settle. "That's why we're here," he continued. "So together we can look at what we are facing. So together we can try to understand what's causing this strange sickness among our people."

A working discussion began among this unique group of people. They were, after all, the most experienced in such matters. These matters were beyond science—beyond health clinics, doctors' offices, and hospitals. These matters were of the supernatural realms.

In comparing recent experiences, they learned that something very unusual was happening, unusual even for them. Something more than regular symptoms was coming forth. And what was needed was more than everyday remedies. What would be required of them now was of a higher order. Greater effort and greater power were called for.

Wesley listened carefully to the ideas that came from the healers at that gathering. And after the talks were over, he asked three people to stay a little while longer. These three had come up with some of the best ideas that day.

The first was a tall older Cherokee man named Elwood. He lived in the eastern part of the Nation. The second was a short middle-aged Indian from down south named Chester. The third was an attractive elderly woman named Wilma. She lived near the city of Tulsa. Through the years, Wesley had heard many good things about all three. He knew he could trust them.

After everyone else had left, he told these healers about a special case he needed their help with. All of them had offered to do anything they could to be of service, so he told them about Chigger. Wesley hoped that the power the four of them had might be able to break through to Chigger.

Whatever it was that formed the barrier around the boy needed strong medicine to melt it away. After they heard what Wesley was up against, all three agreed to help him. They planned to make their move the very next day.

Early the next morning, Wesley got a phone call from Billy.

"Billy, how's the exploration going?" Wesley asked. He was glad to hear from his grandson. "Find out anything yet?"

"Last night in a dream, Grandma told me that Chigger's problem comes from the dark crystal he took out of the cave."

"I'm so jealous and at the same time happy that you get to see Grandma," Wesley said.

"She said you'd be feeling that way," Billy replied. "She also said to remind you that I had to get struck by lightning and die in the hospital to be able to see her."

"Good point," he laughed. "I'll try to remember that."

"The first thing you have to do is get the crystal away from Chigger," his grandson continued. "That won't be easy because the Uktena is connected to the crystal. That means he's also connected to Chigger."

Billy actually didn't remember that piece of information from his dream. It just popped out of his mouth.

"Oh no," Wesley said with sadness. "Who would ever have thought we'd be dealing with the old Horned Serpent in our time?"

"Yeah, who?" Billy asked seriously. "Please don't hurt Chigger," he added after a pause.

"Of course not," his grandpa answered. "We only have Chigger's best interest in mind."

"We'll be down here one more day and then back home," Billy added.

"Remember this," Wesley said. "If you come across the beast, don't look into his eyes."

"Ah, yes—good reminder," he said. "Thanks, Grandpa. Gotta go."

When Billy was off the phone, Professor Stevens gathered the team for an early morning breakfast at a café near their motel. Overnight he had done a simple test on the dark liquid sample he'd collected from the cave.

"It appears to be a concentrated brew of rare herbs and roots," he said. "It's like a tea you might take at night to make you sleepy, but this stuff is strong enough to put a horse to sleep."

Billy thought about that for a moment.

"It sounds like one of Grandpa's herbal remedies," he commented. "Something he gives a patient who's having trouble sleeping. Maybe a medicine man put it in the water."

"When I get back to the lab at the college, I can do a more thorough test," Stevens said as he took his last bite of eggs. "Then I can tell you exactly what the formula is."

"Okay, team. Time to hit the road," Billy's dad announced. "We're due at Spiral Mounds in a few minutes. The park is just down the road."

The four-member team climbed into their van and headed out.

At about the same time, the four healers, led by Wesley, headed to Chigger's mobile home. Armed with the new information from Billy, they hoped they'd be successful.

Chigger's father, Sam, answered the door when they arrived. He'd come right home from his out-of-town job after his wife had called. The tall Cherokee man invited the four medicine people into his humble home. He had never really believed much in traditional Cherokee medicine. But his son needed help from someone, and they were the only ones offering.

Chigger's mother sat on the couch in her bathrobe. Her hair was a mess. She was a mess.

"That's not my boy in there," she said, pointing to Chigger's bedroom. "Something or someone has taken him over. That's the only thing that can explain it."

"He hasn't eaten any of the food we've given him in days," Chigger's father added. "He just throws it at us and curses. He keeps demanding raw meat, but I'm not going to give that to him."

"If you'll allow it, we'd like to go in and check on Chigger," Wesley told the distressed parents. "Just to see if we can do any good."

Sam nodded his permission. He then sat down on the couch next to his wife.

Outside Chigger's bedroom, Wesley spoke to his band of healers. "Remember," he whispered. "As soon as we enter, take up your positions in the four directions. Hopefully, that will prevent him from being able to focus on any one of us and putting up the psychic wall."

They nodded their agreement, and Wesley quietly opened the door. The room smelled of rotting food and worse. They tiptoed in. Chigger was standing in the middle of his bed, entirely focused on the glowing purple crystal in his hands.

"Billy was right," Wesley whispered loudly. "The crystal from the cave has got some power over the boy. We've got to get it away from him."

Chigger looked up from the crystal. His crazed bloodshot eyes darted left and right. The healers fanned out around him in the room. That was when he began speaking in tongues, speaking a language no one in the room could understand. His eyes opened even wider. His head rolled in a circle as he spoke the angry gibberish.

At a signal from Wesley, the four moved in on the crazed teenager. When he could no longer see everyone at the same time, he panicked. At that point Chigger's body jerked in a spasm and he fell back on the bed.

"Hold him down while I grab the crystal!" Wesley yelled.

Pulling a tanned leather bag from his pocket, Wesley used the bag to pry the crystal from Chigger's hands. The elder did not want to come into direct contact with the gem, because he was afraid it might attach itself to him.

That was when Wesley saw the burned, raw flesh on the palms of Chigger's hands for the first time. The gem must have been very painful to hold, but Billy's friend would not loosen his grip on the smooth stone. Then Wesley got an idea.

"Keep holding him down," he told the others and left the room.

"Do you have some raw meat in your refrigerator?" Wesley asked the Muskrats back in the living room.

"Yes, we do," Mrs. Muskrat said. "I was planning on making a couple of steaks for dinner."

"Good," Wesley replied. "Please bring me one of them. And hurry!"

"You're not going to give it to him, are you?" Sam asked. "I don't think that's a good idea."

"I'm going to distract him with it so we can get that crystal away from him," the elder assured him. "In the meantime, please call the hospital and get an ambulance here as quickly as you can."

Molly ran to the kitchen and took an uncooked steak out of the fridge while Sam picked up the phone to call the hospital.

"This shouldn't take too long," Wesley said as he carried the meat toward the bedroom.

Back inside Chigger's bedroom, Wesley approached the bed.

"Look what I've got for you," he said to Chigger. He hoped to attract the creature that was somehow connected to the boy.

Chigger stopped struggling against the three people who were holding him. He looked over at Wesley. When the boy saw the meat, he tried to sit up and reach for it with his mouth.

"If you want it, you'll have to grab it with your hands," Wesley taunted, and sniffed the meat for dramatic effect.

The elder stood holding the raw steak at the edge of the bed. The three healers held the boy tightly so he couldn't reach the meat with his mouth. Chigger had to consider his situation seriously for a moment. Which did he want more, the crystal or the steak? He had a powerful craving for the meat, but the purple gem cried out to be held closely to his chest.

During that long moment, Elwood prepared the leather bag that would hold the crystal.

Finally, Chigger's hunger won out. He released the crystal from his burned hands. Wilma, who was closest to the boy, grabbed the gem using the bedspread as a buffer. Elwood held the bag open as she stuffed it inside. Chester continued to restrain Chigger.

Wesley allowed Chigger to grab the meat in his bare hands. The boy immediately screamed in pain as his burns touched the meat. He dropped the steak and looked down at his scorched hands. That was when he realized he no longer held his precious crystal.

He cried out in agony. He thrashed about against those who held him.

"Sam, come quick!" Wesley yelled, hoping to be heard over Chigger's yelps.

Mr. Muskrat ran into the room, eyes wide with fear. What was happening to his boy?

"Help hold your son down on the bed and talk to him," Wesley said. "Maybe if he hears his father's voice, the real Chigger will start to come back to the surface."

"The ambulance is on the way," Sam said as he took his son's arms in his hands. He began talking to him in a soft voice. It hurt the man to see the burns all over his son's hands, but he kept speaking to him in a calm tone.

Wesley took the leather pouch out the front door and placed it in the bed of his pickup. He would hide the dark crystal in the woods behind his house until he learned what needed to happen next. He hoped Billy already knew what to do or would soon find out.

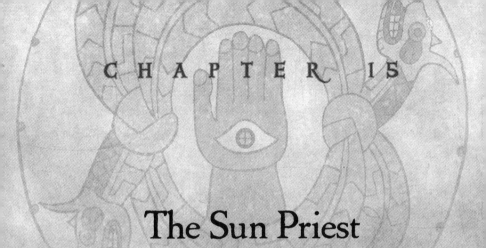

CHAPTER 15

The Sun Priest

S oon the ambulance arrived at the Muskrat home. The emergency medical team had never seen someone in Chigger's condition. He was half-starved and had third-degree burns on the palms of his hands. But these pros worked quickly to get the boy on a gurney and into their vehicle. Then they sped off toward the hospital.

Outside the mobile home, Wesley thanked Wilma, Chester, and Elwood for their assistance. The four healers went their separate ways, but not before Wilma had slipped a note into Wesley's hand.

When things settle down, I'd like to have you over to my place for dinner, the note read. Wilma's phone number was written at the bottom. Wesley looked up and blushed as the woman drove out of the Muskrat's driveway. With a smile, he placed the note in his wallet. *To be continued,* he thought. Awinita had told him over and over again to find someone.

Meanwhile, the expedition team had arrived at Spiral Mounds State Park. They spoke to the park's director, Peter Langford, and he agreed to meet them when he learned that the famous Dr. Stevens was a member of the team.

197

Langford said the damage had been done a couple of nights ago, and the trail left by the vandals came from the river. He showed the team the weird trail of withered plant life. It led from the river into the park. What had caused this trail was a complete mystery to everyone who'd seen it.

"But what's really strange is what happened to our night watchman," Langford said. "He says he was making his midnight rounds through the park. He heard digging, scraping, and grunting noises from the mound I'm going to show you."

"He was able to catch the vandals in the act?" Billy's father asked.

"That's what's so strange," Langford replied. "The watchman claims to have turned on his flashlight when he arrived at the mound. All he saw for a brief second was a pair of large glowing eyes. And there was a bright reflection from those eyes. It sent the light back to him in a flash. He went blind and became paralyzed. Isn't that the craziest thing you've ever heard?"

"Were they like snake eyes?" Billy asked. "You know, with a narrow vertical pupil?"

Langford was stunned by Billy's description. "What would make you say that?" he asked. "That's exactly how the guard described them, but I dismissed this description as the ravings of a man gone mad."

"Is he all right? Can we speak to him?" Billy's father asked. "Whatever he heard or saw before going blind could be useful to us."

"I guess I could give him a call when we get back to the office," Langford said. "But first I'll show you the damage to the mound. We, of course, have been closed to the public since the incident."

No archaeology work had been done around the mound site since the 1950s. At that time archaeologists decided to delay any further digging until new methods and better equipment had been invented. They were sure that the last mound contained very valuable artifacts and important human remains. They wanted to leave those things undisturbed.

"There was another disturbing thing about the whole incident," Langford said. "The damage was done to the least publicly known mound." Langford continued to talk as he led the team toward that mound. "Only a small select group of scientists even knew that there was still one mound waiting to be explored."

"That decision was made to prevent exactly what has now happened," Dr. Stevens confirmed. "We hoped that illegal pot hunters and grave robbers wouldn't break into the park and dig up the place. That's what happened back in the 1930s and 1940s. It's hard to figure how anyone knew where to dig."

The group had almost reached the mound when Billy's dad spoke. "This must be the burial mound that held the bones and funeral objects belonging to the leaders of this community," he said.

"The Sun Priest," Billy blurted out. "He might've been buried here."

Langford, Stevens, and Billy's father just stared at the young man. How did he know this? Their question would have to wait, because they were now looking at the damage done to the burial mound.

A huge ragged hole had been gouged out in the side of the mound. Dried human bones, broken pieces of pottery, and cracked parts of stone and shell carvings were scattered about.

"My god," Dr. Stevens exclaimed. "This is a disaster."

As the digger and the professor examined the scattered fragments, Billy peered into the gaping hole. Intuition told him that something important was still inside the mound. Actually, a throbbing energy was emanating from the mound. Something had been overlooked during the frantic search, because the searcher had been interrupted by the guard in the dark of night.

Billy stepped into the hole in the mound, not knowing what he'd find. He saw stone and bone pieces sticking out of shredded dirt. But a section of a long tubelike object caught his eye. It was partly buried and partly protruding from the back of the hole.

Scraping the debris away from the object, he could see it was a container, apparently made of thick round river cane. Carefully he pulled it away from the dirt and brushed it off. He carried it outside the mound and laid it down on the ground.

Langford noticed what Billy was doing and reacted. "Nothing should be touched or taken from the mound," he said angrily, rushing over to where Billy stood.

"He is a member of my team," Dr. Stevens said loudly. "As such, he's allowed to examine anything that's already been disturbed by the vandals. We have to find out how much damage has been done and what artifacts may have survived."

He moved quickly and stood between Billy and the park director.

"Of course," Langford said as he backed down. "You're right."

"I think now would be a good time for you to contact the night watchman," Billy's father told the park director.

"Right again," Langford replied. "I'll see you gentleman back at my office later."

The team waited until the man was out of sight before doing anything else. Then Dr. Stevens handed Billy a pair of latex gloves to put on. The digger stooped down to see what the teen had found. With gloved hands, Billy carefully opened one end of the hollow tube.

Dr. Stevens pointed his flashlight into the tube but couldn't make out what was inside.

"I'll pick up the tube and tilt it slightly so the contents can slide out," he said to Billy. "You catch whatever's inside. Be very careful."

Then Dr. Stevens, who was already wearing gloves, tilted the tube. A long straight wooden rod began sliding out. Wrapped around the rod was a collection of feathers. They had been tied or sewn together.

"Doug, spread out that sheet of plastic so we can lay this down and unroll it," the archaeologist instructed the grad student.

Once the plastic was down, Billy and Dr. Stevens unrolled the feather-covered rod. The teen couldn't believe what he was seeing: objects that had been hidden away in the mound for centuries. First, astonishingly, there was the feathered cape he'd been wearing in his dream. Then there was the staff he'd been holding in that dream. At the top of the staff was the brilliant diamondlike gem he'd seen as he stood on the tall mound in front of hundreds of people.

"It's the Sun Priest's cape and staff," Billy said, not sure where the information came from. "I'm not exactly sure of the guy's name. It was something like Sun God, Sun Chief, or Sun Priest."

"How do you know any of that?" the digger asked.

"I was wearing this cape and holding this staff in my dream last night," Billy said. "I stood on top of a large flat-top mound. I think I *was* seeing myself as the Sun Priest in that dream. But I wasn't here in this area. It was a much larger space that held hundreds of people who worshipped me as their leader."

"So much of what we know about these ancient people is based on educated guesses," Dr. Stevens said. "So how is it that you seem to know specific details about the Mound Builders?"

"You wouldn't believe me if I told you," Billy answered. "As a matter of fact, I don't expect you to believe anything I say. You go ahead and work with your best guesses. I'm on this expedition for a totally different reason than you are."

Dr. Stevens turned to Billy's father with a puzzled look.

"Billy's right," Professor Buckhorn said. "You have your tasks, and Billy has his. I'm here to coordinate both efforts."

Dr. Stevens had no reply.

"So, Professor Stevens, explain to me how this cape and staff have been preserved so well all these hundreds of years," Billy's father asked. He wanted to change the subject.

As the digger began his explanation, Billy started to hear buzzing in his ears. This was the same buzzing noise he'd heard a few days ago when Awinita introduced him to Uncle Luther.

Billy tuned out Dr. Stevens as he focused on the buzzing.

"It's me again," Awinita's voice said from within the buzz. "I've got someone else for you to meet."

"I hope it's not another uncle I never heard of," Billy thought to himself and then laughed.

"No long-lost uncle this time," Awinita communicated. "Maybe just a long-lost soul who's making a return."

As Billy watched, his grandma appeared in her glowing form inside the hole in the side of the mound. Slowly coming into view beside her, as if a projector were focusing the lens, was a tall, majestic-looking Native American man. Billy was pretty sure no one else saw them.

"Here stands before you the spirit of the man whose bones and belongings are buried in this mound with knowledge he wishes to share with you," Awinita said.

Billy tried as best he could to focus on the spirit man's glowing outline. But the ancient being drifted in and out of view. He was barely able to adjust himself to the physical world.

"It's been hundreds of years since he tried to interact with the world of the living," Awinita said to Billy, "so be patient."

At first, all Billy heard was the muffled voice of a man who was uttering indistinct sounds that might be words. Awinita helped fine-tune and amplify the man's thoughts so they better matched Billy's thought patterns.

No one else on the team heard the interaction between Billy and the Sun Priest. All they saw was the boy standing motionless while looking at the hole in the side of the burial mound. Professor Stevens noticed this strange behavior and began to approach the teen. Billy's father redirected the archaeologist's attention elsewhere, leaving his son to his private supernatural business.

"I'm here to thank you," the spirit man said to Billy in an understandable voice at last. "When you stumbled into the crystal cave chamber, you and your friend broke the curse that held me imprisoned for centuries."

Even though Billy was receiving the spirit man's words as thoughts, his "voice" was deep and sounded almost like multiple voices synchronized to speak in unison.

"But don't forget that we also set the creature free from the lower chamber to go out and wreak havoc everywhere," the teen replied.

"True. You did let loose the dual forces of my ancient culture on the modern world," the translucent being said. "But it was bound to happen sooner or later. Prophecy foretold it."

Billy had to think about that new information for a moment. "What do we do now?" he said.

"The markings you discovered on the beast's prison door at the bottom of the cave are indeed those of our secret holy language," the man said. "Originally that language was only known to the high priests and used in sacred ceremonies, but members of the Owl Nation stole it and bastardized it for their own evil purposes."

Billy couldn't pretend to know what the spirit man was talking about, but it gave him a clue as to why those markings were in the back of Blacksnake's medicine book.

"More to our point," the apparition continued, "what is written on that stone door are the words that must be spoken in order to recapture the serpent and hold him in that prison."

"How will we ever be able to speak those words?" Billy asked. "We do not have that knowledge. We don't know that language."

"When the time comes, I will have to speak them through you," he replied. "But there are many steps that must be taken before that can happen."

It took a moment for that answer to soak into Billy's mind. *This spirit will speak through me?* "What are the steps?" he asked.

"First the dark crystal must be returned to its place on the pedestal near the door. And the person who removed it must be the one who replaces it. Then the bearer of the cape and the staff must find the Horned Serpent. Only the Son of the Sun or his spiritually empowered replacement will be protected from the beast's harmful powers, and only if he is wearing the cape and holding the staff.

"When the creature sees the gem on the staff, he will become hypnotized. That gem is the very stone that was once embedded in his own forehead. He will follow it wherever it goes. You must lead him back into the cave and lure him back into the pit."

"Whoa, hold on," Billy said, interrupting the glowing man. "What do you mean I must lead him back?"

"Your grandmother Awinita told me of your grandfather's proclamation," the spirit said. "Your neck and hand bear the signs that the Sky Beings have chosen you as they chose me a thousand years ago. If that is true, then you are my replacement, my symbolic reincarnation for this age."

Billy suddenly felt the weight of the world settle on his shoulders. But the glowing man continued.

"Once the beast has entered the medicine lake at the bottom of the cave, the words on the door have to be spoken. When the final word is uttered, the door will close and reseal itself. It's all very simple."

Ha, Billy thought. *Simple for you maybe.*

"I will be ready to conduct the ceremony when Awinita contacts me that all is prepared here in the physical realm," the man said. "I will appear where you are and speak the words through you, using your physical body, your voice. Then the creature will be safely secured once more."

The glowing man began to fade at that point.

"Wait," Billy pleaded. "I have so many questions to ask you. Where did the beast come from in the first place? How did you trap him and imprison him? Why is this my responsibility?"

"All will become clearer in due time," the spirit answered as he continued to fade. Soon he was gone.

"I'm sorry, Billy," Awinita said. "That's all for now. Making oneself visible to the living drains us of so much energy. You should return home to visit with Chigger and Wesley. They will have parts to play in conquering the creature. Goodbye for now."

She, too, faded away, leaving Billy with many unanswered questions, many worries and concerns. Most of all, he had many doubts about his own capabilities to do what was being asked of him, to do what needed doing.

Members of the expedition team had work to do and carried out their planned tasks at the site the rest of the day. Dr. Stevens wanted to inventory the artifacts and remains that had been damaged. Then he wanted to make plans for a future dig there.

But all Billy could think about was the whole fantastic string of events that had unfolded over the past couple of weeks. Was this just a series of freak accidents, or was it a sign of the future? Was he at the beginning of a return to the days of miracles and monsters? This had been predicted in some tribal legends, according to Wesley. Or was it all some big delusion he'd been fooled by and fallen for?

He inwardly checked his own intuition on the matter. This is what his grandfather had encouraged him to do, but he didn't like what his intuition was telling him.

At the end of the day, the team loaded their equipment back in the van. Billy took time to speak to his father in private. He wasn't sure his dad would believe him, but the teen told him about the visit from the spirit of the Sun Priest earlier that day.

"At some point, you and I, Wesley, and Chigger will supposedly have to return to that cave with the dark crystal and reseal the Horned Serpent in the lake," Billy said. "And I will need to be wearing the hawk feather cape and holding the priest's staff."

"I was afraid you were going to say something like that," his father replied. "This has all become more real than I'd like to admit. But nothing surprises me anymore when it comes to the things that happen in your life."

"How do you think I feel?" Billy replied. "I don't even know what's real anymore, and I'm pretty sure I can't do the things that are being expected of me."

"I think you're stronger and more capable than you give yourself credit for."

"Yeah, well, what if I'm not? What if I decide I don't want any of it, the medicine journey, the healing formulas, dealing with the Horned Serpent—none of it!"

James saw that his son was getting overwhelmed by what had been happening. "You and I and Grandpa will have to talk more about this later," he said, putting a comforting hand on his son's shoulder. "Let's take it one step at a time. We're all tired, overwhelmed, and feeling like we may be in over our heads."

Billy blew out a lungful of air, releasing some of his tension. "Okay," he said.

"For now, I don't think we should mention anything to Stevens about you needing to have the cape and staff," James said. "He'll probably have a major meltdown over it."

During the drive back to Tahlequah, Dr. Stevens and his grad student sat in the front of the van. They talked a mile a minute about their new discoveries. Billy and James, sitting in the van's middle row, were mostly silent. Mr. Buckhorn tried a couple of times to get Billy talking about everyday subjects. He brought up how much school Billy had missed and asked how he and Sara were doing.

But Billy had no interest or energy for such things. His mind was focused on whether or not his best friend would get well and go back to his old self again. Would Wesley and the other medicine people of the tribe be able to rid the Nation of these troubles? Was he, sixteen-year-old Billy Buckhorn, destined for greatness, or having a gigantic mental breakdown?

Extreme fatigue overtook him as the van rambled across the landscape. The sun set in the western sky. And out of nowhere, the sweet smell of apple cider and pumpkin pie reached his nostrils. This put his mind at ease a little. He wanted to believe everything would eventually be all right. Maybe, even with all the unanswered questions floating through his mind, that was enough for now.

He slept a dreamless sleep the rest of the way home.

CHAPTER 16

What Next?

T he weather turned cold in the days and weeks following the Thanksgiving holiday. That was normal for the Cherokee Nation of Oklahoma. What wasn't normal were the strange things that had been happening recently in Billy's young life.

He'd come to a few conclusions regarding his own role in the unfolding supernatural drama. For now, he'd stay the course, stick to the plan, step up to the plate—he'd used all the clichés to help himself maintain courage, stay on target, and keep on keepin' on.

But the most recurring question on Billy's mind these days was: *Could things get any crazier?*

The teen pondered these quandaries as he drove to the Indian hospital to see Chigger, who was recovering from his own very weird experience. Who could've guessed that the dark purple crystal the Cherokee teen had taken from the cave would put him under a spell? That spell had turned Chigger into an angry, ranting maniac. He had held on to the crystal as though it was his own precious possession. But it didn't belong to him, and it wasn't really Chigger doing those things. Something had been controlling his mind and his actions.

For the time being, the dark crystal was safely hidden away, as were the staff and feather cape that had once belonged to the Sun Priest. Billy's grandfather was keeping the dark gem hidden away at his house. The nearby university's archaeologist, Dr. Stevens, had locked the staff and cape in his underground vault. And they would stay hidden away until the right time came, everything had been arranged, and the master plan could be hatched.

Billy stepped into Chigger's hospital room just as a nurse was leaving. Chigger's mother sat in a chair next to the bed, watching her son. A variety of brand-new comic books lay on the bed, on his movable food tray, and on the nightstand. A typical scene for a normal Chigger.

Billy's friend was sitting up in bed, eating red gelatin from a cup. He was having trouble holding the spoon and the cup because both his hands were bandaged. A third gauze bandage was wrapped around the boy's head, making him look like a scary character from an old horror movie.

"Don't you think it's a little late for Halloween?" Billy said. Chigger and his mother turned to see who had come into the room. "You look like a mummy," he added.

"Billy!" Chigger exclaimed. "I wondered when you were going to find time to visit your oldest best friend." He put the spoon and cup down on the tray.

"We're so glad you came," Mrs. Muskrat said, standing up. "Your mother said you might be stopping by today."

Standing next to the bed, Billy pulled out something he'd been hiding behind his back and presented it to his friend. Chigger was very pleased with what he saw: a comic book, still in its protective clear sleeve, displaying a Native American superhero on the cover.

"A *Brave Eagle* graphic novel!?" he exclaimed. "How'd you get this? It's not even at the comic bookstore yet!"

"I preordered it for you, buddy, after I saw what you'd done to your own comic book collection. It just came in."

"Yeah, I guess I kinda went nuts for a while," Chigger replied, a little embarrassed.

Billy reached out, pulled his friend close, and hugged him.

"This is awkward," Chigger said jokingly when Billy held his friend for what seemed like a long time. "You're going to make Sara jealous."

That made Billy let go.

"I'm breaking up with her," Billy said seriously. "Right after I leave here."

"What? Are you kidding me?" Chigger asked. To Chigger, this was good news, although he'd never say that to Billy.

"I'm serious," Billy replied. "You know how I hate attention and publicity."

"Yeah, I know it all too well," Chigger said. "You've never taken me up on my offer to be your agent and get you on a reality TV show. But what does that have to do with Sara?"

"Well, she's become a social media freak," Billy said. "She's built an online fan club of friends who follow her partly because she's the girlfriend of the famous Lightning Boy."

"How'd you find out?" Chigger asked. "You don't have a Facebook page."

"My mother does," Billy said. "She's online all the time. She told me about it."

Chigger had always known that Billy's mom was on his side. *Go, Mrs. Buckhorn!*

"That's too bad," Chigger said, acting all sad. "You need to be with someone who appreciates you for you, not your special abilities."

"Yeah, well, don't lay it on too thick, Chig," Billy said. "I know you never liked her."

"Whatever," Chigger replied.

"So tell me what happened while you had the dark crystal," Billy said. His tone was serious again. "Grandpa Wesley and I are trying to understand how it works. You're a firsthand witness to its power."

"I'm afraid I can't help you," Chigger replied. "My mind's a blank. The last thing I remember is coming to your house for a visit. You were recovering from being dead. In fact, you were all bandaged up, looking like this." He gestured to his own hands and head.

"That's too bad. I was hoping for some clues."

Then something clicked in Chigger's mind.

"Now that I think of it, I do remember having a sort of weird dream," Chigger said. "It seemed to go on and on forever."

"What was it?" Billy sat on the edge of the bed.

"I was moving through water, just gliding along," Chigger said. "I looked down at my body, and it looked like I was a big snake. I mean really big. Then I saw my reflection in the water. And I had antlers—like deer antlers."

"You saw the beast!" Billy said excitedly. "You were under its spell."

"If you say so."

"Anything else?" Billy asked.

"It felt like I was searching for something," Chigger answered. "Something very important that had been stolen from me. Whatever it was, it belonged to me."

"The gem on the Sun Priest's staff."

"The what on the who?" Chigger said.

"The brilliant gemstone that used to be fixed to the Horned Serpent's forehead." Billy saw the very puzzled look on Chigger's face. "A lot has happened since you and I came out of that cave, Chigger. A lot."

Billy quickly gave him a rundown of the events: The trip back to the cave with the experts. The withered grass and bushes along the trail at the Spiral Mounds site. The curious hole in the side of one of the mounds. The discovery of the Sun Priest's staff and feathered cape.

Chigger was stunned by the report. "If I didn't know better, I'd say you've lost your mind," he said.

"I'd agree if I hadn't experienced it all firsthand," Billy replied. "You need to get well fast, because I want you with us when we return to the cave to recapture the serpent. Maybe we can use the bond you had with the beast to help us draw him back."

Chigger eagerly agreed to help out however he could. Just before Billy left, his friend wished him good luck with Sara.

Now it was time for Billy to face his girlfriend, or rather, his soon-to-be-former girlfriend. They had only been seeing each other since right after he'd saved Sara from the claws of the Raven Stalker in September, and Billy had never had a girlfriend before that. But he'd soon learned that girlfriends expect things—things like time and attention and promises. Billy realized he wasn't ready for any of it. At least not with this particular girl.

"Billy!" Sara yelled when she saw him across the high school parking lot. He'd timed his arrival at the school so he'd be waiting for her when classes were out for the day.

Billy hadn't been in class much lately. His mother had complained about it, but there were too many things to do. Too many people to see. Too many preparations for events to come. Too much on his mind. There would be plenty of time for school later. Or would there be?

Sara ran to the truck and climbed in the passenger door. She leaned over, expecting a kiss. But Billy had other plans. He took a deep breath.

"Sara, I'm breaking up with you," he blurted out.

Sara responded with stunned silence, a rare condition for this girl.

Billy continued. "I saw your Facebook page and read all the Instagram comments you posted," he said sternly. "Over and over, you brag like you're the girlfriend of a big-shot celebrity. You use me to get friends and boost your popularity. It makes me feel like a circus freak. I want out!"

Anger filled her eyes. Panic ran through her veins. How dare he ruin her climbing social status! How could he be so selfish to not think of her needs! Then she realized what exactly she was thinking. She listened to what she was saying in her mind. And she thought of what she'd been doing.

"Billy Buckhorn, you're the most incredible human being I know," she said. Tears began to form in her eyes.

"Sara, don't—"

"Shut up and listen," she demanded. "I will never be half the person you are. All I have are my little shares, likes, and selfies to give to the world. That's all."

"No, don't say that," Billy responded. "I know you've got—"

"Stop interrupting!"

Billy fell silent. Sara recomposed herself.

"I want to be somebody someday," she continued. "This is the only way I know how."

"You saw that thing, that creature, in the plant nursery," Billy reminded her. "You saw how it shifted and changed from a man into an evil bird thing. It was about to suck the very life out of you."

"I know, I know," she admitted, looking away from him. "I try to forget it, but I can't erase those images from my mind. How could that sort of thing really exist?"

"That sort of thing seems to be a permanent part of my life now," Billy said. "There's no turning back for me. For a while I had a hard time accepting it all, but I've come to terms with it. I've been called into action, and I'm going to answer that call. I'm obviously not going to lead a normal life."

Sara looked into Billy's eyes. She saw a depth there she hadn't seen before or had tried to ignore. It was the same depth Billy's father had seen as well. Now she understood. She finally got what Billy was all about.

"Friends?" she asked, putting out her hand. "I mean real friends, not the Facebook kind."

"Friends," Billy responded, shaking on it. Before letting go, he lifted her hand and kissed it. "Thanks for understanding," he said.

Sara raised her index finger to her lips and kissed it. Then she placed that finger in the middle of the weblike scar on the side of Billy's neck, just like she'd done when she had thanked him for saving her life.

Smiling and holding back tears, the girl opened the truck door and climbed out. She waved to Billy and turned away. Then, as her ex-boyfriend drove away, her tears flowed freely. The bottom fell out of her young heart, and she knew there would never be another boy in her life like Billy Buckhorn.

Saturday was Grandpa Wesley's busiest day as a Cherokee medicine man. His doctoring skills were known far and wide. Even though Native medicine men weren't part of the medical establishment, their people called them doctors. Using methods long kept secret, they would prepare, or doctor, herbs to help heal their patients. On Saturdays, people began lining up early in hopes of seeing Wesley. He didn't make appointments. As with most Native medicine people, it was first come, first served.

Billy knew the time was approaching when he would be expected to take over his grandfather's practice. But he still had a lot to learn about Cherokee medicines, spells, songs, and healing techniques. Saturdays were when he often went to help the elder out and get more lessons in the process.

As Billy pulled up in front of Wesley's white frame house, he noticed that the line of waiting patients seemed longer than usual. A few of the patients spotted Billy and moved toward him as he got out of the truck.

He could see the need in their eyes. This used to scare him a little when he came to help his grandfather. Wesley had always taken care of that need. Then Billy had become famous for his psychic abilities and his heroic actions, and people had started turning more of that need toward him. Many would reach out just to touch him as he passed, like he was a saint or a miracle worker to them. That had really shaken him up.

But Wesley had reminded Billy of how healing works. It was a person's own faith that did much of the work. Their own inner belief opened the receiving channels. The healing was already there and available, but faith often allowed a person to accept it.

So this morning Billy allowed the waiting people to touch him. He smiled as he passed, speaking softly to them. *"Osiyo. Tohitsu?"* he said, using a little of the Cherokee he'd recently learned. "Hello. How are you?" he followed up in English. *"Osda sunalei. Tohidu,"* he said to someone else. "Good morning. May you have peace of mind, body, and spirit."

"Words of kindness," Wesley said to Billy as the boy stepped up on the porch. "That's what this world needs." The elder welcomed his grandson into the house. "We'll begin in just a few minutes," he announced to everyone in Cherokee. "Please be patient."

Wesley and his grandson stepped inside the house.

"Well, what did Chigger have to say?" Wesley asked as he poured them both a cup of coffee from a dented old pot. "Could he tell you any more about his experience?"

Billy repeated his friend's sudden memory of seeing things through the serpent's eyes. Wesley agreed that this astounding viewpoint could help them with their plans to recapture the beast.

"I've never seen anything like what's happening in the Nation now," Wesley said, looking out the kitchen window. "A dark force has spread across the land like a heavy blanket. I can see it in people's eyes. They're scared and confused." He turned to Billy. "Can you help me out today?"

"Of course, Grandpa," Billy answered. "What do you need me to do?"

"I have a specific task for you, and it won't be pleasant," Wesley warned.

"I can handle it," Billy said, taking a gulp of coffee.

"All right. I want you to follow Mr. and Mrs. Kingfisher back to their place. They live near Caney Creek on the other side of the lake. Their small dog was attacked by some unknown creature. All that's left of their pet is a pile of bones."

"It was probably just a mountain lion or large wolf that came down from the hills," Billy said. That happened sometimes in the rural areas of eastern Oklahoma.

"There was no blood or body parts left behind," Wesley said. "Just a pile of bones picked clean."

"How's that possible?" Billy asked. "That's *not* possible."

"That's why I want you to go check it out," Wesley said. "Look around and tell me what you see. Put the bones in a bag and bring them to me."

"Yet another mystery," Billy said as he stood to leave.

"Before you go, I want to show you one more thing," Wesley said. "Follow me out to the woods behind the house."

Stepping out the back door, Wesley headed through his backyard herb garden. Billy followed. Seeing the garden reminded him of someone.

"Where's Little Wolf been lately?" Billy asked. "I haven't seen him around."

"I sent him on a special long-distance fact-finding mission," Wesley said. "He probably won't be back for a couple more weeks."

Opening the back gate, Wesley continued across the field behind his house. That was when Billy realized that his grandfather wasn't using his cane. And he was moving faster than he'd ever seen him move.

"What happened to your cane?" Billy asked. "And your hurt leg?"

Wesley stopped in his tracks and turned to his grandson. "You don't know about Wilma, do you?" he said with a smile.

"Who's Wilma?"

"She's one of the medicine people who helped me get the crystal from Chigger," Wesley replied. "She asked me over for dinner the other day. Let's keep moving." He began walking again. "She's quite an amazing woman."

Billy heard a hint of something in the old man's voice that he hadn't heard before. He almost sounded like a teenager. Billy's grandpa had a crush! How interesting.

"Turns out she's not only a medicine woman but also an intuitive physical therapist," Wesley continued. "She located a place on my spine that was twisted. It was pinching the nerve to my leg. She untwisted it, and now I feel like my old self."

They arrived at their destination, a shed that stood at the edge of the woods. Billy had a silly look on his face.

"What?" Wesley asked. "Did I say something funny?"

Billy merely shook his head and smiled. "You mean now you feel like your *young* self, don't you?" he said with a raised eyebrow.

"Whatever," Grandpa replied, ignoring his grandson's inference and turning his attention to the shed. A large padlock hung from a latch that secured the door. Taking a key from his pocket, Wesley opened the lock. He pulled the shed door open to reveal an old bank safe inside. Script letters spelling *Rockwell Bank* had been painted on its side long ago.

"What's this?" Billy said. "Where'd you get it?"

"From an auction in town," Wesley said as he turned the dial on the front of the safe. "It's where I keep important stuff."

"Like what?" Billy asked as Wesley opened the door wide.

"Like the dark crystal we took from Chigger. And the old Cherokee medicine book." Grandpa removed a leather bag from a shelf in the safe. He set the bag down on the ground and opened the bag's flap. "Look, but don't touch," he instructed.

Billy peered into the bag and saw the glowing purple crystal resting at the bottom. "Is it my imagination or is that thing brighter than it used to be?" he said.

"It's not your imagination," Wesley replied. "It's been growing brighter every day." He folded the flap closed and put the bag back in the safe.

"What does it mean?" Billy asked.

"I think it means the Horned Serpent is getting closer," Wesley said. "I think it means we have to act soon, before it finds this."

Wesley closed and locked the safe, and then he closed and locked the shed door.

"That's why I want you to go out to the Kingfisher place with them," Wesley said as he and Billy headed back to the house. "I'm afraid the Uktena got their dog. And that would mean he *is* getting close."

Billy followed Mr. and Mrs. Kingfisher from Wesley's house to their home to see the pile of bones. They lived near a creek that emptied into Lake Tenkiller. Billy knew this lake was connected to the Illinois River and then to the Arkansas River. That river had taken Chigger and him to the cave where the Horned Serpent had been trapped.

Mr. Kingfisher led Billy around to the back of the house. There, in a far corner of the yard, lay the pile of small bones that had once been their little dog. Billy knew at once that the dog had become a meal for the beast. There were telltale signs, including a trail of withered grass and bushes that led from the creek to the yard. It was the same kind of withered trail they had found at Spiral Mounds.

Billy asked the elderly Mr. and Mrs. Kingfisher to come stand with him. Together they formed a little circle around the bones. He said a Cherokee prayer for their dog, which they had named Warrior. Warrior had been their guard for many years, even though he wasn't much larger than a fat house cat. Billy said the prayer to help the elderly couple mourn their longtime protector. He didn't say anything about the beast that had surely eaten their little friend.

Next, he gathered up the bones and put them in a bag to take back to his grandfather. He sprinkled "doctored" tobacco around the area where the bones had been. Then he gave the Kingfishers a packet of tobacco that Wesley had also doctored.

"If you hear anything suspicious back here, offer this tobacco to the four directions and say a prayer for protection," Billy told them. The old couple thanked him for his services, and Mrs. Kingfisher sent him off with a plate of homemade fry bread.

In a short while, he was back at Wesley's to report what he'd seen.

"There's no doubt he's headed this way," Wesley said after hearing Billy's report. "He's coming for the dark crystal. We'd better get together with your father and Dr. Stevens soon. We have to set our plan in motion before it's too late."

Billy agreed to talk to his dad about setting things up when he got home that night. The boy spent the rest of the day helping Wesley look after the physical and emotional needs of his patients. Almost everyone had some strange story to tell—unusual happenings, missing animals, ghost sightings, withered plants, depressed feelings. The list went on and on.

During brief breaks in the flow of clients, Billy studied the book of spells, sounding out Cherokee phrases and memorizing what medicinal plants were used for which ailments. It was a lot to take in and learn.

Drained by the day's activities, Billy arrived home in time to have dinner with his mom and dad.

"Your uncle John wants to come by this evening to see you," Mrs. Buckhorn said at the dinner table.

"Oh no, not him," Billy complained. "I don't think I can handle any preaching tonight."

"He promised not to preach this time," she replied.

"That's what he said last time," Billy countered.

"He knows it will be the last time he sees any of us if he breaks his promise," his mom said. "I think he was really shaken up the last time he was here. Now he wants to apologize."

"That man isn't capable of making an apology," Billy's dad said. "He's too self-righteous to ever do that."

"He's my brother, and I think we should at least give him a chance," Mrs. Buckhorn said. "I promise to kick him out if he even so much as hints at preaching."

Billy just looked at her, rolled his eyes, and sighed.

"I promise," she said again.

"Okay," Billy said as he finished his last bite of food. "What time is he coming?"

Before his mother could answer, there came a loud knock at the front door.

"I guess right about now," she said, getting up from the table.

They all moved to the living room as Billy's uncle John stepped inside behind Billy's mother.

"I've come to ask for your help, Billy," the preacher said. "But first I have something to tell you."

Billy stood across the room, as far away from the man as possible. There was just no telling what he might say or do.

"Jesus said, 'Judge not lest ye be judged,'" the preacher said.

"You said no preaching," Billy's mother complained.

"I'm not preaching," John replied, looking at his sister. "I'm confessing. Just give me a minute." He turned back to Billy. "Jesus told us not to judge other people so we wouldn't be judged harshly by God. But all I've done is judge. You, your father, and your grandfather. I pointed a finger at what I thought was wrong with all of you. I see now that I should've been trying to fix myself."

"Okay," Billy said, not sure where this was going.

"You shined a light on the lie I'd been living with all my life," John admitted. "You revealed the truth about the death of my brother, Luther. I am ashamed, and I ask for your forgiveness. The forgiveness of all of you in this household."

"We can neither condemn you nor forgive you," Billy's dad said. "But we can accept your apology. Right, Billy?"

"Yeah, sure," Billy replied. "Is that all you wanted?"

"No, actually I want to ask you for a favor," John said, "even though I'd understand if you didn't want to do it."

"Grandpa Wesley taught me to always help another Cherokee whenever asked," Billy said. "Now you've asked, so I'll help you if I can."

"Thank you," John said.

He moved farther into the living room. Billy moved a little closer to his uncle as well.

"Can you give my brother, Luther, a message for me?" John asked in a quiet tone. "I'm not sure how your communication with the spirits of the dead works."

"I'm still trying to figure that out myself," Billy replied honestly. "But I will if I can. What would you like me to tell him?"

"Just that I'm sorry," the preacher said. "Sorry that he suffered because of my carelessness. Sorry that I never took responsibility for my actions. Sorry that he never got to live his full life. That's all."

"All right, Uncle. I'll pass along the message the next chance I get. I don't know when that'll be, but I'll get it done."

"Thank you," John replied, rushing to shake Billy's hand. "I'd be forever grateful."

After pumping his nephew's hand a few times and saying his goodbyes to everyone, Billy's uncle left.

"That wasn't so bad, now, was it?" Billy's mother commented. "I think he's a changed man."

"Yeah, but how long will the change last?" Billy's father said. "I'll wait to see how he acts at the next family dinner before letting my guard down."

"I think he's sincere," Billy said. "When I shook his hand, I didn't sense any false feelings or see any bad images."

"I thought your ability to see what was going on inside people had faded," his mother said.

"It comes and goes," Billy replied as he headed back to the kitchen in search of dessert.

What Billy didn't realize was that the message had already passed to Luther. Billy was now an open and active channel to the nonphysical dimension without even knowing it. Ever since his near-death experience, the souls of the departed lingered nearby. Many hoped to one day send messages to their loved ones on earth.

A couple of hours after he went to sleep, Billy woke up to find his grandmother Awinita standing near the foot of his bed. She was in her glowing spirit form, as usual. But she wasn't alone. Standing beside her was the spirit of Billy's great-grandfather Bullseye Buckhorn.

"You can tell your uncle John that Luther got the message," Awinita said, though she didn't actually speak. Her words were again transferred from her mind to Billy's.

"Luther thinks it certainly took his stubborn brother a long time to admit the truth," Bullseye added. "But he was glad John finally did. How are you doing, Billy?"

"Fine, Great-Grandpa," Billy said. "I didn't expect to see you."

"I've been hanging out more with Awinita lately," he replied. "You know she's rather famous on this side for her abilities to bring the living and the dead together. She's kind of like my mentor now."

"Sort of like teaching an old dog new tricks, huh?" Billy commented.

"Well, it's more complicated than that," Bullseye responded. "But yeah."

"So, what's going on, Grandma?" Billy asked. "I know you two didn't show up just to tell me what Uncle Luther had to say."

"I sent your great-grandfather on a scouting trip, and he's here to tell you what he found," Awinita replied.

"I've been to hell and back," Bullseye said with a smile and a twinkle in his eye.

"What?" Billy said and blinked, not understanding what his great-grandfather meant.

"Well, hell isn't really what humans think it is," he said. "Or where they think it is. You see—"

"No time for that now," Billy's grandmother said, interrupting him. "Get on with it."

"Oh, well, maybe another time. Like your grandma said, she sent me on a mission to the lower realms of the nonphysical world. There was a disturbance coming from there that we in the higher realms could feel."

"You can do that?" Billy asked. "Move from area to area?"

"Oh yes," Bullseye said. "Residents of the higher regions can visit the lower layers, not that you'd really want to. But it doesn't work the other way around. It's a matter of energy vibrations, like tuning a radio station to different frequencies."

That went over Billy's head. He was still getting used to the whole talking-to-dead-people thing. And he still didn't really understand much of it.

"Are you going to get to the point, or am I going to have to get there for you?" Awinita insisted.

"I'll make a long story short," Bullseye said. "It's a frenzy of dark energy down there. And the reason is this. When the Horned Serpent awoke, his revived energy was noticed. Ancient minions had been assigned to watch over the beast so they could report any signs of his awakening."

"Minions? What are minions?" Billy asked.

"They're followers," Awinita answered. "They do the bidding of someone of great power. In the Underworld, they're like small dark ghost creatures."

"Okay. Who do these minions answer to?" Billy asked.

"In this case, the Snake Priest," Bullseye said.

"The Snake Priest?" Billy said. "He doesn't sound good."

"He isn't!" Bullseye said. "He led a cult of Horned Serpent worshippers during the Mound Builder period. The Sun Priest threw them out of their villages. He couldn't allow their evil intentions to take hold of his followers."

"Why did anyone follow the guy if he was so bad?" Billy asked.

"The same reason anyone gets involved with the dark side," Awinita answered. "Power. Power over people. Power to make things happen the way you want them to happen. Some call it black magic."

"I get it," Billy said. "Grandpa calls it bad medicine."

"Right," Bullseye replied. "Anyway, the ghost of the Snake Priest has reconnected with the Horned Serpent, and its bad news. He is a dark force, able to guide the beast from the other side and help him along his quest to regain his forehead gem and the purple crystal."

"If his power is anything like what I saw with Benjamin Blacksnake, then it *is* bad news," Billy said. "It's nothing but death and destruction."

"You are so very lucky, young man, that Blacksnake—one of *the* most evil medicine men who ever lived—didn't have a chance to suck the very life out of you," Bullseye said. "Why, he could've—"

"Now you know what's at stake here," Billy's grandmother interrupted. "If the Dark One is controlling the Horned Serpent—"

"And if the serpent's powers are restored through the two gems—" Bullseye continued.

"Then the Uktena will become unstoppable!" Billy concluded.

CHAPTER 17

Slithering Forth

T he Great Snake had grown weary from his travels. It was both exciting and tiring to be out in the world again, free from that liquid prison at the bottom of the cave. Free to roam the land and take what he needed, whenever he needed it. It had been such a long time since he'd had that kind of freedom.

After first leaving the cave, the beast had floated down the Arkansas River. The river current had gently carried him along. Little effort was required, and it was familiar territory. He had roamed this region freely. Long ago, he'd been able to drift downstream until the Arkansas River met the Mississippi River, which, of course, flowed directly to the ocean.

But once outside the cave, he'd immediately felt a strong pull in two opposite directions. The strongest tug had been from the south, so that was where the creature had headed first. He'd been sure that was where the Fire Crystal could be found.

The serpent's attraction to that jewel was really a longing for his past glory. It had once lived in his forehead, and the clear stone was indeed a living thing. It throbbed with a life force. And it had shone brightly when it was in its place. It gave him incredible powers over all living things.

After leaving the cave, the serpent had arrived at the Spiral Mounds in the dark of night. But his eyes were used to the dark. And he knew he had come to the right place. He felt the stone. It throbbed from underground. Like a lighthouse, the treasure sent out its invisible beacon into the darkness.

The beast began happily digging up that gem. But he had to stop when a two-legged one showed up. In the old days, when the faceted rock lived in his forehead, its light would have blinded the man—paralyzed him. But this man carried his own light. When the light from his hand shone on the serpent's scales, it bounced back. Its reflection blinded the man, because the beast's scales contained a little of the rock's power. But the blinding would only be temporary.

Then a loud noise burst forth from all around the mound area. Wailing sounds screeched across the darkness, and an invasion of light ignited the night. The beast was not familiar with modern-day sirens and electric emergency lights.

Startled by the sound and the brightness, the beast was forced to flee the mounds without his prize. He headed quickly back to the safety of the river. Underwater was where he actually belonged, where his ancestors had come from. So that was where he hid until he felt safe again.

That was when, surprisingly, the ghost of the dark priest made contact with the serpent after all that lost time. The beast had been in a deep sleep, unable to see, hear, or feel anything or anyone. Communication had not been possible.

But now the Dark One had finally found a way to contact the physical world. From his mind to the beast's mind, the priest spoke the ancient words. But he could do so only from mind to mind. The dark priest was unable to physically speak the words aloud.

The mental words had only a small effect. He could not fully reunite with the Uktena. The ghost had to be content with crudely guiding the snake in his search for the two precious gems. He was only able to help the snake be a little more sensitive to the signals coming from these stones. He could also watch and wait. Maybe, when the beast found the stones, the dark priest's powers would also be strengthened.

A few days after the first attempt, the serpent returned to the mound. But this time the crystal was gone. It had been taken. Again it had been snatched from him by two-leggeds. The beast felt it move away from that place. Northward it went.

The whole time the beast was in the south searching for his forehead stone, the dark tail crystal also called to him. It was already in the north. The young two-legged one had taken it from the cave. The beast knew it was a young one who had the stone, because the dark priest had used his supernatural force to create a visible connection between it and the beast. The serpent could see through the eyes of anyone who held his precious crystal. And the beast could see who held it as well. It was definitely a young two-legged one. And he saw other older two-legged ones who came. They had come to take that crystal from him.

The young one would not give up the stone without a fight. But finally he was surrounded by four of the two-leggeds with their own weak powers. The four of them together had been powerful enough to steal it away.

The number four. It was indeed a sad day all those centuries ago when the two-legged ones learned the power of four. The number four stood for the four great forces that flowed through the physical world. It had been hidden from the weak humans in the early days. But as the knowledge of the two-leggeds had increased, so had their ability to harness the power of the four directions, as well as their ability to trap the beast.

But at last the time had finally come. Now the precious crystals were near each other. Closer to each other than they'd been in ages. So the serpent had begun his northward journey, swimming upstream, fighting the river current to attain his goal. Soon he would rejoin the Fire Crystal to his forehead and re-attach the purple stone to his tail. Then he would be complete again. Whole.

Of course, he had to keep up his strength during the journey. That was why he would leave the safety of the river from time to time, slithering across the land. A small creature now and then would become a meal. But only the flesh and muscles and tissues. Never the bones. His system couldn't digest the bones, so those were left behind.

And then it was time to move on. Ever onward toward the goal, toward the final reunion with his precious possessions and his power.

And the unseen ghost of the dark priest was there every moment of the journey.

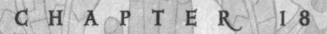

CHAPTER 18

The Missing Piece

The next morning, Billy opened the front door of his house, ready to head out. Standing on the front porch about to knock on that door was a brown-haired Native American girl with dark green eyes. In one hand she held a small writing tablet, and in the other was a pen. Billy was visibly startled by her unexpected presence.

"Oh, sorry for surprising you like that," she said. "I was about to knock."

"Um, is there something I can help you with?" Billy asked. "I've got to be somewhere."

"Okay, I'll try to make this fast," the girl said. "My name is Lisa Lookout, and I'm an intern for the *Cherokee Phoenix*, the Cherokee Nation's tribal newspaper. I—"

"I know what the *Phoenix* is," Billy said impatiently. "And frankly, I'm not interested in any more publicity or sensationalized news coverage."

"I realize that," the girl said. "I don't want to do a newspaper story on you, but I do need to talk to you about your experiences. What it's been like for you to be hit by lightning, to almost die, to take on the Shape-Changer."

"I'll think about it, but right now I've really got to run."

"Let me give you my phone number and email address," Lisa said as she began jotting down her contact information.

As she wrote, Billy noticed a curious spiderlike tattoo on the back of her hand. "What's that on your hand?" he asked. "It looks a little like a spider."

Lisa stopped writing and held the hand out for Billy to see. "It *is* a spider," she said. "Spider Woman, actually. It's a common tattoo for Osage girls and women."

"You're Osage?"

"Yep," Lisa said as she finished writing. Ripping the page from her tablet, she handed it to Billy.

"You say your last name is Lookout?" Billy asked. "And you're Osage?"

"Yes to both."

"I heard the name Lookout recently, but I can't remember where," Billy said. He thought about it another moment or two, allowing his eyes to revisit her face. "Maybe it'll come to me."

He scanned the information she'd written. "You're at Sequoyah High School in the dorms?" he asked. "That's not far from here."

"Yeah, it's my first year at the school. I decided to intern for the newspaper. But like I said, that's not the real reason I want to talk to you."

Billy stepped out onto the porch, closing the door behind him. This put the boy very close to her, because the girl didn't step back from him. Forced to gaze directly into her eyes, he found he was unable to look away. He found a depth there he hadn't expected.

"Well, like I said, I'll think about it," Billy said in a quiet voice. "But I do have to go now."

"Fair enough," Lisa said, also in a quiet voice. "But I hope we can talk soon."

She lingered a moment before turning and heading down the steps. Billy followed a couple of steps behind. At the bottom of the stairs, Lisa headed to the right toward a motorcycle Billy hadn't noticed before. His eyes remained on her awhile before he took a left and headed toward his pickup.

"My grandfather is also a medicine man," she called to him as she reached the reddish-orange motorcycle.

Billy stopped dead in his tracks and looked back at her.

"He wants to meet you. That's the main reason we need to talk." She put on her helmet with the face shield in the open position. "And I think you and I have a lot in common," she added with a smile and closed the shield.

Not waiting for him to respond, Lisa kick-started the bike and rolled out of the gravel drive. As he watched her ride away, Billy found himself thinking about what the Spider Woman tattoo on her hand might look like, or even feel like, resting on the weblike scar on the side of his neck.

Where did that thought come from?

He shook it off as he climbed into his truck. Sensing an unfamiliar, almost electric, feeling throughout his entire body, he paused before starting the engine. Then, taking a look at the pocket watch in the glove box, he realized he was behind schedule.

Billy cranked the truck's engine and drove to Chigger's mobile home to pick him up. The bandages on Chigger's hands were smaller now, and the bandage on his head was gone. All in all, Chigger looked pretty good. No mention was made of the mysterious girl who had appeared on Billy's doorstep.

The boys drove to the college campus so their little group of supernatural explorers could flesh out the plans for their next steps. Billy's father and grandfather were waiting in the professor's office. Spread on the professor's desk were photos and notes taken when they'd explored the cave together.

"The pieces of the cave puzzle seem to be coming together," Billy's dad said as Chigger and Billy sat down. "Grandpa told me about the pile of bones you found."

"Now we need to review what the Sun Priest said about recapturing the beast," Grandpa added. "That way all of us will know what to expect when we try to trap the beast back in the cave."

"Where's Dr. Stevens?" Billy asked. "I thought he was supposed to be here."

"Is he the digger you told me about?" Chigger asked. He hadn't met the archaeologist who had gone with the team to explore the cave and the mounds.

"He doesn't like being called a digger," Billy's dad told Chigger. "It's not a dignified name."

"In case you hadn't noticed, I ain't so dignified myself," Chigger replied. "But okay."

"Anyway, he's probably just running late," the professor said. "I think we can start without him."

"I really don't know what I can do to help," Chigger said. "Each of you has a part to play."

"And you do too," Billy replied. "You have a connection to the Horned Serpent that no one else does. You've seen him from the inside out."

"I hadn't thought of it that way," Chigger said. "Glad to be of service."

Professor Buckhorn shuffled through the photos on his desk, and finally he found the one he was looking for. It was a shot of the stone door that had sealed the serpent in the lake. On its surface were the markings Billy and Chigger had first seen on the day Billy died.

"Tell us again what the spirit of the Sun Priest told you about these markings," the professor said as he handed the photo to his son, "when we were at Spiral Mounds."

"He said the symbols were the letters of a special language used by their holy people," Billy explained, "and what was written there were the words that must be spoken to capture the serpent and hold him in that cave."

"Let me take a look at that picture," Wesley said, not having seen it before. Billy handed him the photo.

"How are you supposed to say those words?" Chigger asked. "You don't speak their language."

"The Sun Priest said he would speak those words *through me* at the right moment," Billy replied. "He said he would take over my mind and body with my grandmother's help."

"You're kidding me, right?" Chigger said in disbelief. "Some dude who died a thousand years ago is gonna show up at just the right time. And then he's gonna use your vocal cords to say some magic words?"

"You're questioning me about what happened at Spiral Mounds?" Billy said with a note of sarcasm. "Oh, that's right. You weren't with us. At that time you were possessed by the power of an evil mythological snake that made you go crazy. And it took four people to get the dark crystal out of your hands."

"When you put it that way," Chigger admitted, "what you said is totally believable."

"Billy was right," Wesley said, and everyone immediately fell silent.

No one spoke for a moment.

"These same markings are in Blacksnake's book of spells," the elder continued, "though I don't have a clue about what they mean, how to pronounce them, or why they're in there."

"Someone from the ancient times must've tried to preserve them," the professor said. "This whole thing gets more mind-boggling by the minute!"

"Well, before those words can be spoken once again, we have many things to do to get ready," Billy said, bringing their minds back to focusing on the task ahead. "First we have to return the purple gem to its place near the stone door. And this is where you come in, Chigger."

Chigger sat up straight in his chair, glad to be an important part of the team.

"The person who removed the gem must be the one who replaces it," Billy said.

Chigger slumped back down in his chair, realizing that he was the one who'd caused this whole mess to begin with. If he hadn't left the cave with that stone, they might not be facing all this trouble.

"Then we wait and watch," Billy's dad said. "The serpent will get a mental signal telling him the stone is back in its place. And he'll probably feel the presence of the diamond in the same area. The combined pull could be strong enough to attract him back to the cave."

"Once the beast is inside, Billy will enter, if I understand the process correctly," Wesley said. "He'll be wearing the Sun Priest's cape and holding the gemstone staff."

"The Horned Serpent's first priority should be finding the dark crystal so he can reattach it to his tail," Billy said. "I'll follow him down the path toward the lake at the bottom of the cave."

"When he sees the crystal on the staff that Billy will be carrying, the beast is supposed to become hypnotized," the professor added. "Billy can lead him beyond the stone door and back into the lake."

"That's when these sacred words must be spoken," Wesley said, holding up the photo of the ancient language. "The stone door will close and reseal itself. The beast will be a prisoner once again."

"It's all pretty simple," Billy said with a smile. "Simple as one, two, three."

"Oh, and there's no way anything can go wrong," Chigger said with his own hint of sarcasm. "You guys are nuts. This'll never work."

"Thanks for your vote of confidence," Billy replied. "Do you—"

Before Billy could complete his sentence, his father's desk phone rang.

"Professor Buckhorn," James said into the receiver, then listened for a moment. "Oh my god," he said finally. "We'll be right there."

He slammed down the receiver. "That was Dr. Stevens. He's been attacked by the serpent, and his artifact collection was destroyed."

Everyone froze in place for a moment. This took them completely by surprise.

"What are we waiting for?" Chigger said as he jumped up. "We gotta get a move on."

Everyone rose from their seats at once.

"We can all fit in my Jeep," James said. "It's parked just outside."

Quickly and silently, they followed the professor out the door.

Dr. Stevens lived east of the college campus in a house that bordered the Illinois River. The river spilled directly into Lake Tenkiller, so the serpent would have had easy access to the house from the water.

When the team pulled up in front of the archaeologist's home, there were no signs of an attack. As they approached the front door, a Native woman in a nurse's uniform opened it and greeted them.

"Dr. Stevens asked me to meet you," she said. "He's resting in his bedroom, but it's all right for you to go back and see him."

"Will he be okay?" Billy's dad asked as the team entered the house. "Is he hurt badly?"

"He's mostly dazed and confused," the nurse replied. "I think—"

The nurse was interrupted by a booming voice coming from the back of the house.

"Billy Buckhorn, I owe you a huge apology," Dr. Stevens said as he came toward them. His face was covered with small cuts and scrapes. One eye was bandaged.

"Dr. Stevens, you shouldn't be out of bed," the nurse scolded. "You heard what the doctor said."

"Yeah, yeah, yeah," Stevens replied. "I can rest when I'm dead. I've got a lot to share with these gentlemen."

"Well, don't be too long," she replied as she turned away. "I'll be in the kitchen if you need me."

"You guys have got to see this," Dr. Stevens said with excitement. "Follow me to my office."

He led them to a door at the rear of the house. As he stepped outside, Billy could see the river flowing about a hundred feet behind it. There was a trail of dead, withered grass and plants leading from the river to the house.

Stevens started climbing down a set of stairs, and the group followed him. They ended up in a basement. It was a total mess. Furniture was overturned, and shelving from the walls lay in pieces on the floor. Shattered fragments of pottery, stones, and baskets were scattered all around.

Ignoring the ruins that were once his office, the archaeologist first addressed the professor.

"We scholars and academics have it all wrong," he said, his eyes wide with astonishment. "These tribal legends aren't just old stories made up by primitive peoples to explain things they didn't understand. Now I know at least some of them must be based on actual truths."

Billy and the others walked carefully through the room. Destroyed Native American artifacts and documents were strewn everywhere.

"What are you talking about?" Billy's father demanded. "Why aren't you concerned about the destruction of your collection?"

"Because I *saw* the Horned Serpent *with my own eyes*," Stevens answered. "What before had been only a curious myth came bursting through that door in real life! I was saved from certain death only because of what I was studying at that moment."

He began searching through a pile of rubble at the back of the room.

"I know it's here somewhere," he said as he sorted through a stack of scattered papers. "Ah, here it is."

He withdrew a large color photo from the pile. It was tattered at the edges and covered with debris and dust. After wiping it clean, he held it up for them all to see.

"It's the eye-in-hand symbol," he said proudly. "This image has been found at many of the ancient Mound Builder sites."

Billy looked at the photo. It showed an image carved into a flat stone. In the center was the open palm of a man's hand. In the middle of the palm was an eye. The hand was encircled by two horned snakes woven together and tied in knots. It seemed to mean the snakes were under control.

"A similar eye-in-hand image has also been found in ancient Jewish and Hindu sites in the Middle East and India," Billy's father observed.

"What does it mean?" Chigger asked.

"My research points to it being a connection between our world and the Upperworld, or what we might call the heavens," Dr. Stevens said. "It's the eye of God, so to speak, and it's in our hands. The serpents are the symbol for the Underworld. They're tied up, so they've been rendered harmless."

"So I've heard you guys talk about the Underworld," Chigger said. "What is it? Is it like hell or something?"

The professor took the lead on this subject. "It's an ancient idea shared by the Hebrews of the Old Testament, other cultures in the Middle East, and many Native American societies. Before anyone came up with the idea of an underground hell, there was Sheol or Hades—cold, dark subterranean areas where the souls of the dead live."

"What does that have to do with serpents?" Chigger asked.

"The Native American version of the Underworld is more about a place where powerful and dangerous spirits and creatures live, under North America, which is viewed as—"

"Turtle Island," Chigger said, finishing the professor's sentence.

"In both Hebrew and Native cosmologies, caves are doorways to the Underworld," James added.

"Okay, so how did this picture of the eye in hand save you from the monster thingy?" Chigger asked, bringing the group firmly back to the present.

"The beast came crashing through those doors last night," Stevens explained. "It moved quickly through the room, turning over objects and breaking my prized artifacts. But I could tell it was looking for something, and it seemed desperate to find it."

"The Sun Priest's staff!" Billy suddenly blurted out. "Of course, the serpent knew it was here. Don't tell me he got it!"

"No, thankfully, he didn't," Dr. Stevens said. "At first, I thought you were crazy when you started talking about the Sun Priest at Spiral Mounds. You said you got some kind of message from the spirit world about the serpent myth. But I decided to hide the feathered cape and staff in my underground vault just in case you weren't totally out of your mind."

"But finish the story of what happened when the beast came crashing in here!" Chigger demanded. "I'm dying to find out."

Dr. Stevens took the eye-in-hand photo from Chigger.

"I was examining this very image as the beast came rushing toward me," he said. "I figured I was about to be killed. But silly me, I held this photo up over my head and crouched down on the floor. I guess it was just instinct to hold something up for protection."

He knelt down on the floor to demonstrate what he'd done.

"It's just a piece of paper, right?" Dr. Stevens continued. "It obviously couldn't have stopped the beast from tearing right through it and biting my head off."

Then he stood up.

"But it *did* stop it," he said calmly. "The serpent was repelled by the image. Its eyes grew wide, and it jumped back. It tried moving to one side and coming at me from a different angle. I swung the photo around and held it like a shield."

"Amazing," Billy's dad said.

"Soon the beast realized he couldn't get to me," Dr. Stevens said. "I even felt a little brave and took a few steps toward him. And he turned and slithered away at top speed."

"This is a missing piece of the puzzle," Billy said with confidence. "From now on, each of us needs to have a copy of this symbol. If we're going to confront the serpent, we should have it on us at all times. For protection."

"So you understand why I'm apologizing," Stevens said. "These are no mere myths. These are warnings. People really experienced some of this stuff. That means at least a few of the tribal legends are true. Details were probably added as the stories were passed along, but they're rooted in reality. I know that now."

Billy was amazed at how both his father and Dr. Stevens had changed their minds about Native legends. These two college big-brains had finally come to believe what he and Grandpa had known all along: that many fantastic ancient Native American stories contained truths at their core.

"Why don't we just shoot the thing the next time we see it?" Chigger suggested. "Or stab it or spear it or cut off its head?"

"If it were only that simple," Wesley replied. "The creature's scales can't be pierced. At least that's what the medicine book says. And so do all the oral stories passed down through the generations."

"It's the perfect monster," Chigger observed. "You can't kill it, and it lives forever. Kind of like Godzilla. Just when you think it's gone for good—*boom*—it resurrects and attacks again."

They all had a good laugh at that one, a much-needed release of the tension brewed by the gravity of their situation.

Before leaving Dr. Stevens's home, the group helped him straighten up his office, at least as much as they could. The archaeologist said that many priceless artifacts had been destroyed, but he didn't focus on the loss like he would have in the past. Now all he wanted to do was be a part of the crew that resealed the beast in the bottom of the cave.

That made the team complete. It consisted of Billy, his dad, his grandfather Wesley, Chigger, and Dr. Stevens, who now insisted on being called by his first name, Augustus.

"What a team," Chigger said as they drove back to campus. "We're like supernatural superheroes. We could call ourselves the . . . What's a good name?"

He thought hard for a minute.

"The Legend League!" he said with enthusiasm. "No, wait. How about the Ghost Guard? Nah, that sounds like we patrol the coastline looking for spooks."

"Give it a rest," Billy advised. "We don't need a name."

"I've got it!" Chigger exclaimed. "Paranormal Patrol! That's it!"

"Hmm," Billy said thoughtfully. "That actually has a nice ring to it. What do you want to do, print up some T-shirts and business cards?"

"No, man, that'll be the name of our reality TV series," Chigger responded.

Soon they arrived back at Professor Buckhorn's office. He had two more topics for them to discuss.

"Chigger, Dr. Stevens insists on being called by his first name," Professor Buckhorn said. "That's unusual for him, but it makes it seem more like we're all equal partners in this."

"That's really great," Chigger said. "You guys are definitely smarter than me, but I have qualities of my own to contribute."

"I'm sure that's true," the professor admitted. "And I guess you can call me by my first name too."

"That's what I'm talkin' 'bout," Chigger responded, jumping up. "Give me five."

He held his right hand up, expecting James to slap it in the classic high-five move. When the man didn't respond, the boy dropped his arm.

"Too soon?" he asked. "Too forward?"

"It'll hurt your hand," James reminded the teen.

Chigger had forgotten all about his bandaged hands.

"And we're working together on a serious project, not hanging out," James replied. "No offense."

"None taken," Chigger said as he sat back down.

"So, team, when do we execute the plan?" James asked the group.

"As soon as possible," Wesley said. "Who knows who or what else might be attacked?"

"It would help me a lot if we could hold off until my classes take their winter break," the professor said. "That way I can focus completely on this."

"When's that?" Wesley asked. "It's already mid-December."

"December eighteenth," James replied. "Not that long off, really."

"That should work," Wesley said. "It'll take me that long to create eye-in-hand medallions for the five of us to wear. We've got to have those before we try to confront the serpent."

"Then it's settled," James said. "In the meantime, we'd better get mentally and physically prepared to meet the monster."

As they stood to leave, Chigger stepped into the midst of them. "Paranormal Patrol dismissed!" he said in a military-style voice.

Everyone ignored him.

Billy drove Chigger home and then headed back to his own place. He felt it was time to check in with his grandmother and maybe the Sun Priest. Chigger had raised a good point earlier that day. Would Awinita and the priest be able to appear at exactly the right time? Would the guy who'd been dead for a thousand years really be able to speak the magic words using Billy's vocal cords? It sounded like some ridiculous fantasy.

There was someone waiting for Billy when he got home: Dr. Abramson, the psychiatrist. He was sipping iced tea and chatting with Billy's mom when the teen walked in.

"Dr. Abramson, what are you doing here?" Billy asked.

"I still have an open mental health file on my desk, which I'd like to be able to close," the doctor said. "We never had a formal exit interview after you were struck by lightning, and then I was never able to reach you after the near-death experience. Even one of those incidents might be enough to leave lifelong psychological scars, but the combination of the two so close together—well, for most people that's a recipe for a mental breakdown."

"I'm fine."

"Could you excuse us for a few minutes?" the doctor asked of Mr. and Mrs. Buckhorn.

They agreed to leave the two alone in the living room. Abramson sat down on the couch not far from the teen.

"Honestly, I really have no mental problems," Billy said in a quiet tone.

"Is that so?" the doctor replied. "Rumor has it that you hear voices, have visions, see apparitions, and talk to dead people."

That pretty well sums it up, Billy thought. Suddenly he had to decide whether to deny everything he'd experienced or embrace it.

"Whatever you say stays strictly between you and me," the bespectacled man added. "Doctor-patient confidentiality and all that."

The teen took another second to make his decision, then muttered, "What the hell."

He stood and began pacing.

"In addition to the things you just mentioned, I have also been able to memorize the Cherokee language and learn school lessons by sleeping on my books, as well as foresee the near future," Billy said. "But that's not all. I've interacted—no, battled—with a Cherokee Shape-Changer and encountered a creature, supposedly mythological, that originally came from the Underworld."

He thought that would be enough to sufficiently shock the shrink. But it didn't.

"Before I came to work for the Indian hospital, I studied up on your traditional culture, you know, investigating the mind of the Cherokee," Abramson said. "I found a remarkable similarity to traditional cultures in other parts of the world."

"Fascinating," Billy replied sarcastically, demonstrating his impatience. "What's that got to do with me and my experiences?"

"I'll get straight to it. The Upper-, Middle-, and Underworlds correspond directly to the layers of the human mind's psychological landscape, and many traditional Indigenous beliefs superbly express those layers symbolically. Do you understand?"

"Sort of," the teen replied. "I see what you're getting at, but the things I've directly experienced go way beyond the symbolic or the metaphorical or whatever academic word you want to use. I could fill a book with the strange things I've seen since I turned sixteen!"

That idea got the psychiatrist up and out of his chair.

"That's a great idea!" he said excitedly as he stood. "You could keep a journal documenting your physical and not-so-physical experiences!"

"Not you too," Billy complained. "My grandfather already has me keeping a medicine journal of the lessons I learn helping him in his healing practice."

"Both journals could be such valuable tools to help you identify patterns in your life or assist you in remembering important information," the shrink argued. Suddenly he remembered something and looked at his watch. "I lost track of the time. I'm supposed to be somewhere right now."

He headed for the front door, then turned back to Billy. "This is a great beginning, young man. I bet it feels good to share those secrets with someone. I hope we can continue this conversation in the very near future."

That's just great, Buckhorn! Why did you tell him all that stuff? He'll never leave you alone.

After the doctor left, Billy went straight to his room, because he didn't want to have to report the conversation to his parents. But the old man was right about one thing. It *did* feel good to vent to someone outside his family. He'd heard that telling your troubles to a stranger could be cleansing. It was what kept bartenders, preachers, and shrinks in business.

He turned out his light and went to bed, but sleep didn't come easily. He woke up several times after disturbing dreams. At around three in the morning, he heard a familiar buzzing in his ears, a sign that Awinita might be nearby. Billy sat up. Soon his grandmother's glowing form came into view at the foot of his bed.

"Your worries about recapturing the beast have reached us," Awinita said. "The Sun Priest has something to tell you."

The glowing form of the much taller spirit priest came into view. Billy had first seen this spirit at Spiral Mounds. At the time, he'd been so amazed by what was happening that he hadn't noticed what the spirit man looked like, but now he could really observe him.

His jet-black hair was framed by a multicolored headdress of feathers. The feathers fanned out on the back of his head, looking like rays of sunshine. An animal skin was draped over his broad shoulders, and he wore a thick necklace made of square shell pieces. A leather belt covered with jewels was wrapped around his waist. The belt held up a short deerskin robe that covered him down to his knees.

"Ancient peoples always paid attention to the stars and planets," the glowing man said. "The yearly timing of movements and star alignments was of utmost importance. Everything we did was governed by the heavens. Our mounds and temples were built to line up with the sun, moon, and certain star constellations at important times of the year."

"So what about the timing for the ceremony to seal the serpent in the underground lake?" Billy asked. "Is there a best time for that?"

"Absolutely," the translucent visitor replied. "The shortest day of sunlight is when it must be done. That day, called the winter solstice, approaches."

"December twenty-first," Billy said. "I only hope the beast doesn't hurt anyone before then. Can't we do it any sooner?"

"I wouldn't advise it," the man said. "The risk of failure is too high any other time. On the winter solstice, late in the afternoon, the sun's rays shine directly into the mouth of the cave. The lower cavern will be well lit then."

"All right, I'll tell the team," Billy said.

"And the Fire Crystal on the top of the staff you'll be holding will be at its most powerful," the priest added. "We'll need as much power as possible to hypnotize the serpent."

"And there's no doubt we can pull this off?" Billy asked, echoing Chigger's question.

"There *are* one or two additional parts to the process you must learn to ensure our success," the priest said. "It was necessary to wait until the proper time to bring it up."

"Waiting for the stars to align, are we?" Billy said jokingly.

"It's good that you attempt humor," the priest said. "You will probably need it to survive in the presence of the serpent."

That statement drained all the humor right out of Billy. "Survival is good," he said nervously. "I like survival."

At that moment, the spirit forms of four more men came into view. Each wore a smaller version of the feathered headdress that adorned the Sun Priest's head. They all wore short robes made of animal skins.

"For step one, you must lie down so that my assistants can perform their duties," the priest said to Billy.

Without knowing what was about to happen, Billy lay down in the middle of his bed. "What are we doing?" he asked.

"Performing the spirit travel ritual," the priest replied. "Your spirit must know how to leave its body for a short time so that I may be imbedded within your physical frame. Otherwise, I can't use your vocal cords to speak the sacred language. The words must be voiced out loud."

"Wait a minute," Billy protested, sitting back up. "The last time I left my body, I was dying. Once was enough for me."

"You'll be just fine, Grandson," Awinita said, glowing brightly. "I won't let anything bad happen to you. Now try to relax."

"Listen to your grandmother, young man," the priest said. "We are only here to help. You are about to learn the art of spirit travel, and soon you will take part in returning the beast to his underwater prison. Once these two rarest of tasks are achieved, you will be the only medicine man living to have done so."

Billy was now realizing the full meaning of the events he'd been part of. At the stomp grounds last September, he'd had a vision of climbing a ladder. Grandpa Wesley had said that ladder represented the steps he would take to become a Cherokee medicine man. Billy could never in a million years have imagined where those steps would lead.

He lay down on his bed, tried to relax, and waited for what was to come.

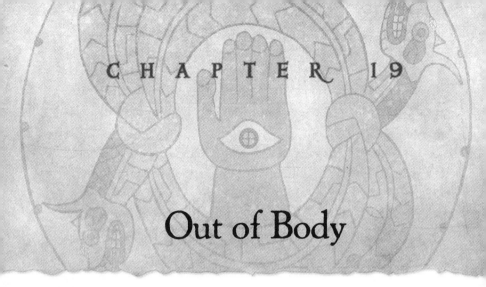

CHAPTER 19

Out of Body

Billy heard buzzing, which gradually grew louder and louder. As it did, it sounded more like humming. The four helpers moved to the four corners of Billy's bed. Billy realized the humming was coming from them.

The humming soon turned into a melody, a song that sounded vaguely familiar—a lot like one sung by Cherokees every year at the Live Oak stomp grounds, where he and Wesley went on Labor Day! The old medicine man in charge of the stomp dance said it was one of the oldest songs Cherokees knew. And here it was again being hummed by the spirits of thousand-year-old Mound Builder Indians. Wow!

The four helpers reached out toward Billy. One placed his hand under the boy's right foot. Another hand moved under his left foot. The two spirits near Billy's head reached under his shoulders.

At that point the humming moved into Billy's body. It became physical, making him feel like his body was now humming the song. Strange. Soon he could feel the vibration getting faster and louder. The teen thought he might come apart at the seams at any minute.

Then the Sun Priest began speaking. No, it was more like chanting. The chanting was in a strange language Billy had never heard. It wasn't Cherokee, but it did contain a few words that seemed a little familiar.

At a signal from the priest, the four helpers lifted Billy from the bed. The teen felt himself rise up, supported by the hands of the helpers. He continued to rise and rise until he almost reached the ceiling, and just when Billy thought he was about to smash into the ceiling, he passed through it. That was when he realized his physical body was still in bed.

The teen began to panic. He was just about to try to escape from the helpers when he saw his grandmother floating beside him. That calmed him down. She smiled, and soon he and Awinita floated above his house. The helpers turned him over so he could look down at the ground below him. That was when he saw the Sun Priest up ahead of him. Immediately Billy and the other six transparent forms began racing away, heading south.

Soon they slowed down above a river. Billy looked closely and saw that they were about to reach the cave that once held the serpent captive. The flying group dropped down to the ledge at the mouth of the cave.

Continuing to move, they drifted into the cave, quickly reaching the fork in the path that divided it in two. The right path led down to the dark lake that once held the Horned Serpent. The left path led upward through the white crystal room. The four helpers guided Billy along the upward path. They moved along the path rather than pass directly through the solid cave walls to help orient Billy to his surroundings.

When they reached the white crystal room, the priest and Awinita were already there, waiting.

"We've brought you here, Billy, for a reason," the priest said. "Look upon these images that you and your friend discovered."

Billy looked again at the images scratched into the walls that showed two groups of people separated by a central figure. The figure in the middle of the two groups was half man, half hawk, which Billy now knew was the Sun Priest dressed in his ceremonial outfit.

"Why do the people on the left side look sharp and clear?" Billy asked. "And why do the people on the right look all fuzzy? Chigger and I couldn't figure that out."

"The people on the left are physically present on earth," Awinita answered. "The people on the right are souls in the spirit world. The figure in the middle is communicating between the two."

Billy thought about that for a moment. Then he realized something.

"That's what you and I did when Luther brought a message for Uncle John," Billy said to his grandmother excitedly. "That's sort of what happens every time you visit me too."

"Now you've got the picture," Awinita said.

"That was always part of the job of spiritual leaders in our ancient communities," the priest said. "I believe people in modern society call it being a medium."

"A medium—I've heard of that," Billy said after a moment's thought. "I remember seeing a woman on TV who does that all the time."

"At the time of my earthly death, I was visiting Spiral Mounds to perform one of our important annual spirit rituals where departed loved ones visited with their earthly relatives," the priest said. "As you step into your spiritual role, this will become one part of your regular activities as well."

"Wait. What?"

"Before, I hinted that you are destined to become unique among today's medicine men," the priest said, "combining those powers and abilities exhibited by your grandfather with the powers, abilities, and responsibilities I had to manifest in my time."

Even though he wasn't sure he fully understood what the spirit man was saying, the weight of the Sun Priest's words nevertheless made Billy feel heavy. His spirit body went through a series of color changes that reflected the revolving emotions he was experiencing.

Understanding what was happening to her grandson, Awinita radiated a surge of golden glowing energy that coursed through him. That settled Billy down and allowed him to stabilize his own energy.

"You'll have plenty of time to process these ideas after we take care of the serpent," the priest said. "Before we leave this room, though, I want you to focus your attention on the ceiling here."

Billy looked up at the ceiling of the small space they were in. There, etched in the ceiling of the little room, was that same symbol, the eye-in-hand image he'd seen in the photo in Augustus's office.

"Your Dr. Stevens did indeed make an important discovery," the spirit priest said. "This symbol, the Eye of God in the Hand of Man, is one of the most powerful and universal symbols of positive energy there is. Surely it will protect you, if you place your faith in it."

With a simple nod of the head, the priest indicated to his helpers that it was time to move on.

"Now we'll take the cave's other path to the lower regions," he said as the group moved away from the crystal room.

As they reached the stone door, Billy began feeling odd. In his mind he saw flashes of his physical body back home in bed, which seemed to be calling to him. It apparently needed something.

"You are getting a signal from your physical body," the spirit priest observed. "We must get you back. But before we go, there is one more thing for you to see."

Billy tried to focus on his immediate surroundings.

"The markings on this door represent the words I will speak through you when the time is right," the priest said. "For that to actually work, you must practice speaking them so that your mouth, tongue, and vocal cords will become familiar with their unfamiliar sounds."

"How am I going to do that?"

"By doing what your grandfather asked you to do," the priest replied. "Studying and memorizing the magical phrases in the book of spells."

"What does that have to do with this?" Billy asked.

"Everything."

As Billy watched, the priest created a translucent ball of focused energy and propelled it toward the surface of the stone door. The seemingly hard surface began to waver as if it was really a liquid. The markings transformed from their almost alienlike form to recognizable letters of the Cherokee syllabary.

"No way!" Billy blurted out.

Then the Sun Priest sent a similar energy ball toward Billy, and the teen felt a warm wave pass through him.

"You now possess the translation key that will allow you to study your father's photo of the markings, see them as Cherokee letters, and practice speaking the syllables."

"No way!" Billy blurted out again.

"You really have to work on your positive belief system and cease with the negativity," the priest said, then smiled. "Think of it as homework. I believe you can sleep on your homework and memorize the pages overnight."

"My ability to do that has been fading lately," Billy replied.

The priest sent another energy thought-ball to Billy. "Try it again tonight," he said.

Billy could feel a new wave of knowledge somehow fill him, and it prompted him to ask a new question.

"We've been calling you the Sun Priest, but I bet you have a name," he said.

"My birth name is Shakuru, which means 'Sun' in my tribal language. It would be pleasing to hear that name spoken again."

"Shakuru, Shakuru," Billy said, committing the name to memory. The teen's energy body quivered, momentarily losing strength. "I can feel my energy fading. I think my physical body is calling to me."

"Time to go," Awinita said.

"Make sure your grandfather finishes those medallions before you return here to face the serpent," Shakuru said. "Their power is real."

With those words, Billy felt himself being pulled back to his physical body. Within seconds he felt himself merge with the flesh. He lay still for a few seconds, trying to sense what it was that was so important. He finally realized what had called him back. He had to pee.

"Really, Buckhorn?" he said aloud, talking to his own body as he got up to go to the bathroom. "You made me leave the most incredible experience of my life so I could drain my bladder? That's just pathetic."

While scanning the newspaper the following morning in the family kitchen, Billy's father asked about the boy's recent conversation with Dr. Abramson.

"He's just doing some follow-up with me," Billy said. "No big deal."

Professor Buckhorn seemed satisfied with that answer.

"More importantly, Pops," Billy continued, "I know when we're supposed to recapture the serpent in the cave!"

Billy's father looked up when he realized what his son was saying. "Did you have a visitation last night?" he asked.

Billy nodded as he poured himself a cup of coffee.

"Don't keep me in suspense," his father said, dropping the paper. "When?"

"Winter solstice," Billy answered between sips of the hot liquid. "The afternoon of December twenty-first."

"That's perfect," the professor said after doing a few mental calculations. "We'll be on winter break at the college. That's good for Dr. Stevens too. Uh, I mean Augustus."

"What's good for Dr. Stevens?" Billy's mother said as she entered the kitchen and headed for the stove.

Billy repeated what he'd said to his father. "Mom, I need you to sit down," he then said in a calm voice. "There's something I have to tell you."

Puzzled, Mrs. Buckhorn sat down next to her husband at the breakfast table. Then Billy proceeded to tell his parents about his visit from Awinita and the Sun Priest. More specifically, he repeated what the spirit had said about his own future.

Both parents were silent. *Maybe they don't believe me,* he thought. *Or maybe they weren't paying attention.*

"I held my tongue when I first heard the wild tale about this big snake monster," his mother said. "And again when your father said he believed this story. I didn't express my opinion or my feelings."

Billy and his father just looked at her. Where was this going?

"But a woman who is a mother and wife has to speak when she hears that her husband and son are planning to confront this dangerous creature," she concluded. "Now I must ask if you two have gone absolutely mad."

"Rebecca, you don't seem to—" her husband began.

"Never in my life have I heard such crazy talk!" she said, interrupting him. Standing up, Rebecca loomed above her seated son and husband. "I don't know if this creature is a figment of your imaginations or if you've been eating too many of Wesley's funny herbs from the garden. But this stuff has got to stop!"

She gave them both a harsh look and then stormed out of the room. Father and son were silent for a moment.

"She'll come around," Billy's dad finally said. "Look at me. I was once a die-hard materialist, only able to believe what the senses could perceive or what the instruments of science could measure."

"I'm not so sure she will," Billy replied, pouring himself another cup of coffee.

"She'll eventually learn to accept it, just like Augustus has," the professor said. "Especially when she sees the video and pictures I'm going to shoot as the serpent comes back to the cave."

Billy looked at his father and smiled nervously, thinking about the task ahead of them.

On the day before the winter solstice, four of the five members of the Paranormal Patrol gathered at Dr. Stevens's house. The team had gear to pack and plans to make. Chigger, who was nervous and excited, chattered a mile a minute.

"I knew you guys would come around," he said. "Paranormal Patrol is the perfect name for this group."

"We're using that name as a joke," Billy said with a laugh. "It's too ridiculous to take seriously."

"Joke or not, it's what the professor and the scientist are calling us," Chigger said. "Isn't that right, Digger?"

"Please call me Augustus," the archaeologist said as he packed supplies in a box. "I don't like the name Digger."

"I like it, though," Chigger replied. "Augustus is too long and sounds like you're the king of Rome or something. Digger rhymes with Chigger, so it sounds like we could be pals."

Augustus thought about that for a moment and then reached a conclusion. "All right then, young man," he said at last. "You may call me Digger. The rest of you," he said, speaking to the group, "shall continue calling me Augustus."

Chigger reached out his hand toward the man. "I'm happy to make your acquaintance, Digger. I'm Chigger."

The two laughed as they shook hands.

"To answer your question, I've labeled all the gear we're taking with the letters PP, for Paranormal Patrol, for one reason," Augustus said. "It's easy to write and takes up less space on the labels."

"See?" Chigger said in a childish taunting voice. He was looking at Billy.

"But we would never use that name in public," the professor said as he finished packing a box. "It's a silly name."

He carried the box out to the van, which was parked in back of the house next to Dr. Stevens's boat.

Chigger looked absolutely deflated.

"Well, I still like it," he said as he finished stuffing freeze-dried food packets into a backpack. "Paranormal Patrol is just the greatest name in the history of names."

"Now we're ready to load the most important items of all," Augustus said. "The hawk cape and gemstone staff."

He removed a large piece of the floor near the back of his office, revealing the hidden space underneath. A metal ladder led down to an underground vault. He climbed down the steps and turned on a light. The rest of the team watched from above.

"This is why the serpent couldn't find the stone," Augustus said.

Turning around in the tight space, he reached out and spun the dial on a combination lock. Although this safe was built into the wall of the space, it reminded Billy of the safe in the shed behind Wesley's house.

"As soon as we're loaded up here, we'll head to Grandpa's house," Billy said. "He's expecting us in about an hour."

With one final spin of the lock, the safe was opened. Augustus pulled out the long tube that held the cape and staff that he'd stored there. He handed the tube up to Billy.

"Ever since I was attacked by the serpent, I've stored the cape and staff in this new tube," Augustus said as he climbed back up the ladder. "It's lined with lead, and I think that has made it hard for the beast to home in on it."

"Good idea," James said as he carried the tube to the van.

Within half an hour, the team had the van loaded and the boat trailer hooked up.

"Over the river and through the woods to Grandpa's house we go," Chigger said excitedly as he jumped in the van.

When they arrived at Wesley's place, the elder was not waiting out front as expected. Billy tried the front door and found it open. He stepped inside while the rest of the team waited on the front porch.

"Grandpa," Billy called several times as he walked through the old house. As he passed through the kitchen, he heard the faint words "out here" coming from the backyard.

Stepping out the back door, Billy saw his grandfather in the field in the back of his house. The elderly medicine man was picking up broken pieces of wood that were scattered through the tall grass and stacking the pieces in a pile.

Then Billy looked toward the woods farther away. There, where Wesley's shed once stood, was only the bank safe lying on its side. Scratch marks scarred its surface.

"What happened?" Billy yelled as he ran toward his grandfather. "Are you okay?"

"Yeah, I'm fine," Wesley replied as Billy reached him. "What a mess. Good thing I finished making our eye-in-hand medallions." He pointed toward the safe using his lips, as many older Natives did. "Our serpent friend put in an appearance this morning. He was after the dark crystal."

"He didn't attack you, did he?" Billy asked as he helped Wesley pick up pieces of wood.

"No," his grandfather answered. "I was just finishing up the last medallion when I heard a loud crash from back here. Still holding the piece in my hand, I ran to see what had happened. That's when I saw him."

For the first time, Billy noticed the withered trail of grass heading off to the east.

"He had already destroyed the shed and was trying to break open the safe," Wesley continued. "He heard me coming and spun around to face me. Boy, is he big! And scary!"

"What did you do?" Billy asked.

"The same thing Dr. Stevens did," Wesley replied. "Without thinking, I held up my hands as if they could somehow protect me from the beast. I forgot I was holding the eye-in-hand medallion. The beast quickly pulled back. That's when I realized I was holding the piece. The serpent tried to come at me from the side. When I turned the medallion toward him, he pulled back again."

"So that image really does repel the thing," Billy said. "It's like a magic amulet or something."

"After that, he just gave up and slithered away," Wesley said, completing his story.

Just then, Billy's dad approached from the house. "What's going on out here?" he asked. "We need to get going."

Billy gave his father a quick summary of what had taken place.

"I think we should load up and get out of here before it comes back," Professor Buckhorn said. "We'll come back later and help you clean up after the beast is no longer a threat."

Agreeing with his son, Wesley opened the overturned safe and took out the pouch that held the dark crystal. Then the three Buckhorns went back in the house. Wesley grabbed his overnight bag and his medicine satchel. After a quick look around the house, he locked the front door. The team was now complete, and off they went in the van.

Wesley's report of the beast's latest attack caused the group to ride in silence for a while. The dangerous nature of their expedition was sinking in. Was this going to be harder than they had imagined? What if the beast had other powers no one knew about?

Wesley began singing an old Cherokee warrior song. The words spoke of strength and victory. In the old days, the men in a war party would sing this before facing an enemy. Billy recognized the song. It was one he'd heard his grandfather sing before. He joined in. Billy's dad also remembered hearing Wesley sing it long ago and followed along as best he could.

Wesley kept singing the song over and over. Chigger and Augustus picked up on the tune and hummed along. Wesley was the only one who knew exactly what the words meant, but all of them felt the song's strength. And each one of them became more certain of his mission with every passing mile.

Arriving at the boat landing on the river, the team transferred their gear to the vessel. Quickly they shoved off, heading south down the river once again, and they reached the campsite near the cave in the middle of the afternoon.

Everyone on the team was eager to get started setting up.

"Hold on, everybody," Wesley said as he took his medicine satchel out of the boat. "First things first. Let's form a small circle."

He set his bag down on the ground and opened it. The other team members gathered around him.

"All great endeavors should begin with prayer," Wesley said as he removed his pipe and tobacco from the satchel. "We are here by the river, so when we've finished, we'll purify ourselves in the water."

Augustus, the scientist, was not sure what to expect. He didn't begin most of his projects with a prayer. But, as a loyal member of the Paranormal Patrol, he followed along.

Wesley placed a small amount of natural tobacco in the pipe and lit it. Then, in the Cherokee language, he prayed on their behalf, asking Creator to bless their task and protect them from harm. After taking four puffs of the pipe, he passed it on. And so it went around the circle.

When all the tobacco had been smoked, Wesley and Billy sat down and removed their shoes. The others did the same. Wesley and his grandson waded into the shallow part of the river. The others watched.

"Cherokees call this 'going to the water,'" Wesley said. "It purifies us inside and out."

He and Billy demonstrated the process. Each of them cupped their hands together and scooped up a handful of water. Then, as Wesley recited another Cherokee prayer, they threw the handfuls of water over their shoulders. This was done four times. The rest of the team did the same thing. When they'd finished, the elder just looked at the unusual team—two teenagers, two college professors, and an old man.

"Now we're ready to do this thing," he said with confidence and led them back to the riverbank.

The first task was to have Chigger remove the dark crystal from its case and carry it around for a while. The team hoped this would reopen the beast's connection to the boy. While everyone else unloaded equipment and set up camp, Chigger walked around holding the gem. It wasn't long before he started feeling weird.

"I think something's happening," he said in a loud voice. "The stone is getting warm and beginning to glow. And I'm beginning to feel light headed."

"Good," Wesley said. "Hopefully, the serpent has learned of the gem's new location. Now for the next step. Time to put the dark crystal back in its original place."

With Chigger and the crystal in front, the team climbed up the steps that led to the cave. They stood on the ledge at the cave's mouth and turned on their flashlights. The boy looked down at the purple stone.

"You're going back home, buddy," Chigger said with longing in his voice. He looked back at Billy. "Feels like I'm saying good-bye to an old friend," he said with a slight sneer. "A close friend who values me above everything else."

Alarmed by Chigger's words and demeanor, Billy couldn't speak.

"We'd better get this done as quickly as possible," Wesley advised, also alarmed. He shined his flashlight into Chigger's eyes, which seemed to wake the boy up.

"This stone is already beginning to get hot in my hands," Chigger said, sounding more like his usual self. "And the burn scars are starting to hurt."

Refocused, Chigger headed into the darkness. The other four team members felt an additional sense of urgency as they walked down the lower path and headed for the stone door. The purple gemstone obviously still had a powerful pull on Chigger's mind.

Once they arrived at the door, Wesley took a quick peek at the markings on the door.

"They do resemble the characters in the back of Blacksnake's medicine book," he said.

Then the group turned their attention to Chigger as he stood beside the pedestal. He seemed reluctant to release the gem. In fact, his determination to accomplish the task wavered. How quickly the bond reasserted itself. For a moment, Chigger stood frozen in place, unable to finish the job.

"Chigger, put the stone on the pedestal!" Billy commanded. "Now!"

He made a quick move toward his friend. The sudden action took the teen by surprise, and he dropped the stone into place. Everyone breathed a sigh of relief.

Once the stone was out of Chigger's hands, it seemed as if he woke up fully.

"Oh, look at that," he said. "The stone's right where it should be." He looked at his fellow Paranormal Patrol mates, seeming oblivious to what had just taken place. "Well, what are you waiting for? Let's get out of here."

"Uh, we were just waiting to see if anything happened as a result of the gem being back in place," Billy's father said. "Nothing did, so you're right. Let's get going."

The team headed back to their camp. Little did they know that something *had* actually happened. An unseen signal had gone out from that dark stone. The bats that had lived in the cave felt it. So did the serpent. And so did the ghost of the Snake Priest.

For the bats, it was like a homing beacon. They somehow knew it was time to return to their old roosting haunt. For the dark priest, it was a signal to guide the serpent back to gather up the stone. After all, it did belong to the serpent. And soon the serpent would once again do the Snake Priest's bidding.

As for Billy and the team, they could only hope that the beast would show up at the right time. But they had to be ready in case it came earlier or later than planned. They set up a twenty-four-hour watch schedule. Each member of the team would take a four-hour shift. Around the clock someone would be on the lookout for the beast.

Before the first shift began, Wesley passed out the eye-in-hand medallions.

"Wear this at all times until we've completed our mission," he instructed. "Don't take it off to sleep, eat, or go to the bathroom."

Billy volunteered for the first watch. That way he'd be able to sleep most of the night and get plenty of rest. He had to be ready. Who knew when the serpent would actually show up? Who knew how soon he'd have to allow the spirit of the ancient Sun Priest, Shakuru, to possess him?

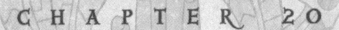

CHAPTER 20

The Spell Is Cast

Billy's watch shift was uneventful. A rising moon in a cloudless sky shone brightly over the darkened landscape. The lookout position they used was the ledge above the campsite. From that spot, they could see both upriver and downriver for several miles.

Chigger took the next watch. He came to the ledge carrying an armload of snacks and his flashlight.

"All's quiet," Billy said as he watched Chigger take his seat in the dirt. "Are you okay?" he asked his friend. "I thought for a minute we'd lost you again back there in the cave."

The questioning look on Chigger's face indicated he wasn't sure what his friend was talking about. "What do you mean?" he asked.

"Forget it," Billy responded and headed down the cliffside steps.

Back at the camp, he took a few bites of a protein snack before setting up his memorization station for the night. He placed the photo of the ancient markings on the pillow in his sleeping bag, then crawled into the bag. First making sure his head was resting on the photo, he closed his eyes. He hadn't realized just how tired he was, and he quickly conked out.

Around midnight, the teen started dreaming. The Sun Priest came into view, along with two of the priest's helpers. Also, Cherokee words from the photo he'd been sleeping on floated in the space around him.

"Am I dreaming?" Billy asked.

"Yes and no," Shakuru answered. "You need to mentally absorb the ceremonial words and practice leaving your body one more time."

The priest began humming. It was the same song Billy had heard the first time he left his body. The teen hummed along this time as the helpers moved in closer. Everyone was humming, and the sound vibrated throughout his body. At a peak moment, they lifted Billy's energy body out of his physical body and held him above their heads.

Then all four of them floated upward. Looking down, Billy saw he was hovering over his own physical body. He was beginning to get used to this experience.

"That's the idea," the priest said. "The more you practice, the better you will become."

The priest nodded to the helpers. The two slowly removed their hands from under Billy's arms. He continued to float. The helpers moved a little farther away. Billy continued to float.

"Now what?" he asked.

"Now you begin to learn the skills of spirit travel," the priest said. "You practice the art of leaving and returning to your body. You practice the art of moving from place to place. It all takes practice."

Billy tried flapping his arms like a bird. He felt silly, and he didn't move an inch. Then he tried to swim through the air like a swimmer would move through water. After a few useless strokes, he still hadn't moved an inch. He looked to the priest for help. The man was grinning from ear to ear. He enjoyed watching the newbie flailing around.

"It won't be like physically moving," he said. "It is all about focusing your attention."

Billy didn't get it.

"Think hard about a place you want to go or someone you want to see," the priest advised. "Picture that in your mind."

Billy shut everything out. Then he thought of Chigger sitting at the lookout point. Immediately he felt a blur of movement. It wasn't like flying. It was more like stretching. One part of him instantly floated near Chigger. The rest of Billy caught up a split second later. Looking around, he found he was floating out in front of the ledge. Chigger sat at the mouth of the cave—fast asleep. Billy tried to wake him up.

"Wake up, sleepyhead," he said, but got no response. "I said, 'Wake up!'" he shouted.

Still no response.

"You're supposed to be watching out for the beast!" he yelled as loud as he could.

Still nothing.

"He can't hear you," the priest said. He was watching the whole thing from a few feet away. "You are invisible to him. You are yelling with your thoughts, not your voice."

"Oh yeah," Billy said. "I forgot."

"Now you know why I must take over your body and your vocal cords to speak the sacred words," the spirit man said. "The words must be spoken aloud in the physical realm."

"Got it," Billy replied.

"These words form an ancient secret spell used only by me and a handful of spiritual leaders," the priest said. "It may be used to hypnotize any person or creature and control their actions. Someday in the future it may be useful to you."

To Billy, this made learning the spell even more important.

Next the priest's helpers moved Billy's spirit body to another location. In two quick blinks, they were standing on an ancient mound site. A thatched-roof building stood on the mound's flat-top surface. Billy looked out over a vast grassy area where hundreds of smaller thatched-roof homes stood. They were neatly arranged in a grid along straight paths.

"Where is this place?" Billy asked as they settled down on top of the mound.

"The question is not only where but also when," one of the priest's helpers answered. "Time and place have different meanings in the nonphysical world. This is the Temple Mound at the center of Solstice City."

Once again Billy did not understand what he was being told, but he noticed that the Sun Priest was no longer with the group. "What happened to the Sun Priest?"

"The reason he can't yet return to the Solstice City locale is a long story he will explain at another time."

Now Billy was doubly confused.

"There will be plenty of time to grasp these ideas later," the priest's assistant said. "You will learn all there is to know about spirit travel and the other worlds. For now we must focus on the job at hand."

"Of course," Billy said, still curious about Shakuru's status.

The helper sensed Billy's continuing concern. "He's still back near the cave, but he can pick up on our thoughts. A portion of the ancient curse is still unbroken. You and your friend partially broke the curse when you entered the upper crystal room, but another part of the curse keeps him tied to the Spiral Mounds area. He is unable to return to the Solstice City area until that spell is fully broken."

"Who or what could cast such a spell?"

"They called themselves Night-Seers of the Owl Clan," the helper replied. "Evil people making bad medicine. Shakuru's own brother joined them, but that's a story for another time."

Billy's energy body began fading.

"You may return to your body now," the helper said. "I think you are ready for the ceremony to recapture the serpent. The Sun Priest must also prepare."

With that, Billy zoomed away to the campsite. He jolted awake, back in his physical body in the sleeping bag. Feeling a little dazed, he sat up. Everyone else was asleep. He thought of Chigger, who he now knew was also asleep at his post.

Billy climbed up the steps in the face of the cliff. He stepped onto the ledge in front of the cave. There was Chigger, fast asleep, just as he'd seen him earlier.

"Wake up, sleepyhead," he said again to his friend.

No response.

"I said wake up!" he shouted as he'd done before. This time there was an immediate reaction.

"What? Where?" Chigger said as he jumped up off the ground. "Who's there?"

Billy broke into a big belly laugh that went on and on. Then he said, "You've been sleeping on the job."

Chigger finally woke up enough to realize what was happening. "So I fell asleep," he admitted. "It's not that funny." Then a thought struck him. "How did you know I was asleep?"

"I was up here earlier, and I saw you sleeping," Billy said, still chuckling. "I even tried to wake you up, but you couldn't hear me."

"Why didn't I hear you?" Chigger said. "I heard you just now. Why wouldn't I have heard you before?"

"Because I wasn't in my body," Billy said. "I was practicing spirit travel."

Chigger blinked. He was trying hard to get what Billy was saying. Then his eyes lit up.

"You were spying on me?" he said as he realized what Billy could do. "You can spy on people without them knowing it?"

"I hadn't thought of it like that," Billy answered. "I guess I can."

"Do you know what the government would do if they knew about this?" Chigger said.

"Down, boy," Billy said. "You're having another fantasy attack."

"No, I'm serious," Chigger protested. "This could—"

"Enough already," Billy interrupted. "I'm going back to bed."

He reached into his back pocket and pulled out a small can of energy drink he'd brought with him. He handed the can to Chigger.

"Maybe this will help you stay awake," he said and climbed back down the stone stairs.

The Paranormal Patrol team members took turns keeping watch the rest of the night. Nothing much happened except that clouds rolled in. Billy awoke to gray skies. No sun. And it was the big day: winter solstice.

Billy's father had explained that the summer and winter solstices were often tied together in tribal cultures. During a ceremony on the summer solstice, some tribes used a clear crystal to capture the sun's rays. That was on June twenty-first, the longest day of sunlight. People believed the sun to be most powerful at that time of year.

That crystal would be stored away until time for the winter solstice. During a ceremony on or near December twenty-first, those rays would be released from the crystal on the shortest day. This would ensure that the sun would begin its new cycle. Its power would increase as the days got longer.

"The weather forecast didn't say anything about clouds for today," James said. "I hope it doesn't hamper our plans."

"The Sun Priest said the gemstone in the staff was most powerful on this day," Billy said. "I think the ceremony will still work."

Augustus finished his turn on watch. He came down to the camp to have breakfast.

"Nothing much to report," he said as he ate his freeze-dried eggs. "Just that I started seeing bats before sunrise this morning."

"What?" Billy sat up straight, alarmed by this news.

"They came from all directions," Augustus continued. "In little groups. I had to stay low to keep from getting hit as they flew into the cave."

"Why didn't you call us?" Wesley asked. He was also alarmed.

"I figured it was normal for bats to enter the cave at sunrise," Augustus replied. "Nobody ever said anything about bats. I was just watching for the serpent."

"Oh my gosh," Billy said as he stood up. "We'd better get ready."

Everyone but the scientist stood up.

"What's going on?" he asked with a puzzled face. "What did I miss?"

"The return of the bats means the beast is on its way," Chigger said. "They haven't been back to this cave since the day the serpent left. Everyone knows that." He shook his head as if this was the most obvious thing in the world.

Chigger grabbed the binoculars from near the campfire. Then he scrambled up the stone stairs as fast as he could. He stood on the ledge and looked upstream. He could see no signs of the serpent. What the team hoped to see was regular movement in the middle of the river, a water trail that showed where the snake was swimming.

"No sign of it yet," Chigger yelled to the camp below.

"Keep watching," Wesley called up to him.

"Get behind that rock so he can't see you," Billy's father said. Then he began preparing his cameras in hopes of recording the event. Chigger hid behind a large rock on the ledge. He peered through the binoculars.

The professor had brought two video cameras and one still camera with him. Everything was digital. He had already set up one video camera on a tripod. It had a wide-angle lens, so it pictured everything from the river's edge to the mouth of the cave, and he could start recording using a little remote control he kept in his pocket.

Wesley and Billy made their way to the upper crystal room inside the cave. Augustus had hidden the storage tube there so the cape and staff would be handy when needed. The team had also placed a cot in that room as part of their plan.

Wesley helped Billy put on the cape. Then the teen lay down on the cot. When the final signal came, he would begin the process of leaving his body. He hoped. The elder left the staff inside the lead-lined tube. The gem was to remain hidden from the serpent until the creature had reached the bottom of the lower path.

Then Wesley made his way back down the upper path and took up a position just inside the mouth of the cave so he'd hear Chigger's signal. He made sure he was out of sight.

Augustus took up his position as well. Even though he'd been told that bullets couldn't pierce the serpent's scales, he wanted to try. He had created a camouflaged hunting bunker at the edge of the river. This was located out of the way but near where the serpent would slither to reach the cave. The archaeologist did a final check of the ammo for the handgun and rifle he'd brought. They were locked and loaded. He planned to shoot the beast if it escaped from the cave, which would only happen if the Sun Priest's ceremony failed.

All was ready for the Uktena to arrive. The only thing the team needed now was some sunshine. That would guarantee their success.

Time passed. Everyone waited and watched. Chigger peered through the binoculars. The clouds continued to cover the sun. Wesley waited just inside the cave for the signal.

At around two o'clock in the afternoon, Chigger checked the binoculars one more time. Starting in the water near their camp, he moved his view slowly upriver. He caught sight of a swirl of water. He paused to take a closer look and saw a turtle pop his head up. Chigger moved on.

About a hundred yards farther upstream, he saw another swirl. *Probably another turtle,* Chigger thought. He focused the lenses. The swirl continued to move downstream. Moments later a few shiny scales appeared just under the water's surface. Then there was a long line of scales.

Suddenly the serpent's head rose out of the water. A few sprigs of underwater plants hung from his antlers. He licked the air with his very long tongue.

Chigger jumped and nearly dropped the binoculars. He put his fingers to the corners of his mouth and tried to whistle. That was supposed to be the signal to let the team know the beast had been spotted. But he couldn't make his mouth whistle. All that came out was a spitting noise. He tried again, but this time it only sounded like he was passing gas.

He turned toward the cave.

"It's coming!" he said in a loud whisper. "I saw it. It's coming."

Wesley nodded that he'd heard Chigger's warning and then headed immediately to the upper path to tell Billy.

Meanwhile, Chigger looked down toward the camp and repeated his warning. Billy's dad stood up from his hiding place and gave the teen a thumbs-up. Augustus did the same.

Chigger immediately headed for his designated hiding place. The plan called for him to help Billy's dad with the cameras. James turned on the first video camera, the one on the tripod. He held on to the other one so he could follow the beast into the cave. He gave Chigger the still camera.

In the upper room, Billy lay down on the cot and began humming the song the priest had taught him. In order for him to escape his body, he had to completely relax and wait for the vibrations to begin.

Soon the familiar humming sound came to his ear. This told him Awinita was standing by. Soon she and the Sun Priest faded into view. Beside the priest were two spirit assistants. Again the assistants hummed their song. That started the vibrations that allowed Billy to leave his body.

The priest chanted, and the assistants moved in to lift Billy's spirit body up. Once Billy was out, he waited with Awinita. What they witnessed next seemed very strange. Stranger yet than anything else either one had experienced.

From out of nowhere, a ghostly being appeared in the upper room. He looked a little like the Sun Priest. His spirit clothing was similar. His face was similar but seemed distorted. His spirit body, however, was deformed. He seemed to be a poorly constructed imitation of the Sun Priest, a malformed twin.

This figure's appearance took the Sun Priest completely by surprise. Billy watched as the two spirit beings confronted each other. Then Billy saw a flicker of recognition pulse through the Sun Priest. He knew who the intruder was!

"Monkata, my brother, how are you here?" the Sun Priest asked.

"The Night-Seers freed me at long last from my hellish prison, Shakuru. Whether you like it or not, the Snake Priest has returned!"

Before the Sun Priest could move or do anything else, the intruder thrust himself into Billy's physical body. Billy understood that the dark priest intended to possess him. Billy's spirit body began to feel heavy. His energy was draining. Awinita saw and felt what was happening to her grandson.

Quickly, acting in unison, the Sun Priest, his helpers, and Awinita surrounded Billy's body and moved in on the intruder. Humming a higher-pitched version of the Cherokee song Billy knew, their combined energy wrestled with the shadowy ghost.

Then the humming vibration grew even stronger, and the light generated by the Sun Priest's team became brighter.

With so much energy swirling around him, Billy felt quite ill. Was it his spirit body or his physical body that felt that way? He couldn't tell, because the two were mingled together. As the struggle continued, he remembered the warrior song his grandfather had sung in the van. With all the energy he could muster, he began humming that melody. Awinita felt it and joined in. She glowed more brightly, sending strong energy to Billy.

With this extra spiritual strength, Billy also began pushing against the unwelcome guest. That extra push was what was needed. The intruder was thrust from Billy's physical body, and the Sun Priest quickly formed an energy bubble around the body, blocking the trespasser from reentering.

And then suddenly a bright ball of fiery energy shot out from the Sun Priest's chest. It hit the Dark One like a cannonball. The deformed entity flew backward, crashing against the cave's crystal wall. Without hesitating, the Sun Priest threw a sort of energy rope toward the intruder, and the brightly glowing lasso wrapped around him. To Billy it was almost like a cowboy roping a calf.

The Sun Priest streaked up and away, dragging his brother behind him. The two disappeared momentarily. Within a matter of seconds, Shakuru reappeared alone.

"What just happened?" Billy asked.

"No time for explanations," the Sun Priest replied. "We have to begin the ceremony now."

Without further delay, the Sun Priest's spirit body began shrinking, reducing to the size of Billy's body. Then he lay back on the cot, merging himself with Billy's body. Billy's spirit body somehow felt what the physical body was feeling. It looked and felt as though the priest had put on Billy's body like a suit—a Billy suit.

Then Billy's physical body made an attempt to stand up, moving awkwardly at first. But then the body seemed to enlarge somewhat, to grow bigger, stronger. The priest's powerful presence seemed to actually be affecting the molecules in the teen's physical body.

The physical Billy began chanting the same chant the Sun Priest had chanted before. At first, the words weren't clear. The priest's spirit was adapting to being inside a physical body for the first time in a thousand years, and it took a little getting used to. Billy and Awinita were both amazed that this actually worked.

Wesley handed the tube that held the staff to the priest in the Billy suit. Moving stiffly at first, the boy took the tube and slung the strap over his shoulder.

And then everyone waited.

Down close to the river, Augustus, Chigger, and James began to smell a foul odor. At about the same time, they heard splashes in the water. The Horned Serpent had arrived. The three humans froze in place and held their breath. They dared not move.

Soon the beast's head came up out of the water. He hissed loudly as he studied his surroundings. He saw nothing that made him suspicious. The video camera sitting on its tripod was odd looking to the beast, but it wasn't threatening. He ignored it and looked up toward the cave. That was where the unseen signal had been coming from. The dark crystal called to him from there. *Finally, the gem will be returned to its rightful place,* he thought.

This was the first time either Chigger or Billy's dad had seen the creature. Its scales seemed to constantly change colors. Sometimes they were white; other times they seemed iridescent blue or green. And the antlers on top of his head almost looked like those of a deer. In the middle of the beast's forehead was an indentation where the Fire Crystal used to sit. On either side of the indentation glowed a red eye. The eyes were burning, seemingly filled with death.

Before exiting the water, the serpent extended his tongue and licked the air. As with all reptiles, this was where he had his sense of smell. That was when Chigger saw the beast's fangs and teeth, sharp and yellowed and dripping with saliva. The teen shuddered at the sight.

Luckily, everyone in the Paranormal Patrol had rubbed themselves with dirt and green leaves to prevent the serpent from detecting their human scent.

Satisfied that the coast was clear, the beast slithered out of the water and up the craggy cliff. Its scales gripped the uneven cliff surface like suction cups as it climbed.

That was when Chigger finally remembered to send the second signal up to the crystal room. Dr. Stevens had run a small black wire from the campsite up the cliff. It continued into the upper room. To one end of the wire was attached a small trigger. On the other end of the wire was a red light. Chigger pushed the trigger, which turned on the light inside the cave.

The Sun Priest, wearing Billy's body, saw the signal and knew the serpent was entering the cave. Time for action! He quietly moved down the path toward the lower cavern.

Once the serpent had entered the cave, James and Chigger quietly climbed the stone stairs. They followed the beast into the darkness. But they had no trouble knowing where the beast was. Its fiery eyes glowed red. And as it slithered along, its scales made a crunching sound against the loose dirt on the cave floor. James began videotaping in the cave, using the camera's night vision feature.

Downward the beast moved toward its precious dark crystal. At last the stone was within reach. Soon it would be rejoined to his tail, where it belonged.

At the same time, the Sun Priest in Billy's body stepped out on the ledge. He removed his royal staff from the tube. The physical feel of the staff in his hand brought back glorious memories from a thousand years ago.

Holding the staff up over his head, he turned toward the west. He silently called to Grandfather Sun, asking the old man to appear. Then, loudly, he began to speak his ancient language. Again, he asked the grandfather to shine forth.

Suddenly a wind arose from the west. The clouds above began churning and swirling. To the amazement of James and Chigger, layers of clouds began to part. Darker ones moved away, replaced by fluffy white ones, but they didn't fully part. Although the sky was brighter, direct sunlight was still blocked from view.

Thankfully, enough light reached the gemstone to activate it. It began to glow dimly.

At the same moment, down at the bottom of the path, the beast suddenly turned. He, too, felt the power of that gem as its brightness grew.

Quickly the Sun Priest carried the staff down the lower path. As he did, he loudly proclaimed the sacred words, the words that had been etched into the stone door in ancient times. Upon seeing the brightly shining stone and hearing the ancient words, the serpent fell under a spell, the same spell that had captured him so long ago. He stopped moving.

Billy hovered nearby in his spirit body, watching the action. It was very odd to see himself, his physical body, doing things without him. He was in two places at the same time! Until that moment, he'd believed that was impossible.

Chigger thought this would be a perfect time to take a picture. He pressed the camera's button, and because it was an automatic camera, the flash unit popped up. A second later, its bright light flashed in the darkness. This startled everyone— including the serpent.

It awoke from the spell and looked around. Quickly the creature saw the gemstone in the staff and headed toward it. Hoping to counter the beast's actions, the priest in the Billy suit started chanting the spell faster and louder.

Suddenly, up in the sky, the clouds completely parted. Rays of bright sunlight streamed at just the right angle directly into the lower area of the cave. A few of those rays struck the Fire Crystal, and the gem ignited as if it had been set ablaze. A golden heavenly brilliance filled the cavern.

The refracted light reached the Horned Serpent and filled his eyes. He grew still as the chanting and the unearthly radiance filled his mind. The priest drew closer to the beast, chanting more powerfully with each step. Soon he was dangerously close to the monster. But by then the beast was back under the priest's spell. The serpent stared blankly at his surroundings.

The priest continued his chant and headed down the path. The beast remained fixated on the stone and followed the priest each step of the way. The priest led the beast through the open stone door, and turning to the right, he walked along a raised platform next to the lower lake. The beast slithered into the dark liquid with ease. There he floated in a daze.

The priest made his way back to the stone door and stood in front of it. Reading from the symbols carved into the stone, he began the sealing ceremony. Billy's rehearsals of those words paid off as his commanding voice echoed throughout the cavern.

Chigger looked up at the ceiling and saw that the bat colony had settled back in its place. The bats, too, grew still and quiet as the chanting came to an end. Just before voicing the final words of the spell, the priest stepped back from the door. He completed the ceremony with a closing word.

"*Aho*," he said, the way generations of Native people had ended prayers and rituals down through the ages.

With that, the stone door swung shut all by itself. A sucking noise flowed from around the edges of the door as it sealed itself closed once again.

"It is finished," Billy the priest said, uttering words in English for the first and only time.

The Sun Priest immediately vacated Billy's body, and the staff fell from his hand to the cave floor. Billy's unconscious body collapsed on the ground beside it as the Fire Crystal ceased to glow.

James and Chigger were enveloped in darkness and engulfed in utter silence. Neither one moved for a long moment. Finally, Chigger pulled a flashlight out of his pocket and turned it on. His first concern was the condition of his friend.

"Billy? Billy!" he called as the beam of his light searched the floor. Momentarily, the light swept over the purple crystal. Chigger let the light linger on it for an extended moment, remembering the sense of power it had given him.

The professor's voice broke the silence. "Billy!" he yelled as his own flashlight beam found his son's unmoving body.

Rushing to him, James felt for a pulse on his son's neck. He touched the spiderweb scar left on his son by the lightning strike months earlier. The scar was hot to the touch. Upon a closer look, he saw that it was glowing. It looked like a hot net of lava had splattered on Billy's neck.

"Help me get him out of here," James yelled at Chigger. "We've got to see what's wrong with his neck."

Chigger snapped his wandering mind back to the here and now, and finally he sprang into action. Together, the two struggled to carry Billy up the path and out of the cave. They set him down on the ledge. Wesley and Augustus joined them as James frantically felt for a pulse on the boy's wrist and then his neck. Finally, the man relaxed.

"I found a pulse," he reported. "It's weak but regular."

He looked more closely at the pattern on his son's neck. It had stopped glowing, but it was still reddish colored. It looked like it had looked right after the lightning strike.

A few moments later, Billy stirred. He opened his eyes and found himself surrounded by the members of his team. He tried to get up, but his father prevented it.

"Don't rush it," James said. "Give yourself a few minutes to get collected."

The teen lay back and looked up at the team. "Now that was some strange stuff," he said with a smile.

"Do you feel okay?" James asked. "The scar on your neck was glowing."

Billy reached up to feel the scar.

"Ow!" he yelped. "It's sore. It feels like it did when I was recovering in the hospital. Energy from the Sun Priest must've caused that."

He sat up, then slowly stood under his own power, and everyone breathed a sigh of relief. But Billy was somehow different on the inside. Physically, he felt a tingling sensation from head to foot, like he'd been electrified—not electrocuted but electrically charged. And, on top of that, his clothes felt tight against his skin.

Noticing his son's apparent discomfort, James thought there must be something wrong.

"Nothing's really wrong, Pops," Billy replied as if his father had spoken.

"How did you know what I was thinking?" James asked. "I didn't say anything."

"But I heard you, clear as day."

That was when Billy noticed he could see energy fields radiating out from his companions. Looking down at his own body, he saw his own energy field as well.

"This is bizarre," Billy remarked. "We've all got some sort of electrical energy radiating out from our bodies. Can you see it?"

Of course, no one else could.

"That's the way it was in the old days," Wesley said. "Some of our most powerful and knowledgeable healers saw people's auras, though that word wasn't used."

"Whoa," Chigger said, drawing out the word dramatically. "That's heavy."

Billy didn't tell anyone that his friend's energy field seemed to have breaks in it, like it wasn't fully connected to his body the way everyone else's field was.

The crew was quiet for a moment as another, more immediate, realization settled in.

Their mission was complete. The plan had actually worked! There'd be time to think about auras and energy fields later.

Meanwhile, the feeling of tightness in Billy's clothing increased until he couldn't stand it anymore, so he stretched the muscles in his back and shoulders. *Rip* came the sound of the seams splitting in his shirt's shoulders.

"What happened?" Billy asked as he reached up to feel the torn seams.

James touched the torn seam, confirming the presence of the tear.

"Yep, it's definitely torn," he said. "You just outgrew the shirt that fit you fine when you put it on this morning."

Another quiet moment overtook the group as each member of the Paranormal Patrol came to the conclusion that there might be other aftereffects awaiting them.

"I've had enough of this place," Billy said, trying to shake off his new reality. "I think it's time we get out of here."

"First we have to decide what we're going to do about this cave," Augustus said. "We can't just leave it for someone else to accidentally discover."

They all knew he was right. The serpent must never be released again.

"Can't we dynamite the cave entrance?" Chigger suggested. "That should do it."

"We can do that right after I retrieve the center crystal from the pedestal in the upper crystal room," Billy replied.

"What for?" Chigger asked.

"I'm supposed to put that crystal to use when I communicate with the dead—to help focus the interdimensional energies."

"That's right," Wesley said. "Billy's going to reconnect people to their loved ones who've died, just like the original Sun Priest did. Billy is now his apprentice."

They all looked at Wesley.

"And you know this how?" James asked his father.

"You forget that I've been connecting with the spirit world for a long time," Wesley reminded him. "Not like Billy, but in my own way. The Sun Priest's ability to communicate from the spirit world to our world has gotten amazingly strong."

"Grandpa's right," Billy confirmed. "They're expecting me to carry on that work. It's a little like what they've been doing at the Live Oak during the stomp dances."

"But this is more powerful," Wesley continued. "It's from the original source."

The Paranormal Patrol was again silent. They needed time to absorb all these new ideas. Quietly they set about the task of packing up to head back home. The decision about resealing the cave would have to wait.

CHAPTER 21

Of Men and Monsters

When the team got back to Dr. Stevens' house, they took time to review the photos and video that had been shot. James played back the tape from the tripod-mounted video camera. Oddly, there was nothing on the tape but washed-out, snowy images. It looked like the tape had been placed near a magnet.

On the other video camera, there were only distorted, grainy shadows. James and Augustus were heartbroken. They'd expected to have visual proof of the creature to show the academic world. Now there was nothing.

"Let's check the still camera," James said with a hint of hope.

A quick check of that camera revealed only a single image. It was the one Chigger had taken inside the lower cavern when the camera flashed. What it showed was Billy wearing the hawk feather cape and holding the Sun Priest's staff. The frame didn't include the Horned Serpent.

But as they looked more closely at the image, they did realize one thing. Billy looked a lot like the half-man, half-bird image that had been etched into the wall of the upper crystal room, and he seemed somehow larger and more majestic than usual. Plus, his eyes were on fire! It wasn't the usual camera red eye caused by the flash. His eyes glowed with golden energy.

"The Sun Priest's energy was radiating from Billy's body," Wesley said. "His power is a supernatural force that changed Billy's physical appearance for a while, maybe for good. Very rare."

"Speaking of the Sun Priest, I'm confused about who the guy is—or was," Chigger admitted. "Was he a good version of our Birdman, Ravenwood or Blacksnake or whatever his name was?"

"From what I could piece together, he was nothing like our Birdman, who was a shape-shifting witch," Billy answered as he seemed to drift into a trancelike state. He took a deep breath, and a flood of words rushed out of his mouth.

"His name was Shakuru, which means 'Sun' in his tribal language. A thousand years ago, he was the Sun Priest at a place called Solstice City, where twenty thousand people lived. It was the capital of a vast empire that included hundreds of Mound Builder cities and villages spread all over the country. Shakuru's own twin brother became the Snake Priest, head of a cult that worshipped the Horned Serpent. The Snake Priest and his followers tried to take over Solstice City, and the Snake Priest was killed in battle. Then, later, Shakuru temporarily left Solstice City and went to Spiral Mounds to perform an annual winter solstice ceremony in honor of people who'd died during the past year. While there, he was assassinated by members of his brother's cult in revenge, and a league of dark medicine people cursed the Sun Priest, which kept his spirit trapped within the nearby region in some sort of spirit jail."

The rapid flow of words suddenly stopped, and he snapped out of whatever state of mind he'd been in. He took another breath.

Bewildered by what he'd just experienced, Billy said, "I don't know where all that came from. I don't even remember hearing half of that stuff."

Unable to process the information overload that had just been dumped on him, Chigger simply replied, "Oh."

No one was really sure how to respond, but to get back on track, Augustus said, "Well, with no photos and no video, we have no proof of any of it. I think it must be a sign."

"A sign of what?" Billy asked, seemingly back from who knows where.

"A sign that some things in this world are best kept secret," James said, realizing what the scientist was getting at. "There'll be no press conference to announce the greatest archaeology find in modern times. We won't be writing any reports to publish in academic journals."

"Your father and I have come to respect what you and Wesley are doing," Augustus said, continuing with the idea started by James. "And you need to operate without a lot of media attention. It works best that way."

Another moment of silence settled over the group. Each person was lost in his own thoughts.

"As archaeologists, though, we did make a couple significant finds," Augustus said, looking at the photo Chigger took. "The Sun Priest's hawk feather cape and gem-topped staff, which were amazingly well preserved."

"I had forgotten about those things," James said. "Don't those have to go back to the Spiral Mounds collection?"

"Eventually," the digger answered. "For now, it can be on loan to the university for further study, under my supervision, since I was the senior archaeologist on the dig."

"Technically, we didn't dig those things up," Chigger observed. "The Horned Serpent did."

"But he doesn't exist," Billy added. Then a realization hit him. "Won't the Spiral Mounds night watchman have to report what he saw that night?"

"I think Mr. Langford, the park director, has convinced the watchman of the wisdom of keeping the unbelievable incident to himself," Augustus answered.

"Okay, there's one last thing that's been bugging me ever since we found out the Horned Serpent was more than a legend," Chigger said. "Who created it? Where did it come from?"

"Every culture has its stories of monsters and dragons and frightful giants that lived long ago," James said, sounding every bit like the college professor he was. "They're often part of a creation story where a cultural hero vanquishes one or more beasts so humans can live on the earth. Some scholars posit that these mythological creatures are symbols of humanity's own darker nature, our shadow selves."

"Sounds a little like what Dr. Abramson, the shrink, told me," Billy offered.

"Or maybe humans believed these things for so long that they came into being," Chigger, who was not known for great mental feats, said proudly. "What can be conceived and believed can be achieved."

Three pairs of surprised eyes stared at Chigger.

"What?" the boy asked defensively. "I watch self-improvement TV shows," he added with a slight touch of hurt in his voice.

Wesley broke the silence. "According to the Old Testament of the Bible, God created a great and terrible sea monster called the leviathan."

"When did you start reading the Bible?" Billy asked.

"When your grandma Awinita died," Grandpa answered. "It's hers. I keep it on the nightstand next to my bed. I read a little every night. You'd be surprised by what can be found in there."

"I thought you only believed in Cherokee religion and culture," Chigger observed.

"Spiritual teachings come from many places," Wesley replied. "But Cherokee ways are still closest to my heart."

"I learn something new about you every day, old man," James said with admiration. "What *does* the Old Testament say about this leviathan?"

"'In that day, the Lord with his great and powerful sword shall punish leviathan, the piercing serpent,'" Wesley quoted, "'even leviathan, that crooked serpent; and he shall slay the dragon that is in the sea.' Isaiah 27. There's another one from the Book of Job I could give you."

"No, no," James protested. "That one is plenty."

"Then there's a Cherokee legend that says the Horned Serpent was created by an angry medicine man who turned a human being into the Uktena and banished him to the Underworld," the elder continued.

"Stop, you're hurting my brain," James pleaded. "I've seen and heard more than enough the last few days to completely rearrange my view of the world. I need a break."

Yet another moment of silence came upon the team. In their minds, they were all updating their views of the physical world as well as the spirit world. Meanwhile, exhaustion was overtaking all of them.

After they unloaded all the gear from the van and the boat, the team broke up. Each one headed back to his normal life. But none of them would be the same.

When Billy and his father walked through their front door, Mrs. Buckhorn was waiting. She immediately noticed there was something different about her son.

"Billy, you've changed somehow," she said. "I'm not quite sure what the difference is, but you seem . . . a little larger, more . . . robust." She paused and looked him over again, noticing the ripped seams in his shirt. "I'm not imagining it, am I? Tell me what happened."

James and Billy gave her a condensed version of events, leaving out certain details that would be too hard for anyone to believe.

They felt it was better to spare her these details for now. No one outside the Paranormal Patrol was to ever know about the very real but unbelievable appearance of the legendary beast.

Alone in his bedroom later, Billy opened the deerskin pouch Wesley had given him. Peering inside, he saw the clear quartz crystal he'd retrieved from the upper cave room. Like the purple crystal on the pedestal at the bottom of the cave, this gem also gave off a glow the teen hadn't noticed before. But unlike its counterpart, this stone radiated a faint golden glow and an accompanying sense of positivity.

A thought occurred to him. *This crystal and the purple one are twin opposites, kind of like the Sun Priest and his twin brother, the Snake Priest. Shakuru said we awakened the dual forces of his culture when we entered that cave, but Blacksnake and the Raven Stalker had already been awakened before then. Are the returns of these creatures isolated events or part of something larger? Is something happening to increase the powers of the Underworld?*

The thought made Billy shiver.

As the teen got ready for bed, he set aside his torn shirt and too-tight jeans, realizing he might need to move up a size in clothing.

"Time for a trip to Walmart," he said of the store where most of his clothes came from.

It was then that he began to notice that his very bones ached and his skin itched—all over. He remembered that when he was about thirteen, he'd gone through a period of time when his bones felt this way. His mother called it growing pains.

Strange changes are afoot, he thought, echoing a phrase Wesley had said at the stomp dance last September.

Then, unexpectedly, the image of Lisa Lookout standing on his front porch popped into the teen's mind. Something about the Osage girl certainly intrigued him. Was it her spider tattoo? Or was it those deep green eyes?

Then he remembered something.

"Ethan Lookout," Billy said out loud.

A rapid flow of thoughts followed. *That's where I heard the Lookout name before. Augustus said he was one of the few Native American archaeologists. And he's Osage. And he studies Mound Builders. He has to be related to Lisa.*

Before climbing into bed, he opened the top drawer of his nightstand. The piece of paper she'd written her phone number on was still where he'd left it. That was reassuring. *Maybe it's time to call her,* he thought. After all, she'd said they might have a lot in common. And her grandfather *was* a medicine man. It couldn't hurt to give her a call.

As he began falling asleep, Billy heard a familiar humming in his ears. Soon his grandmother's transparent form came into view at the foot of his bed. And his great-grandfather Bullseye showed up too.

"I'm very proud of you," Awinita said. "Your victory has created a positive ripple effect throughout our worlds."

"So why did the Snake Priest want to take over my body so badly?" Billy asked.

"The Sun Priest explained that to us," Bullseye answered.

"A thousand years ago, the Sun Priest's brother was the Snake Priest, the leader of a cult that worshipped the Uktena beast," Awinita said. "It's a long story, but the short version is that the Sun Priest's twin brother was exiled from Solstice City, and the two brothers became mortal enemies."

"So he was trying to control the serpent once again," Billy said, putting some of the details together in his mind. "Maybe he thought he could beat his brother this time."

"Very good," Bullseye said. "Fortunately, this evil twin spirit has only limited powers here. Hopefully, you won't be hearing anything from him anytime soon."

Billy thought hard for a long moment as he tried to absorb and understand all that had occurred. "Who would have ever thought a sixteen-year-old Cherokee would be involved in such things?" he said. "I'm still trying to get used to all of this."

"In time you will," Awinita said. "This *is* just the beginning."

"What happened to the Sun Priest?" Billy asked. "He just sort of disappeared after the door was resealed."

"He had other places to be, things to do," Grandma said. "He told me he'll meet you, if he can, at the top of the Temple Mound in Solstice City on the summer solstice—but there are a couple of hurdles he has to clear first."

"That's the mound I saw in my dream, isn't it?"

"That's the one," Awinita answered. "Do you know where it is?"

"No, I don't," Billy admitted. "When I asked him where it was, he said I should also ask *when* it was."

"That mound was the center of his civilization a thousand years ago," Grandma said. "Now it's a state park not far from St. Louis, Missouri. In his time, major ceremonies were held there for thousands of people."

"I'm supposed to meet him there on June twenty-first?" Billy said.

"Yes," his grandmother said. "And that's all I know about it. You'll have to go there yourself to find out the rest."

"I still have so many questions," Billy said as fatigue began overtaking him. "Like what happened to the Mound Builders? Why did their civilization disappear?"

Billy was now feeling tired all the way down to his bones. He yawned a big yawn as his ability to maintain contact with his grandmother began fading.

"There'll be plenty of time to search for answers to those questions," Awinita said. "For now, sleep well, young man."

"I see quite a future ahead of you, boy," Bullseye added.

And both apparitions dissolved into nothingness.

As he drifted off to sleep, the teen's thoughts turned not to visions of Solstice City, the Sun Priest, or the crystal cave but to the brown-haired girl with the dark green eyes. What about her intrigued him so?

"That's something you definitely have to investigate in the very near future, Buckhorn," he said out loud.

What Billy Buckhorn didn't know was that this girl was the key to his future.

BIBLIOGRAPHY OF SOURCES

Conley, Robert J. *Cherokee Medicine Man: The Life and Work of a Modern-Day Healer.* Norman, OK: University of Oklahoma Press, 2005.

Diaz-Granados, Carol, James R. Duncan, and F. Kent Reilly III, eds. *Picture Cave: Unraveling the Mysteries of the Mississippian Cosmos.* Austin, TX: University of Texas Press, 2015.

Garrett, J. T. and Michael Garrett. *Medicine of the Cherokee: The Way of Right Relationship.* Rochester, VT: Bear & Company, 1996.

Jefferson, Warren. *Reincarnation Beliefs of North American Indians: Soul Journeys, Metamorphoses, and Near-Death Experiences.* Summertown, TN: Native Voices, 2009.

Kilpatrick, Alan. *The Night Has a Naked Soul: Witchcraft and Sorcery among the Western Cherokee.* Syracuse, NY: Syracuse University Press, 1997.

Kilpatrick, Jack F. and Anna G. Kilpatrick. *Friends of Thunder: Folktales of the Oklahoma Cherokees.* Norman, OK: University of Oklahoma Press, 1995.

Little, Gregory L. *The Illustrated Encyclopedia of Native American Indian Mounds and Earthworks.* Memphis, TN: Eagle Wing Books, 2016.

Little, Gregory. *Path of Souls: The Native American Death Journey.* Memphis, TN: ATA Archetype Books, 2014.

Mooney, James. "The Sacred Formulas of the Cherokees." *Seventh Annual Report of the Bureau of Ethnology*, 1886, 301-397, Bureau of American Ethnology.

Monroe, Robert A. *Ultimate Journey.* New York: Doubleday, 1994.

Pauketat, Timothy R. *Cahokia: Ancient America's Great City on the Mississippi.* New York: Penguin Books, 2009.

Zimmerman, Fritz. *The Native American Book of the Dead.* Self-published, 2020.

ABOUT THE AUTHOR

Gary Robinson, a writer and filmmaker of Cherokee and Choctaw Indian descent, has spent more than thirty years collaborating with American Indian communities to tell the historical and contemporary stories of Native people in all forms of media.

His most recent books include *Native Actors and Filmmakers: Visual Storytellers* and *Be Your Own Best Friend Forever*, both published by 7th Generation in 2021.

His historical novel series, *Lands of Our Ancestors*, portrays California history from a Native American perspective. It is used in many classrooms in the state, and has been praised by teachers and students alike.

He has also written several other teen novels, including *Thunder on the Plains*, *Tribal Journey*, *Little Brother of War*, and *Son Who Returns*. His two children's books share aspects of Native American culture through popular holiday themes: *Native American Night Before Christmas* and *Native American Twelve Days of Christmas*.

He lives in rural central California.

Look for **Billy Buckhorn and the Rise of the Night Seers**, *the next book in the Thunder Child Prophecy Series available January 2024.*

"I've come to a conclusion," Billy said. "After being through everything I've been through, plus just now being soul-trapped by the worst group of the medicine makers in Indian Country, why would I consciously choose to become the main target for this bunch of evil-minded, soul sucking, shapeshifters? It sounds like a total suicide mission, to me, and I don't want any part of it."

Personal peril comes to the forefront in *Billy Buckhorn and the Rise of the Night Seers*, book two of the Thunder Child Prophecy Series, when members of the centuries old Owl Clan begin using their mastery of the dark arts against Billy and his loved ones. As details of their plans to regain control of the Middleworld become clearer, Billy steps into his role as the Chosen One, destined to save humanity from the designs of the denizens of the Underworld.

7th
GENERATION

For more information, visit: **nativevoicesbooks.com**
Book Publishing Company • PO Box 99 • Summertown, TN 38483 • 888-260-8458
Free shipping and handling on all orders.